I0670494

# SpellSlinger

## The Veil War: Book One

# By Eric Garner Johnson

# Copper Veil Publishing

For permission requests, write to the publisher at:
Copper Veil Publishing LLC
Email: Copperveilpublishing@outlook.com
Website: Https://www.copperveilpublishing.com

Patreon-
https://patreon.com/EricGarnerJohnson?utm_medium=unknown
&utm_source=join_link&utm_campaign=creatorshare_creator&ut
m_content=copyLink

This is a work of fiction. Names, characters, places,
and incidents are either the products of the author's
imagination or are used fictitiously. Any resemblance to actual
persons, living or dead, or actual events is purely coincidental.

Cover design by Copper Veil Publishing
Edited by Eric G. Johnson
Interior design by Copper Veil Publishing

First Edition: 2025

ISBN: 979-8-9936573-0-1
Printed in the United States of America

# Dedication

This book—and pretty much everything else I do in life—is dedicated to my wife, Sharon. She is the toughest person I know, and she's kept me moving long after most would have given up.

I'm going to say something here that I've rarely said out loud: I admire her. Greatly.

For those who don't know, my wife is very sick—the kind of sick that doesn't get better. She was diagnosed years ago and has already outlived more than ninety percent of those with the same illness. I think part of that is sheer defiance. She's so fierce, so gloriously angry at the world, so full of unrelenting fire that even Death must've taken one look and said, *"Screw that. I'm taking the day off."*

I love her more than I can ever put into words. So much, in fact, that the Sharon in this story is based on her—steadfast, methodical, and always ready to kick someone square in the ass if that's what it takes to get things done.

She's more than my better half. She's my everything. She is, in fact, the reason you are reading this book now.

All thanks to her.

# The Stand

You never know when it's coming.
Your test.

That moment where you put up... or
shut up.

No help. No mercy.
Just you. Alone.

Some run.
Some crumble.
Some just give up.

But a few—
They stand.
They walk into the fire.

No matter what it costs

# Savannah

# Chapter One

Idaho Territory, 1874.

Her father's screams had only just stopped when the Comanche warrior looked in her direction. Savannah had been huddled in on herself, trying to make as small a target as possible, hopefully to be forgotten entirely. He had a knife in hand, the same knife he had used to slice away portions of her father's face, and both of his hands were covered in blood. Her father's blood.

Savannah was nine, too young to understand what he meant to do, but not too young to recognize death when it came for her. His war paint was all jagged black and red, crude slashes over skin, and he did not hesitate. He was the one who had tortured her father for a day and killed him slowly, methodically, while she watched. All because her father had killed one of the brave's family. Now he was coming for her. Fear crushed the breath from her lungs, left her trembling, hollow, small.

Then something in her snapped. Not fear breaking, something deeper.

Rage rose in its place. Sharp. Blinding. Cold. Rage at the man who'd destroyed her family, at the world that had let it happen. And in that moment, she stopped trying to run. She faced him.

As the warrior reached out to her, she became aware of a buzzing in her ears, a warmth, the taste of blood in her mouth. Instinct took over, causing her to raise her hand, fingers splayed. She reached into herself as her hand appeared to reach for the warrior, and pure power erupted from her, a blue-white gout of flame that jumped from her open hand to the warrior, who suddenly realized his death had arrived.

As the fire left her hand and took root in the warrior's blood, Savannah felt a wave of weariness that almost sent her into unconsciousness. The fire clung to him, burning him to the bone in an instant. He never even had time to scream as his body ruptured from steam pressure. In a second, Savannah was covered head to foot in his blood, and the shock of it all took her away from the world for a time.

The fire was still burning when they found her, kneeling between the blasted and burned body of the Comanche brave and a large stake that had been driven into the ground, with a pitifully burned body hanging from a chain driven into the wood. They were all veterans of the Apache Comanche wars and could easily recognize the signs of torture. But the Comanche warrior, who was still on fire? That was horrifyingly different, down to the blue-white fire that was still burning from the ruptures in the warrior's body. And different was dangerous.

Not the kind of fire you build to cook meat or warm your hands. Not even the kind that comes from a torch or a burned wagon. This one hissed. It ate. It clung to the body like it had a taste for bone. What was left of the Comanche warrior had already stopped resembling a man.

Now he was just a blackened heap of something brittle and steaming, crumpled in the dirt like a broken shrine. The skin was gone. The eyes had boiled. His ribs showed through a split in his side, charred and glistening. Metal ornaments melted into the muscle. His knife had fused to the belt buckle he'd taken from a dead cavalryman a year ago.

And at the edge of the blast radius, untouched, they could see the girl. She was barefoot, legs folded under her, knees scraped, arms limp in her lap, palms turned up, still caked with grit and blood. Her hair stuck to her face in burnt locks, one braid fully scorched off at the end.

She didn't blink, didn't shiver. Didn't cry.

She just stared at the dirt between her knees. There was a small rock there, white quartz, shaped like a bird skull. She studied it like it might explain something. Like it owed her an answer.

The riders came in slow, hooves soft, no war cries, no laughter.

They weren't Comanche. That mattered. But her body didn't react.

She heard the tongue, Apache, fast and hard-edged, but her mind was too far gone to track the words. They surrounded her in a loose circle, boots crunching the burned earth, hands near bows or rifles. No one dared get closer than ten feet. She could feel them all watching her.

And behind their silence, one thought: How is she alive?

One of them broke rank, a younger man, sharp-shouldered, sinewy from years in the saddle. His voice came hot through the dry air. "She's a witch. That's what this is. That thing she burned—it wasn't normal. She's Comanche-tainted. We should end it now, before she brings more death on us."

A few murmured in agreement. One spit. Then another stepped forward. Older, slower, but no fear. Eagle Feather, a shaman of advanced years.

He didn't say anything right away. Just walked up to the edge of the circle and stopped a few paces from the girl. The wind caught the red fringe on his shoulder wrap and flared it out behind him like wings. He looked at her for a long time.

Then, without turning his head, he reached to his belt and drew a long, curved knife, bone-handled, with a ridge of obsidian laid down its back like a spine. He held it out by the blade. Offered the handle to the younger warrior.

"Then do it."

The younger one froze. "What?"

Eagle Feather still didn't look away from the girl. "You said she's a threat. If you believe it, kill her now. Make the world safer."

The younger man hesitated.

Eagle Feather's eyes finally cut toward him, just briefly, and then pointedly down at the corpse behind the girl. Still hissing. Still smoking. The air above it wavered with heat, and a smell like burned coins twisted in the wind. "That was a grown man," Eagle Feather said. "Armed. Strong. Not alone. She didn't run."

The younger man took a small step back, without taking the knife.

Eagle Feather's expression never changed. But something in his mouth twitched, almost a grin. He sheathed the blade. Crouched beside the girl. His knees cracked as he lowered himself, slow and deliberate, no sudden movements.

She didn't look at him.

He studied her face. Eyes blown wide, lips cracked. Dirt in the corners of her mouth. One of her earlobes was burned black. Her dress had once been blue. Not anymore.

With a soft grunt, he shrugged the red blanket from his shoulders. It was sun-faded, frayed along the edges, the wool stiff with years of use. He draped it around her shoulders, not gently. Not unkindly, either. Just… like it was the next thing to do. She didn't resist. The weight of it slumped around her like a second skin. It smelled of campfire and horsehair and wind.

Eagle Feather stood. Faced the rest. "She killed the man who meant to own her," he said in Apache. "She wasn't traded. She wasn't given. She was taken, and she killed him. That makes her free."

The younger warrior opened his mouth to speak but then thought better of it.

"She's not one of us," someone muttered.

"Not yet," Eagle Feather agreed. "But she's not one of them either." He looked back at the girl, still unmoving under the blanket. Her eyes were half-lidded now, unfocused. "She's ours."

They didn't talk to her on the ride back. Didn't give her a horse, either. Just let her walk.

She didn't complain. She wouldn't have known how.

The blanket dragged behind her like a flag in the dust, frayed red picking up burrs and cinder ash. Her bare feet moved slow, stiff, each step a conscious effort to keep from falling. She didn't fall. She never did. She kept her eyes down. Her mouth closed.

Someone offered her water, an older woman, skin tough as leather, eyes like coal, but Savannah only stared at the canteen. Not out of pride. Just… didn't seem like it would help. You're still alive, she told herself. Not like her father. For an instant, her mind danced around the edges of a thought that threatened to drive her over the edge. Her father... cut, beaten, burned, finally, to death. She shook her head violently, shoving that thought down deep. That should've meant something. But it didn't feel like anything. Just facts.

She noticed how the men walked around her. None stayed close. Most gave her a wide berth. She was in the center of a loose circle, like a prisoner, except no one had drawn a weapon. It wasn't that they feared her. It was what she represented.

One of them behind her said something low in Apache, a sneer of a joke, just crude enough to carry. "Comanche bride's ready for a new husband."

Savannah didn't understand enough Apache to know exactly what he said, but she did understand the word for 'bride'. She stopped walking. Just stopped. The joke died in the air. She turned, not fast. No fire. No anger. Just turned, slowly, until her eyes met his. Not blinking. Not searching. Just looking. Three heartbeats. Four. The warrior's grin faltered. He shifted his weight. Looked away. She turned back. Kept walking. Didn't say a word. She didn't need to.

Ahead, the hills gave way to a shallow basin, rimmed with brush and stone. Lean-tos and hide tents scattered across a packed stretch of ground near the river's bend. The sun had nearly gone. Just a glow left along the ridge. Camp. She paused without meaning to.

It looked like safety. But she didn't trust the feeling.

A blur of movement, a child running past, laughing, dragging a stick in the dirt. He skidded to a halt when he saw her. Not fear, not surprise. Just stopped. Watched. Then turned and bolted the other way. A dog barked once. Then went quiet.

Eagle Feather came up behind her. Didn't speak. Didn't prod her forward. Just stood there, presence like iron. That gave her the push to keep walking.

A woman drawing water from a basin tightened her grip on the jug, knuckles whitening. She didn't stop working, but her eyes never left Savannah's face.

In a nearby ring of children, someone whispered her name.

"Tł'óól," said a voice. Witch. The circle rippled with nervous laughter. One of the braver girls spat into the dust.

Savannah didn't react. She kept walking, one foot in front of the other, until she reached the edge of the main fire circle. She didn't step inside. Just stopped. The silence around her thickened. Even the fire seemed to shrink away from her.

They gave her food that night. Bread and beans, simple, charred around the edges. One of the women left it in the dust a few feet from her. No words. No eye contact. Savannah didn't move.

She sat just outside the reach of the main fire, where the shadows wrapped the blanket tighter than her arms ever could. Her knees were pulled up, bare feet tucked beneath the cloth, elbows balanced on bone.

She stared at the flames. Not into them. Not past them. At them. Like she could burn them back.

Camp life moved around her, warily. Voices kept low. No one laughed. No one came close. Children were called inside. Dogs slunk behind wagons. Even the fire seemed quieter on her side of the ring.

At one point, someone tried to leave a second piece of bread nearer her side of the circle. They took one look at her face and walked it back to the edge.

That's when the girl showed up. She didn't announce herself. No one did, in this place. But Savannah noticed the movement. Soft steps. Small shape. She expected a child. She didn't expect one who sat down beside her like it was normal.

The girl crossed her legs. Set something down—half a boiled egg, wrapped in paper. She leaned back on her palms and tilted her head up to look at the stars. She hadn't said a word for a long time.

Savannah waited. Because that's what you do with strangers. You wait to see who they really are.

The girl didn't twitch. Didn't glance over. She just sighed. "You ever wonder if stars are just holes in the world?"

Savannah blinked. "…What?"

The girl pointed skyward with one dirty finger. "Up there. Looks like a hide stretched over the sky. Stars are where something poked through. Blood light."

Savannah didn't answer. She wasn't sure how.

The girl glanced at her, taking in the blanket, the soot. The eyes.

"You look like someone who knows about blood."

Savannah stared. Not offended. Not frightened. Just surprised. "Who are you?"

"Ahyoka," said the girl. "My mother says I talk too much. My father said I was born with a knife in my teeth. But he died a long time ago, so maybe it fell out."

"Why are you here?"

Ahyoka shrugged. "You looked like the fire was winning."

Savannah looked at the egg. Then at the girl. "I don't need help."

"Sure," said Ahyoka. "But you look like someone who's about to bite a rock out of spite." She said it with a little grin, not cruel, not mocking. Like it was a challenge. Like she expected Savannah to live up to it.

Savannah didn't laugh. But the fire behind her eyes cooled half a degree. "You always like this?" she asked.

"No," said Ahyoka. "Sometimes I'm worse." Then she stood. Walked away. Didn't say goodbye. Didn't say you're welcome. She left the egg. Savannah didn't eat it. Not then. But she picked it up. Held it for a long time.

And for the first time since the flames, the voice in her head, the one that had said "Not today", was silent.

The blanket was stiff by morning. Dried blood and soot turned the wool coarse, heavy with sleep and memory. Savannah woke under it, lying beside a cold firepit, her arms crossed beneath her head like she hadn't moved once through the night.

She hadn't dreamed. Thankfully. Her brain still wasn't ready to process everything that had happened, all that she had lost, in just one day. The burn scar on her left calf was enough to remind her what the dream would have been.

Footsteps approached, two sets. She didn't look. Eagle Feather's voice came low. "Up."

Savannah pushed herself upright, slower than she wanted. Her body was starting to feel again—blisters on her soles, bruises on her ribs. Every joint felt like it had been packed with stone dust.

But she stood. Eagle Feather didn't explain where they were going. She didn't ask.

They crossed the camp in silence, cutting through morning cook smoke and the hiss of boiling water. People moved out of their way, not fast, not obviously, but always enough to mark her.

They arrived at a small tent near the edge of the trees. Hides stretched tight, marked in red symbols. A circle of white stones lined the front. The smell of herbs and smoke hung thick in the air. Healer's tent. Savannah hesitated, not because she feared pain, but because she feared being seen.

Eagle Feather held the flap open. "Inside."

She ducked in. The tent was darker than outside, lit only by the yellow flicker of a single oil lamp hanging from a hook. The walls were lined with bundles, sage, cornflower, juniper, dried teeth and talismans. In the center sat a woman. Bent with age, hands knotted like old roots, eyes sharp as obsidian points.

She said nothing. Just gestured to a woven mat. Savannah sat.

The old woman shuffled closer, knees popping with each step. She didn't greet her. Didn't ask her name. She pressed fingers to Savannah's throat. Her jaw. Pulled down one eyelid, then the other. Tugged the blanket away from one shoulder and pressed knuckles into the skin beneath. A bruise there made Savannah flinch. The woman paused, watching. "You are cursed," the healer said at last, voice like a kettle lid scraping stone.

Savannah didn't answer.

The healer ran two fingers down her forearm, stopping just above the wrist. She muttered something low and fast in a dialect Savannah didn't catch. "Do you know what you are?"

Savannah met her eyes. "Alive."

The old woman's face cracked. Not a smile, more like a warning line through granite. She turned. Took a pinch of red dust from a bowl and threw it into the fire pot. The air snapped, blue sparks dancing. For a moment, the space between them shimmered like heat on stone. The healer squinted at the air like she saw something Savannah didn't.

Then—

A cough at the tent flap. Ahyoka's head poked through. "She done yet?"

The old woman didn't look away. "Why?"

"Because I want to show her where not to step if she wants to keep her feet."

The healer gave no signal. No permission. Just turned away and went back to her bowl.

Eagle Feather's voice came through behind Ahyoka. "Go with her."

Savannah stood. The blanket shifted as she moved. The firelight caught the edges and for a second, Savannah looked like she was walking through smoke.

As she passed, the healer's hand darted out. Not to strike. Not to grab. Just to place one rough palm against Savannah's heart. A beat. A whisper of pressure. "It's not done with you," the healer murmured.

Savannah paused. "What isn't?"

"The voice." Then she pulled back, sat again. As if the moment had never happened.

Savannah stepped into the light, out of the tent, where Ahyoka waited.

The girl gave a grin. Not all teeth. Just enough. "Come on, blood light. Let's get you a real blanket. That one makes you look like a corpse. You smell like scorched piss and war." Ahyoka said that cheerfully.

Savannah didn't look over.

"Thanks."

"That's not an insult. That's just how I know you're not weak." She tapped her nose. "Most of the weak smell like fear. You smell like someone who bit the devil and liked the taste."

Savannah gave her a sideways glance. "You talk like that to everyone?"

"No. Just the interesting ones."

They passed between two fire pits where several families were preparing breakfast—tortillas and roasted beans, smoke curling low and gray in the still morning air. Adults turned to look. Children froze mid-play.

The silence rippled outward as Savannah walked through it.

Ahyoka didn't seem to notice, or didn't care.

"Anyway, I figured if I didn't show you around, you'd step on someone's sacred bone pile or fall into a sweat lodge naked and backward. We've had that happen. One time a Navajo trader tried to—"

"I don't need a babysitter," Savannah muttered.

Ahyoka snorted. "This isn't babysitting. This is community service."

She led her past the water barrels and down a dirt path lined with hides hung for drying. Savannah felt every eye on her. Not hatred. Not fear. Something heavier. Like a crowd watching a caged mountain lion and wondering if the bars would hold.

They turned a corner toward the horse pens. A young boy—maybe eight, maybe ten—stood in the path ahead, arms folded. He didn't move.

Ahyoka slowed. "Uh-oh. That's Little Chaska. He thinks he's braver than he is. Just... let me do the talking."

Before she could say more, Chaska bent down, scooped up a stone, and hurled it. It hit Savannah square in the chest. Hard. Enough to sting.

Everything stopped.

Savannah didn't flinch. Didn't blink. She stepped forward. One pace. Two.

Chaska took a step back.

A third step—and Savannah crouched, slow and deliberate. She picked up the stone. Turned it in her fingers like she was inspecting it for value. Then she tossed it, underhand, back at the boy's feet. "Try again," she said flatly. "You missed my face."

The boy stared.

Ahyoka gave a low whistle.

Around them, the watchers reacted—not with words, but with the smallest shift in posture. A lean forward. A tension easing. The kind of shared breath that passes through a village when something *unexpected* happens.

Chaska turned and ran.

Savannah stood straight again. Not proud. Not smug. Just… standing.

Ahyoka grinned. "That was *deeply* unsettling. I think I love you."

They kept walking. Behind them, someone whispered again.

But this time the word wasn't *Tł'óół.* It was **"Ghost."** And for once, Savannah didn't feel the need to correct them.

Some of them called her Tazhi by the end of that year. Swift One. Not because she ran fast. Because she *learned* fast. And fought faster.

Not every warrior liked it, not every elder approved, but no one stopped her.

And Ahyoka? She bragged to everyone. "That's my sister," she'd say. "She will set the world on fire. And I will help."

The other girls rolled their eyes. The elders groaned. Savannah… she just smiled. For once, it wasn't made of ashes.

The girl they called Tazhi didn't smile often. But when she did, it was real now.

# Chapter Two

She stood barefoot on warm rock, bowstring drawn, eyes fixed on a jackrabbit crouched between two thorn bushes across the wash. The breeze tickled her hair. Somewhere behind her, Ahyoka muttered, "You're too slow."

Savannah released.

The arrow hit just behind the ear. The rabbit didn't twitch.

Ahyoka whooped, skipping down the slope like she'd scored the kill herself. "About time," she said, crouching beside the rabbit. "Last week you couldn't hit a sleeping cow."

Savannah snorted, lowering her bow. "You're a terrible teacher."

"I'm the best teacher," Ahyoka corrected, grinning. "You're just a stubborn white girl with slow fingers and no butt."

Savannah kicked a pebble at her. "Say that again."

"You heard me."

They laughed, the sound bouncing off rock walls and running wild down into the brush. It was easy to laugh with Ahyoka. Always had been.

The sun climbed overhead as they skinned and cleaned the rabbit, smearing their hands with blood and dust. Ahyoka talked constantly—about nothing, about everything. Which boys were handsome. Which elders were idiots. What kind of tattoos they'd get when they were older and meaner and far from here.

Savannah only half-listened. Not because she wasn't interested. But because the quiet beneath it all—the safe kind of quiet, the kind that comes when you trust the person beside you—was louder.

She had never thought she'd feel that again. Not since the fire. Not since the screams. Not since the ride into dark country with Comanche blood on her feet and a broken heart in her chest. Not since her family died.

But here she was, eating a rabbit she shot herself, with dust in her hair and dirt under her nails and someone at her side who *saw her*. Who *chose her*.

They returned before dusk, with meat in their bags and pride on their faces. The elders didn't nod. Didn't smile. But they didn't scowl either.

That was progress.

Eagle Feather met them near the fire pit. He said nothing, just laid a hand on Savannah's shoulder—brief, solid, heavy with approval. It was the closest he ever came to affection. She held her breath until he walked away.

"You're winning them over," Ahyoka whispered. "Slowly."

"They still think I'm cursed."

"They still think *I'm* cursed," Ahyoka grinned. "Difference is, you're useful."

Savannah rolled her eyes. "Thanks."

Ahyoka bumped her shoulder. "It's true. You're faster than most of them now. Smarter, too. Tazhi fits. Even if it does sound like a nickname for a squirrel."

That night, Savannah lay under her blanket staring at the stars. Ahyoka was beside her, already half-asleep. The fire crackled. Insects hummed. And for the first time in two years, Savannah didn't dream of blood.

She dreamed of home.


The hawk was dead when they found it.

It lay outside Savannah's lodge, wings sprawled, head turned unnaturally sideways, black eyes open to the morning sun. No blood. No wound. Just stillness.

Ahyoka frowned. "That's not good."

Savannah crouched beside the bird, touching its feathers. They were warm. No rigor yet. "It wasn't here last night."

"Something killed it. Something quiet."

They burned it on a small stone altar behind the far huts. Smoke curled like a question into the sky.

That night, the fire wouldn't light. No matter how much kindling, no matter how strong her flint, no matter how softly she whispered the ignition glyphs Eagle Feather taught her—nothing.

She sat in the cold while Ahyoka grumbled and tried to get warm off shared body heat. "You've pissed off something," the other girl muttered, eyes half-lidded. "Probably me. Maybe the mountain. You keep making that face. The mountain hates that face."

"I'm not cursed," Savannah said, but it came out flat.

"Didn't say cursed," Ahyoka replied sleepily. "Just weird."

Two days later, Savannah overheard them. The elders sat in the far tent. She hadn't meant to listen. She was only coming back from the creek, arms full of wood. But then she heard Eagle Feather's voice. Low. Tight.

"She is no longer just a guest."

Another answered. "She is dangerous. You saw what she did. That... flame. The air around her moves wrong. She should not have that kind of power."

A pause. "She doesn't *use* it."

"Not yet."

Another voice. "The brasscoats will come. Or worse. What if she draws them to us? What if she's marked?"

"She is one of us," Eagle Feather said. "We took her in. We gave her a name. You gave her a name. She earned it."

A hard silence followed.

Savannah backed away slowly, heart pounding. She didn't hear the rest.


That night, she didn't sleep. Ahyoka noticed. "You heard something."

Savannah didn't answer.

"You're not leaving."

Savannah glanced sideways.

"I said," Ahyoka repeated, "you're *not* leaving. You're mine now, White Girl. You're my shadow. I go—you go. We're a pair. Sisters from another mother. A terror on four feet. If they try to send you away—"

"They won't," Savannah said quietly.

"No." Ahyoka leaned over, poked her forehead. "You're too useful. Also, I'd miss the way your nose wrinkles when you lie."

Savannah tried to smile. Couldn't. But she reached out and hooked her pinky around Ahyoka's. It wasn't a promise. Not quite. But it was something.

The riders came at dawn. Five of them, dusty blue uniforms under patched leather. Two carried rifles, one had a sword, and one rode tall with silver braid on his shoulder—a rank Savannah didn't recognize. The fifth was the worst of all. A SpellSlinger. You could tell without seeing the gloves.

His coat was darker than the others. Black buttons, copper etched. He sat too still in the saddle, like his body was waiting on orders from something colder than thought. His eyes swept the village like he already owned it. A brasscoat.

They didn't come out here. Not unless they were hunting something.

Eagle Feather went out to meet them, bare-chested and alone. He left his knife sheathed. Held his hands where they could be seen.

Savannah and Ahyoka watched from the ridge above the camp, crouched behind the rocks. The morning sun lit the village golden, quiet. Too quiet.

"He shouldn't go alone," Savannah whispered.

"He has to," Ahyoka murmured. "If we go down armed, it's war."

"They'll kill him."

"They're here to talk. Look. They're not—"

The SpellSlinger raised a hand holding an ornate revolver, silver and copper, gleaming in the light.

It was slow. Calm. Not a threat. He wanted Eagle Feather to see it coming. To recognize death.

When he triggered the shot, a bright blue bolt of lightning sizzled between them, lancing through Eagle Feather as if he didn't exist.

And Eagle Feather was blasted back, to land in several pieces. He never had a chance. After all, there had been no warning, no reason that either girl could see. Other than simply swatting an annoying insect. Where he stood, only a black scorch mark remained. A few ashes floated up and scattered on the breeze.

Savannah didn't scream. Couldn't. Ahyoka did.

The cavalry turned, rifles up, as if they had been expecting trouble. One fired.

Savannah grabbed Ahyoka's hand, dragging her back toward the brush. They ran like hell. Dust kicked up around them. Bullets zipped low. They cleared the slope, breath ragged, legs pumping.

Ahyoka's grip loosened.

Savannah turned and saw her stumble. Her leg buckled under her. She tried to take a step, then crumpled. No sound. No cry. There was blood blooming beneath her ribs. Savannah dropped beside her. "Ahyoka! Ahyoka!" Ahyoka blinked slowly. Her lips moved. Nothing came out.

Savannah pressed both hands to the wound. It was already too much. The blood poured like it wanted to leave. Like it *knew*. "No," she whispered. "Not you. Not you."

Ahyoka exhaled—and didn't inhale again. Savannah stared at her face, at the half-smile still there, at the way her hand was still curled into Savannah's sleeve.

The wind shifted and Savannah stood, hands dripping red. Her face did not move. Her heart made no sound. She turned back toward the ridge, toward the gunfire, toward the riders, toward the brasscoat—

And **everything burned**.

She didn't remember what happened after the fire, not exactly.

One moment, she was standing above Ahyoka's body, her hands slick with blood, her soul hollowed out by something that felt too big to be grief. The next—everything was burning.

Men screamed. Horses bucked and fled without riders. The sky bled red as buildings cracked like old bones. Savannah moved through it, untouched, silent, watching the world unravel.

She didn't feel the heat. Didn't smell the smoke. Just walked.

And when it was done—when the fire had nothing left to eat—she stood alone in a sea of ash and scorched stone. The only thing she carried was Ahyoka's body, limp in her arms, head tucked against Savannah's chest like she might still be asleep.

No one else had survived. Not Eagle Feather. Not the children. Not the elders who had, as it turned out, been correct to fear her, none of the youth who had trained beside her.

The Apache village was gone.


**Three days later,** they found her wandering the flats beyond the Chuska ridges, barefoot, sunburned, body streaked in soot and dried blood. Her eyes were black, obsidian black, no iris, no white, just black.

She didn't speak, didn't flinch when they raised their rifles. She didn't blink when Cyrus dismounted and approached with slow, cautious steps. "What in the hell happened to you, girl?" he asked softly.

She didn't answer. She just stood there, holding Ahyoka. And in the heat-shimmered silence between them, Cyrus saw something old looking back through that girl's eyes—something not quite human anymore.

He stepped closer.

She let him. Very gently, he reached for Ahyoka's body. Savannah didn't move, but the wind did. It rose like a breath held too long. Cyrus hesitated. "I'll help you. But you gotta come with me. Understand?"

A beat. Then two. She nodded. Her eyes slowly faded from solid black to a very pretty, bright blue. And finally, she spoke one word. Quiet. Final. "Tazhi."

The carriage pulled up to Melville House two weeks after Cyrus found her. It was late morning. Bright. Summer heat already rising off the stone walkway in visible waves. Savannah sat inside, knees drawn up, watching the world pass through narrowed eyes. She hadn't spoken since the desert. Not really.

Cyrus didn't press her, just concentrated on driving.

Melville House loomed like a palace—stone walls, brass fittings, three towering spires and not a speck of dust on the flagstones. The symbol of the Concordium hung above the gate— spiral sun, etched in gold.

Savannah stared at it like it might blink.

When the doors opened, they were greeted by silence. Students stopped what they were doing—reading on benches, practicing air glyphs, sparring on the green. All of them turned and stared.

Cyrus stepped down and turned to offer her a hand. She ignored it, climbed out on her own.

Her boots were scuffed. Her coat was Apache leather, stiff with blood and travel. Her eyes moved slow, assessing. She didn't look scared. She looked *ready*. Behind her, Cyrus sighed. He'd known this day would come. He just hadn't expected it to look like a goddamn gunpowder keg in a silk ballroom.

He leaned down beside her. "Listen to me, Tazhi. These people… they don't see the world like you do. They don't understand it. And what folks don't understand? They poke at. Or they try to break."

When she didn't answer, didn't acknowledge his words at all, he straightened, looked up at the prim, polished Headmistress approaching across the green like she'd swallowed a straightedge.

"This is Savannah. She'll be staying," he said before the woman could speak. "And I'd strongly advise briefing your students on the cost of disrespect."

The headmistress arched a brow. "Is that a threat, Warden?"

"No ma'am," Cyrus said, tipping his hat. "That's a mercy."

Savannah walked past them both without a word. And as she did, every privileged eye tracked her, some in curiosity, some in disgust. One boy, tall, blue-blood handsome and smug as a summer rooster, gave a theatrical cough. "Don't they have cages for wild animals?"

Savannah stopped. Turned. Looked him dead in the eye. And smiled. It wasn't a smile of amusement or of friendliness. It was the kind of smile wolves wear when they find something stupid limping too far from the fire.

The boy blinked, looked away. Hard.

Cyrus caught up to her with a shake of his head and a twitch of his lip. "For the record," he muttered, "I warned 'em."

## Interlude

### [CONFIDENTIAL – INTERNAL COMMUNICATION]
Concordium Record No. 4489-A
Filed: 4th of August 1874
Subject: Savannah Blackwell (Unregistered Magical Minor)
Status: PRESUMED DECEASED

To: Archivist Marleigh Tern, Bureau of Wandering Talents
From: Inspector Volen Kaye, Field Division No. 3 – Western Reach

Concerning the occurrence of July 29th in the Idaho Territory: reports confirm that a Comanche raiding party was utterly destroyed, together with severe desolation of the surrounding ground. Our riders were dispatched forthwith, yet upon arrival found the site already reduced to ash and ruin. Not a living soul remained.

The force employed is believed to have been blood-wrought in nature, in keeping with the known aptitude of Subject Savannah Blackwell, aged nine years, previously marked for observation under Classification W-M4 (Wildcard Minor: High Potential, Untutored). Said subject was last observed under passive watch in the Boise Sector. Her kin are accounted deceased. Surveillance was discontinued on the presumption the child herself perished in the raid.

No remains have been secured. The traces left upon the ground bear marks of combustion most unnatural, though corrupted by the taint of blood magic. All customary means of divination and scry returned naught. A secondary sweep was ordered; its results remain inconclusive.

**Status of file amended to: PRESUMED DECEASED.**

**Recommendation:**
Close the ledger upon this case and reassign the men. Mark for future note: blood-worked manifestations continue to befoul the Concordium's instruments and frustrate our tracking. Further inquiry to that matter remains ongoing.

# William Clinton Black

# Chapter Three

Kansas City, 1879.

It didn't smell like hope. It smelled like soot and piss and horses that had been dead three days before the wagon carried them off. Eight-year-old Clint Black knew better than to look for hope here. What you looked for was bread. Meat. Water that didn't make you sick later.

His mother had died in February—fevered, delirious, shaking the little apartment walls with her screams. His father followed ten days later. And by spring, the landlord had tossed Clint out with a broken toy and a single wool blanket. The toy went first, traded for stale crackers. The blanket came second. After that, Clint learned what mattered.

He wasn't the biggest kid on the street. He wasn't even the meanest. But he was the one who didn't give up. When his nose got broken, he reset it himself. When someone tried to steal his boots, he bit down on the boy's neck hard enough to draw blood. When he went four days without eating, he stole a whole chicken from a traveling preacher and ate it raw in an alley, feathers and all. He was skin and bones and a hundred splinters of angry steel.

There were others like him, kids the world had tossed away. They clustered in packs sometimes, but Clint stayed alone. The pack had rules. Clint didn't like rules. Not anymore.

He slept where the rats didn't. Fought when he had to. Hid when he couldn't win. And every morning, when the frost made his breath curl like smoke, he'd whisper to himself the same words: *Get up. Get moving. Don't die today.*

That was all there was to it. One brick at a time, the wall began.

He was ten when it happened. Two years on the street had stripped the softness out of him. Clint didn't cry anymore. He didn't flinch when people shouted. He didn't blink when he saw someone die in the gutter, and he never ran from the screams in the alley. That was just background noise in Kansas City. Like the church bells or the whimper of coal trains.

He'd grown harder. Meaner. Quieter. By now, Clint had figured out all the hiding spots, all the trash bins worth checking, which kitchens had a back door, and which cooks would throw a cleaver at a thief. He could tell the difference between a drunk who would swing wild and a man who wanted to make an example out of a street kid.

It was late fall, cold enough that the breath came out in clouds, and Clint hadn't eaten in three days. He was thinner than he'd ever been. His ribs stuck out like rafters. And he was tired, bone-tired, the kind of tired that makes bad decisions look like good ones.

As he rounded the corner into Cutthroat alley, he could see a child ahead, younger, smaller, holding something in his hand, like found treasure. He was standing by a broken crate, hunched down so he wouldn't be seen easily from the street. Clint had learned to move quiet, like his life depended on it, because it generally did. Without thinking, he scooped up a fist-sized piece of brick, drew back, ready to smash the kid's head in. The boy turned, and Clint froze. He was younger than he had first appeared, maybe eight or nine, sickly, and had the appearance of a beating victim. Big brown eyes. Cheeks hollow from hunger. And a piece of moldy bread clutched tight in both hands like it was treasure. The kid froze. Clint froze. For a second, the street went quiet.

Then the boy offered him half. Clint's stomach growled so loud it hurt. But his arm dropped. The brick fell to the dirt. And

31

something inside him snapped, not like a twig, but like a rope that had been holding too much weight for too long. He grabbed the boy, shoved the bread into his own coat, and half-dragged him toward a healer's post two streets over.

The healer was a wrinkled old SpellCaster with bad teeth and worse manners, but she saw the blood, saw the bruises, and didn't ask questions. She healed the boy's fever, mended a broken rib, and gave Clint a sideways glance like she was seeing through him.

"You're lucky," she muttered. "Most don't come back from the edge."

Clint didn't answer. He just nodded once and sat in the corner until the boy could walk again.

He left before the sun rose.

That night, he found a new alley. And for the first time in two years, he didn't sleep with a weapon in his hand. Because he had found it, he wouldn't cross the line.


Clint didn't want to go to the Kansas City Orphanage. He didn't go quietly, either. It took two officers and a binding spell to haul him out of the alley where he'd been living, wounded and feral, guarding a trash can fire like it was sacred flame. He spat, clawed, and bit until one of them cracked a rib, and only stopped when they promised food and warmth.

The orphanage wasn't a refuge. It was a proving ground, a crucible. The building was all brick and grime, older than the war and twice as cruel. Inside, the beds were rusted, the windows barred, and the food measured by the ladle. Children weren't nurtured there, they were sorted. The strong rose, the weak vanished into the walls.

Clint recognized the law of the place immediately. It was the same code that ruled the gutters: survival. The strongest kids ran the bunkrooms like warlords, trading safety for obedience. A few older boys noticed the lean muscle and the glare Clint never bothered to hide. They threw him scraps, tested his reaction. One handed him a knife with a grin and a nod, as if passing a torch.

Clint didn't flinch. He took it, turned it over in his hand... and then handed it back.

The first time he saw a smaller boy getting kicked in the ribs for a half-biscuit, something inside Clint snapped sideways. Not because he cared about the biscuit. Not even the boy, really. But because he remembered what it felt like to be smaller, hungrier, more alone than the world seemed able to measure.

He stepped in, didn't speak, didn't threaten. Just moved. The beating he took that night left his nose broken again and one eye sealed shut. He didn't complain.

The second time, he used a mop handle.

The third time, he used fists, fury, and teeth.

He didn't fight clean. He fought to end things. He knew every dirty trick the streets had ever taught him, and he added a few of his own. The older boys came at him in groups. He sent them limping to the infirmary. One lost two teeth and another cried in the dark for three nights before disappearing altogether.

Clint didn't enjoy the violence, but he never stopped it, either. Not until the message sank in pick on someone your own size, or bigger, if you're stupid enough. But if you mess with someone smaller, you will have a problem.

After a few months, the fights slowed. The younger kids started following him at a distance. Watching and waiting. He didn't ask for it, never asked for anything. But some of them started sitting closer during meals, sleeping closer to his bunk. Like they knew he wouldn't let anyone touch them.

He didn't call it loyalty. He just called it necessary.

That's when the SpellSlinger arrived.

The man was tall and straight-backed, with weather-worn skin and eyes like flint. His long coat was patched in a dozen places, and the spell shooter at his hip looked like it had seen more wars than presidents. He came on a Concordium writ, inspecting orphans for latent talent.

Most flinched when he tested them. Some ran. Clint stood still.

He matched the sigils and read the glyphs. When handed a blank crystal, he squeezed it in his fist until it glowed white-hot and cracked in half.

The 'Slinger arched one brow. "You don't scare easy."

Clint shrugged. "Doesn't help much."

"You've got more than aptitude," the man said, scribbling something on a parchment. "You've got instinct. Anger. Guts. You want out of this place?"

Clint's eyes narrowed. "What's the catch?"

"Apprentice contract," the man said. "Seven years or until you pass your trials. Room, board, education. Combat magic. The Concordium takes care of its own. Or you can stay here, keep knocking heads and hoping you don't catch a fever next winter."

Clint didn't answer right away. But he took the scroll when it was offered, not because he trusted the man, not because he believed in second chances, but because it was a door.

34

And Clint Black never forgot what it felt like when every door in the world slammed shut.

The SpellSlinger dormitory at Fort Sangre was nothing like Clint expected.

He imagined secret labs and mystical libraries, duels at dawn and strange artifacts glowing behind locked doors. What he got instead was a squat granite building with a leaky roof, a no-nonsense house matron named Elsie who made grown men cry, and a daily routine built from five things: wake, study, train, clean, and shut the hell up.

It suited him.

SpellSlingers weren't like the 'Casters. There were no meditations, no chants, no careful weavings of health and light. Slingers didn't heal. They didn't bless. They enchanted spellshells, they loaded, they aimed, and they fired.

If Casters were gardeners and builders, Slingers were butchers. Fighters. *Warriors.*

Clint fit right in.

His first year was hell. Not because the coursework was difficult—it was—but because he couldn't fake deference. He didn't bow. He didn't flatter. When a dorm instructor tried to haze him with a live-fire drill, Clint responded with a glyph grenade that leveled half the obstacle course. He was beaten for that, hard. But the beatings stopped after he rebuilt the glyph blindfolded and explained how to make it *worse.*

He was sixteen when he passed the first-tier trials. Most take until eighteen. But Clint learned faster than most because he refused to be *worse* than anyone. Not better—he didn't care about being admired. He just needed to know that if a fight ever came, he wouldn't be outgunned.

That was the year he found the wall. Not a literal wall. A philosophy.

There was an old instructor, Grey Ronan, who had once held the line at Devil's Gate Pass. Held it alone, against something dark and hungry. Ronan lost most of one leg and all of his men. But the town behind him lived.

When Clint heard that story, something clicked. You didn't have to win. You just had to *stand*.

He started watching how people folded under pressure. Not just opponents—friends, teachers, even the occasional visitor. Most people broke. Clint made it his mission not to. Ever. Pain was noise. Fear was static. What mattered was holding the line.

By year four, his name was whispered through the dorms, not fondly. Clint had no friends, not really. He didn't laugh with the others. Didn't drink. Didn't tell stories at the mess hall tables. But there were whispers, especially about the time another youth tried to mess with him, tried to make him look bad in front of the instructors.

Scuttlebutt was, Clint caught the other youth alone and put the barrel of his 'shooter in the kid's mouth. Told him he was going to be the test subject for a lightning bolt round. When the hammer fell and nothing happened, the boy had pissed himself and was never a problem for Clint again.

Every time a test came—written, magical, or physical—he passed it. And every time a fight broke out, he finished it.

No one liked him, but they all respected him. In fact, deep down, some of them were starting to *depend* on him. And that scared the hell out of Clint. He wasn't ready to carry people. Not again.

So he stayed sharp. Stayed quiet. Let others talk. Let others *assume.*

He worked the spell matrices longer than required, learned to tweak the standard combat rounds until they did things that weren't in any manual. He found out early that there were more effective gemstone combinations than they taught directly. Some were off the charts better. His instructors gave him extra credit and worried behind closed doors. Because what Clint was building wasn't a career.

It was a weapon.

And when, at nineteen, he walked into his final trials with a handmade shooter, a palm full of trick rounds, and a calm, unreadable stare, the examiners sat a little straighter in their chairs.

No flash. No flair. Just precision, power, and a grim silence.

He passed, top marks. No celebration.

He left the testing chamber, didn't wait for applause, didn't even change into his formal uniform. There was no need, since he didn't bother to attend the graduation. He walked out of Fort Sangre and into the world, one bag over his shoulder, shooter on his hip.

Now he was officially what the world feared, and loved, most: A journeyman SpellSlinger. One who didn't just survive the crucible.

One who *built* one of his own.

Getting his journeyman certification didn't mean the world flung its doors open.

It meant Clint Black was legally permitted to sell his services as a licensed SpellSlinger, but the parchment and wax seal might as well have been written in invisible ink for all the good it did him.

He drifted south from Fort Sangre with a light kit and heavy expectations. The instructors hadn't said much when he left, just a nod, and a warning to stay clear of frontier settlements until he was sure of his footing. They didn't tell him how few contracts would come. They didn't explain that out here, on the line between wilderness and law, people didn't want new blood. They wanted *reputation*.

He didn't have one.

Instead, he had a Spellshooter, already getting darker with every spell shot, on his hip and two dozen homemade spell rounds, half of which wouldn't kill a rabbit. The instructors had emphasized precision. Restraint. His nonlethals were clean, practical—sleep charms, flash bursts, a mercy tap with a tingle like a lightning rod up the spine. He had smoke, concussion, and two immobilizers that could freeze a grown man mid-sprint.

And then there was the inferno round.

Buried deep, tucked away in his oilskin roll, it hummed with wrongness. A forbidden thing. No instructor had taught him how to make it. But he'd read, and practiced, and studied burn patterns in Daguerreotypes. When he forged it, it had taken three tries not to lose a finger. Hell, the fire opal he used as the anchor cost him every single bit of coin he had at the time. It still scared him. But he kept it. He might need it.

After two weeks, he'd traded warding services for a roof over his head, fixed a cracked caster rail for a grain silo, and taught a merchant's daughter how to reinforce a weather spell with stabilizer runes.       All honest work. All underpaid. None of it made him feel like a SpellSlinger. He wanted a field test. He needed to *know* what he could do.

That's when he saw the flier: a ripped parchment tacked to the board outside a rail station cantina, curling in the wind. *Caravan needs protection. Copper Creek to Carson City. Two-week run. Pay negotiable, by the trip. Slingers preferred.*

It wasn't glamorous. Wasn't even tempting. But it was *something.* Clint tore it down, folded it in quarters, and stuffed it into his coat.

That night, he paid for a bed he didn't sleep in. He sat at the edge of town, tuning his spellshooter, checking glyph fuses, rerunning pressure calibrations. The weapon was steady. Familiar. Like breathing or eating.

The next morning, he found the caravan master, an older man with tobacco stains on his shirt and the patience of a snake, and signed the contract with a fountain pen he borrowed from a clerk.

The ink barely dried before Clint regretted it.

But he didn't walk away. He should have known better.

Should have seen the cracks in the wheels, the sloppiness in the escort formation, the fact that the caravan master never once looked him in the eye.

Clint glanced at the wagons, all tarped and chained down like a prison convoy, and couldn't help himself. "I'm surprised you don't just ship it out by rail."

The Caravan master barked a laugh. "Nearest station's Carson City — two days east if the road's good, three if it's not. And that's before you factor in the badlands."

Clint raised an eyebrow.

"Badlands will chew up a train as quick as a wagon," the man went on. "Twist the rails, wash out bridges, and sometimes…" He glanced to the horizon. "Sometimes it's not the weather that does the damage."

Clint decided not to ask. Instead, he took the job. Because it was time. Because no one ever got better hiding in safe jobs and comfort zones. Because sooner or later, the only way to know what you're made of… is to bleed for it.

He holstered his shooter and rode out at dawn.

# Chapter Four

The sun sprawled across the desert like molten copper, the heat dragging everything into a slow, suffocating lull. Clint Black rode point, his duster stained by travel and suspicion, the cargo behind him shimmering—ten wagons loaded with raw, gleaming ore. They should have felt powerful, commanding, the guardians of fortune rolling toward civilization. Instead, silence rotted through the convoy.

Dust clung to sweat-slicked skin. The guards fidgeted—too many hired hands, too little discipline. Clint had tried drilling them, had barked orders on the early ride out from Copper Creek, but cohesion was brittle. Now, as the desert stretched endless and empty around them, the brittle shell cracked, revealing the soft, fragile men beneath.

They were at the mouth of Carrion Canyon, a smallish ravine that cut through the Nevada terrain like God's own gash. The air was hot and dry, dust on the wind, crows in the air. Clint felt a certain tension in his neck and shoulders, a sixth sense that had helped him several times in training. He had one hand on the butt of his spellshooter, shielding his eyes from the ever-present sunlight with the other. A voice called from the rear, uneasy. "Black—"

Then, absence. No wind. No insects. No sound beyond the shallow rasp of Clint's own breath. The caravan tensed as if every man felt it at once, a moment stretched too thin, vibrating at the edge of breaking.

And then it broke.

Green fire tore through the center wagon, a beam so bright it left spots in Clint's vision even as wood splintered, metal shrieked, and flesh ignited. A heartbeat later, the air filled with screams. Horses thrashed, their high-pitched cries merging with the sharper, agonized wails of men.

Clint's training kicked in. He shouted, orders that crumbled even as they left his lips. The guards were already scattering, their movements useless, frantic. A boy named Mallory fumbled for his pistol, sprinting, his face frozen in raw panic. The second blast caught him mid-stride. His body convulsed violently before slamming into the dirt, smoke rising from the deep, blackened gouges in his flesh.

Another surge of spellfire detonated the ground by the third wagon. The shockwave peeled the earth apart. A man screamed as his leg twisted through the air, separating mid-flight before thudding wetly into the dust. Blood misted, an ugly spray that coated wagon wheels and horse hides.

"COVER!" Clint roared, but his voice was lost in the noise.

He dove behind the towering basalt outcrop, the rock ancient and split by time, its black surface a haven against the slaughter. Gunshots echoed. Spell bolts screamed through the air. The convoy wasn't fighting back; they were dying. He spoke to himself, a moment of wry humor. "Dammit, I thought wagons were supposed to be SAFER...".

Clint pressed himself against the stone as a razor-edged shard of ice shattered above him, showering him with frozen splinters. He ignored the sting, steadying his breath. This wasn't battle. This was butchery.

A glimpse beyond the rock showed the architects of death. Two figures stalked the ridgeline—casual, poised, sweeping destruction across the caravan with effortless precision. One, a lean woman with stark white hair, laughed as she fired, her amusement somehow worse than the carnage. The other, broad-shouldered with skin like hammered bronze, calmly reloaded his spell shooter, scanning the wreckage for survivors.

They weren't attacking. They were showcasing.

Clint exhaled slowly, steadying his nerves. His fingers brushed the lined pouch at his belt—smoke rounds, force shells, a shock charge if he had the time. He wasn't dead yet.

And if they wanted a spectacle, he'd damn well give them one. Clint counted his heartbeats, one, two, then slipped two dull gray smoke shells into his SpellShooter's chamber.

He fired twice.

The rounds landed just beyond the basalt rock, their muted pops barely audible amid the carnage. But the hiss that followed was thick, swallowing sight and sound in a swirling green-black fog.

Clint crouched low, ghosting into the smoke, each step controlled, measured. The gunfire shifted, hammering his former shelter, the enemy still convinced he was pinned behind stone. A blast of kinetic energy struck where he'd been seconds before, cracking the basalt and scorching the haze.

He slid into a shallow ravine, pressed tight against a charred cactus, listening. He could hear movement beyond the smoke, and his mind showed him where they likely were. So far, they were behaving exactly as he would have expected, and he was preparing to go to war. SpellSlinger training was quite thorough and covered many different scenarios.

A shout pierced the smoke. "Got 'im!"

Clint grinned, grim and sharp. Not yet, you bastards. He flipped open his cylinder, sliding in the round he'd been saving, a deep crimson shell lined with intricate gold runes. His inferno round. Expensive, powerful, horrifying. Not anything he would use if he had a choice. But he intended to make it back. No matter what he needed to do.

As the smoke began to thin, Clint saw them—three men emerging from behind a boulder, their faces twisted into casual grins, counting the dead like tally marks in some grim ledger. Others followed, their movements loose, cocky. It made it easier, their cockiness, but still not easy. Old Farrell, his first 'Slinger instructor, told them all that taking a life should never be easy, or the first choice. Most of the apprentices had barely paid attention. Clint, fresh out of the orphanage, drank in every drop.

He aimed and fired, willing the spell into the configuration he desired.

The inferno round hit the ground between them and detonated with a scream—raw, furious, a newborn dragon's cry. Fire bloomed in a perfect burst, consuming them instantly, the mouth to Hell, open for a fraction of a second. Their laughter died as their bodies incinerated, ash choking the air.

An instant after the detonation, Clint felt the first whispers of guilt. That was the first time he had ever killed anyone. Even as a boy, fighting for survival, that was one line he had never crossed. He would spend some sleepless nights sitting around the campfire, thinking about how easily he had taken lives.

The survivors turned wild, firing blind, shrieking curses. The panic felt different now, genuine.

Then, lightning. It snaked through the haze, precise, a needle of blue-white energy threading toward Clint's crouched form. He felt nothing at first, not sure it had gotten past the protection of his copper vest. Just a sudden cold where his left hand was. He looked down. His fingers were gone. His wrist ended in scorched flesh, raw but cauterized.

Clint collapsed into the dust, breath shallow, vision wavering. He wouldn't panic. Couldn't. He used every ounce of mental discipline to hold the agony at bay, dragging himself forward, ignoring the blood seeping from his ruined arm.

He reached the far end of the ravine. Charred bodies smoldered nearby, unrecognizable in death. The bandits were enraged now, firing wildly, shouting obscenities. Undisciplined.

Above him, the ridgeline loomed—sharp, sheer, steep. That's where the slingers were. That's where this ended. For a single second, an instant in eternity, he considered just giving up, giving in to the pain, going to sleep. An instant, that's all. Then his eyes snapped open and he snarled. There was no WAY he was going to let them get away with all of this!

Clint holstered his SpellShooter, forcing his body forward despite the pain, despite the heat, despite the cost. He followed cover to the edge of the ravine, right up to the wall. There were handholds aplenty, though it would have been much easier had he still possessed two working hands. He shook his head slightly. No time now to mourn his missing limb, in the heat of combat. There would be time for that later, if he survived. If he didn't, it wouldn't matter anyway.

The rock was hot. His muscles screamed. His stump bled freely now, exertion ripping open the wound. But Clint Black climbed. His duty and identity would let him do nothing else. The pain was terrible, but not as terrible as losing, abandoning his contract. Those were worse.

The climb took, at most, a minute that felt like an hour. He crested the edge, collapsed forward onto sunbaked stone, and lay there, chest heaving, vision swimming. The sky was too bright, the air too thin, the world too damn loud in its quiet.

Below him, the caravan was dead or dying. Wagons burned, men sprawled in broken heaps, blood pooling in the dust like wine spilled at a funeral feast. A few remaining bandits fired into the smoke, wasting bullets on corpses.

And there—exactly where a man who orchestrated slaughter would stand—was Nate Jackson. Clint dragged his focus forward. Jackson stood behind a brass spyglass, watching, detached, unreadable. Not reveling, not grieving, just witnessing.

Not far away, the two SpellSlingers lounged beneath conjured shade. Relaxed. Careless. Confident. Foolish. No one is untouchable.

Clint forced himself to move, body protesting. He slid back from the ridge, opened his SpellShooter with slow, deliberate motions. His fingers trembled, but the ritual steadied them. His mind narrowed.

Slot one: Sleep spell—opal-wrapped, delicate sigils of binding.
Slot two: Mercy Tap—an electro burst sharp enough to paralyze, not kill.
Three through six: Force beams.

The last of his arsenal.

He inhaled, sharp, painful, then crawled. Through loose shale, through brittle brush, through a world that no longer welcomed him, moving from slight cover to slight cover. They didn't see him anyway, focused on the scene below. Clint shook his head again. By now, they should have begun questioning why there was no return fire, looked around, at least. Soft, he thought.

At ten feet, he fired. Click. The sleep round hummed. The male SpellSlinger jerked once, then slumped sideways, snoring before he hit the ground.

The female Slinger looked around, startled, then locked eyes on Clint. Her eyes widened, and she opened her mouth to yell, or scream, or curse. It didn't matter, really. Click. The mercy tap struck the woman's forehead, cracking blue light through her skull. She convulsed, teeth clacking, and collapsed in a heap beside her partner.

Clint barely registered it. His body begged for stillness. He ignored it. Jackson was next.

He dragged himself through the last stretch, belly-down, buried in shadow. His arm shook. His vision blurred. He had seconds—just seconds left.

Jackson was frowning now. His eye had left the scope. His head tilted, then it snapped around. Their eyes met.

Too late.

Clint fired. The force beam struck Jackson square in the chest with a concussive *thump*, lifting him bodily into the air. He flew backward, arms flailing, and disappeared over the ridge with a *crunch-thud-thud-snap* as he tumbled downslope like a sack of meat.

"Jackson's down!" His men panicked, running for cover, firing wildly at the ridgeline. Clint stood, wavering. He calmly aimed at the men in the ravine below. They hadn't recognized that circumstances had truly changed. He could see all of them at once, and none of them had adequate cover.

One soul, either braver or stupider than the rest, aimed at Clint and fired, missing slightly to the left. Clint calmly took aim and triggered his second to last force beam, and the man ceased to be a problem. That took the fight out of the rest. "Goddammit— stand down! STAND DOWN!"

Clint stood on the rim, holding himself upright by an act of sheer willpower. He shouted, "I am offering quarter to those who are smart. Anyone who won't take it, I have six shells left, and I will use them. You choose."

The gunfire stopped. Weapons dropped. Men stepped out, hands high, surrender plain in their eyes. Clint didn't move. He couldn't, not yet. He sat back, half dazed, half dead, letting exhaustion settle like lead in his bones.

Behind him, the female SpellSlinger stirred with a groan. Clint turned, spellshooter low, voice scraped raw. "Easy. Just leave the 'shooter on the ground."

She blinked at him. "...You didn't kill us?"

"Nope. No reason." Clint leaned back for a second, more tired than he had ever been before in his life. The male moaned from the dirt. Clint steadied himself. "You were under contract. By the Accords, Jackson answers for your actions. You're prisoners—but you get quarter. Take it, and live."

The woman swallowed. Looked at the battlefield. Then at Clint, bloodied, broken, but still standing. She nodded. "Deal." She sounded grateful, a woman who was very aware she had used up her chances and had miraculously been given another.

And just like that, it was over.

But Clint felt no triumph—only weariness.

Smoke curled above the pass, though the killing had long since ended.

Clint sat against a half-burnt wagon, his right arm stiff with dried blood, his left arm ending just above the wrist—bandaged, ruined, a new kind of weight. Every breath hurt. Every motion sent pain lancing through his ribs. But he remained. He had won. Now came the hard part.

There were no horses left. The ones that hadn't bolted were dead, twisted under wreckage, spellfire, chaos. The wagons were shattered, half the copper lost to the desert, gleaming in the sun like some god's abandoned treasure.

He had gathered the prisoners—twelve survivors, plus the two SpellSlingers and Jackson—corralled them in the canyon's narrow throat, where shade gave respite, where escape was impossible.

Jackson had fought against consciousness, then against reality. But reality always won. And when Clint leaned close, voice flat and unforgiving, and said, "Try anything and I'll bury you where you lie. The Accords don't protect fools," Jackson had simply grunted and fallen silent.

Now, two days later, they were all still there.

Clint had made a sling for his ruined arm using strips of burnt canvas. Leya—the female SpellSlinger—had dug through wreckage to find herbs for a crude poultice. Gorran—the male— kept the prisoners in line, kept rationing what little remained. Not that a line of beaten men who understood that they shouldn't have come out on the other side were interested in giving anyone a problem.

By the Accords, their lives were Clint's responsibility, and the SpellSlingers knew that. So he carried them.

He carried them as he fetched water in dented tin buckets, even as his body begged for rest.
He carried them as he sat up every night, teeth gritted against exhaustion, trading watch shifts.
He carried them as he forced food down, despite the bitterness curling in his gut.

They saw it. And slowly, reluctantly, respect followed.

# Chapter Five

Jackson stirred in his sleep. His back was propped against a boulder, hands bound at the wrist, a strip of rough linen tied between them and a nearby iron ring sunk into stone. His breathing had been steady most of the night—slow, even. Almost meditative.

Then it changed.

Leya looked up from the half-burned branch she'd been prodding. Her eyes flicked across the prisoners, settling on Jackson. His chest now rose too fast, a hitch in the rhythm. His lips moved, muttering something too quiet to catch.

At first, she thought it was a dream. The others had nightmares. Screamed, wept, begged. Trauma was a bitter wine, and they'd drunk deep.

But Jackson's voice didn't tremble. Didn't waver. He was *chanting.*

A slow, low murmur. Words that didn't belong in any spellbook she'd studied. Rough, grinding syllables. Wrong, in that way instinct understood before language did.

Leya stood slowly, hand moving to the haft of her spellshooter. The words slipped away as she approached, the chant dissolving into a slow, sharp inhale.

Jackson's head lolled slightly, then stilled. His eyes opened.

Leya froze.

He stared up at her—not startled, not confused, just blank. His pupils were *huge*, the black swallowing almost all the color.

51

Then, as if a switch flipped, he blinked and frowned. "...Did I say something?" he asked, groggy. His voice was thick with sleep, but that frown deepened.

"You were dreaming," Leya said carefully.

He nodded, closed his eyes, and went back to sleep.

Leya didn't move. She stood there a long moment, watching the shadow Jackson cast against the stone behind him. Watching how it twitched when he didn't.


By the morning of the second day, dust rose on the far ridge, sunlight gleaming off badges and rifles.

Clint stood.

Marshal Michael Slay crested the hill, ten riders behind him, rifles up. He scanned the wreckage, the prisoners, the soot-streaked man swaying from exhaustion, arm bound, expression unreadable.

Clint raised his one good hand.

Slay rode forward, squinted, and muttered, "Well, hell. I heard the caravan got hit. Didn't expect to find the whole damn gang gift-wrapped."

Clint gave a lopsided shrug. "Took me a few tries."

Marshal Slay dismounted with measured caution, his sharp gaze flicking between Clint, Jackson, and the spellcasters. Dust settled in slow, lazy waves, curling at his boots.

"Alive?" Slay asked. He didn't sound surprised, merely assessing.

Clint nodded once. "Quarter. Formally."

Slay studied him, silence stretching between them. Finally, he exhaled and gave a short nod. "I'll make sure the judge knows." One of the riders snorted, half-laughing, half-disbelieving. Slay turned to his men. "Get them rounded up. Hands tied, mouths shut. Treat 'em like prisoners, not animals."

The posse moved in, securing chains, speaking in clipped orders. Jackson passed close to Clint, his hands already bound. Their eyes met, and for the first time since this began, Jackson smiled—small, almost thoughtful.

"You're not what I expected," he murmured. "Good job, son. You handled yourself well."

Clint only stared as Jackson was led away. He didn't want the man's respect. He wanted to go home.


Carson City loomed three days away.

They moved slowly, the battered and bleeding forcing the pace. Clint rode in the saddle longer than he should have, accepting Slay's horse only after the pain in his ruined arm became unbearable—sharp, white-hot agony crawling through his bones with every jolt of the trail.

He kept the wound bandaged tight, tucked against his chest, but the phantom weight of missing fingers haunted him. He felt them when he wasn't thinking. Expected them when he reached. Missed them when he tried to forget.

Jackson's men rode in chains but held their heads high. The spellcasters kept their word. Leya dressed Clint's arm twice, professional and impassive. Gorran rode near the front, quiet, thoughtful, watching the landscape pass.

None of them had been treated like animals, and it mattered. To them, and to Clint.


By the time Carson City's gates rose against the horizon, Clint swayed in the saddle, fever pressing behind his eyes. He'd held himself together for the journey, but the moment civilization returned, his body threatened collapse. But Clint Black didn't know how to quit.

Slay was the one who dragged him upright, half-hauling him toward the Factor's office.

George Abernathy was already pacing when they arrived, his polished boots tapping rhythmically against the wood floor. Word of the capture had spread ahead of them. When Abernathy stepped onto the porch, handkerchief in hand, he paled at the sight of Clint's state. "Sweet mother of mercy," he muttered, nearly dropping the monogrammed linen. "You—you brought them all in?"

Slay tipped his hat. "He did."

Abernathy blinked, gaze darting between them. "But your hand—?"

Slay shook his head. "Happened in the fight. And he still finished the job."

Abernathy hesitated, then motioned them inside. "We'll settle accounts. Immediately."

The office was a haven of polished wood, oil lamps, and heavy rugs. Clint sank into the nearest chair and nearly blacked out.

Abernathy rummaged through a desk drawer, retrieving two pouches—one heavy, one heavier.

"Per the contract," Abernathy began, placing the first bag on the desk, "you were set for two hundred dollars upon successful escort. However—" He dropped the second pouch beside it. "This is bounty. Eight hundred. We posted it three weeks ago when Jackson was confirmed in the territory. Bringing him in alive? Well, the Consortium values testimony."

Clint stared at the two bags as though unsure what to do with them.

Abernathy leaned forward. "You've earned it, Mr. Black. Every last coin."

Clint finally nodded, slipping both into his duster. "Thank you."

Slay clapped a firm hand against Clint's shoulder. "Now let's get that arm looked at before you pass out and ruin the rug."

The dormitory bar buzzed like a kicked beehive. Word had spread—first contract, full caravan defense, impossible odds, Jackson alive, two SpellSlingers captured.

Clint had meant to order one drink. One, then just sit in the quiet. Forget. He stepped across the threshold, under the brass plaque **Kin Before Coin,** which was in every Dormitory and Melville House, everywhere.

The moment he stepped inside, the room silenced.

Dozens of copper-rimmed gazes turned toward him. Veterans. Instructors. Journeymen. Their eyes swept over him—

one-armed, bloodstained, barely upright. Someone whispered,
"That's him!"

Then the room erupted.

A drink was pressed into his good hand before he even
reached the bar. Someone clapped him on the back. Another
barked, "You knocked Jackson off a damn cliff?"

Clint winced. "Ridge," he muttered. "Technically."

The stories twisted with each retelling. Somewhere between
his first and second drink, someone had painted him as a one-
handed gunslinger who grinned in the face of firestorms.

He didn't correct them. He was too tired.

Somewhere in the haze of conversation, someone called
him **The Wall**. It stuck.

Clint hated it. He never understood why people needed to
make symbols out of ordinary men doing their best in a bad
situation.


The corridors of the Carson City Dormitory were quiet,
candlelight flickering against the stone walls of the Master Warden's
study. The flame in the hearth crackled softly, casting warm
shadows against stacks of parchment.

Eland Marron sat with his sleeves rolled, fingers wrapped
around a low glass of dark liquor. Marshal Slay's report lay before
him—short, direct, official. Beside it, Clint Black's own account,
scrawled in precise but slightly shaky script.

When Second Warden Aven Rusk stepped inside without
knocking, Marron merely gestured toward the empty chair.

56

"Heard he made it back," Rusk said, settling in. "With all of Jackson's crew tied up like sheep. And two Slingers breathing."

Marron nodded. "He did."

Rusk exhaled. "He kill anyone he didn't have to?"

"Not one."

Rusk leaned forward slightly, elbows on knees. "That's rare."

"Very." Marron took a slow sip, eyes unreadable. "First contract. Green as cut grass. Walks out of a canyon ambush with one shell left, no backup, no hand, and fifteen prisoners. Alive."

Rusk frowned. "Should've bled out."

"Should've died screaming, you mean," Marron replied. "But he didn't panic. He moved. Dropped smoke for cover, reloaded with his damn teeth. Found terrain. Crawled behind them. Took down two trained SpellSlingers without a sound and spared them when he didn't have to."

"That's not just skill," Rusk murmured. "That's restraint."

Marron nodded. "You know how rare that is at his age. Hell, any age."

Rusk sighed, rubbing his jaw. "He's gonna make people nervous, isn't he?"

Marron smiled faintly. "He already has. The Concordium has already asked for a full report. Both from me and from Fort Sangre."

Rusk hesitated, then said, "I know someone. Mage-engineer out of San Francisco. She doesn't make replacement limbs. She makes weapons people wear. She might take an interest."

Marron considered, then nodded. "Reach out. Discreetly. Whatever the cost, put it on our books."

Rusk rose, stretching. "You really think he's that rare? Is he worth that kind of effort?"

Marron glanced at Clint's report once more, running a thumb over the last few lines. Then he exhaled. "He killed those he had to," Marron murmured. "And no one else." He looked up. "Any fool can kill indiscriminately. That's the difference."

The sky above Carson City hadn't yet decided what kind of day it would be. The sun stayed hidden behind dull gray cloud, coal smoke curling from unseen chimneys beyond the dormitory walls.

Clint Black sat on the edge of a narrow cot, awake long before the hall stirred. The oil lamp on his desk flickered, casting weak light over a battered trunk and the travel-worn revolver that had kept him alive when skill alone should not have.

His left sleeve was pinned just above the wrist. Dark fabric. Burned through. He flexed out of habit. Nothing answered.

His SpellShooter rested beside him, loaded with simple utility shells. Smoke. Force. Light. Nothing elegant—just enough to survive.

The real weight hadn't hit him in the canyon. Not during the fight. Not even in the silence afterward. It came now, when there was no danger left to outrun.

The door creaked. Clint turned, expecting Slay.

58

Instead, Second Warden Rusk stepped inside without ceremony, cloak still wet with rain. "Didn't mean to wake you," he said, already knowing he hadn't.

"You didn't," Clint replied.

Rusk crossed the room and set a small, cloth-wrapped bundle on the desk beside the revolver. "I need to speak with you."

Clint eyed it. "I'm listening."

"I know a mage-engineer in San Francisco. Independent. Best at what she does." Rusk paused. "She builds replacement limbs."

Clint lifted a brow. "Sounds expensive."

"No," Rusk said. "Covered."

"By who?"

"Slingers from three chapters. And London." Rusk's mouth twitched. "One of His Majesty's representatives offered to pay personally. Said it would be an honor to put a brick in the Wall."

Clint snorted tiredly. "I ain't the Wall."

"Not yet," Rusk said. "But you acted like one."

Clint didn't answer. He unwrapped the bundle slowly. Inside lay a schematic etched in mage-script—clean angles, copper-chased lines. The outline of a hand. Elegant. Purpose-built. Unmistakably permanent.

"I don't even know what I am yet," Clint said quietly.

Rusk crouched beside him. "You offered quarter under fire. Followed the Accords when most men forget their own names. That makes you different."

"That supposed to help?"

"No," Rusk said. "But it makes you worth the effort."

A long silence settled.

"You'll never be green again," Rusk said as he stood. "But you're not broken either."

Clint studied the schematic once more. Then he nodded. "I'm in."

At the door, Rusk paused. "Think about what you want the hand to be." Then he was gone.

Clint picked up his SpellShooter, balanced it in his good hand. Then he looked again at the design on the desk. He wouldn't be whole. But he'd be ready.

# Chapter Six

The sun hung low over the Nevada sky, casting long copper shadows across the scorched earth of the ambush site. A thin wind whispered through the pass, stirring dust and brittle fragments of wagon debris. The heat had faded days ago, but the place still smoldered with something deeper than fire.

Slay stepped carefully over a blackened axle, boots brushing soot from stone. A pale-blue memory crystal hovered near his shoulder, pulsing softly as it recorded the scene.

The stench clung thick in the air—charred wood, cold smoke, cooked meat. Death.

Some bodies had been buried in haste. Others—those caught mid-stride by Clint's inferno—had left only scorched silhouettes on the stone.

Clint stood nearby, one boot on the splintered remains of a wheel. His duster shifted in the wind. His right hand hovered near his SpellShooter.

"Don't know why," he muttered, eyes tracing the canyon walls, "but I feel watched."

"You are," Slay said. "Have been since we arrived."

Clint followed his gaze.

Six crows lined the rocky ledges above them—spaced evenly, motionless. Silent.

"Birds?" Clint asked.

Slay shook his head slowly. "I've walked more killing fields than I care to remember." He hesitated. "This one's wrong."

The memory crystal's faint hum suddenly felt too loud.

Clint crouched near the scorched outline of a fallen bandit. A faint distortion rippled in the air, warping like heat shimmer despite the cool evening. He felt it in his teeth. Pressure. Even the SpellShooter at his hip seemed to hum in response.

The wind shifted.

Every crow lifted its head at once.

Slay exhaled. "Let's not stay longer than we have to."

"I've got first watch," Clint said.

They made camp quickly. No fire burned long—just a tight circle of cold ash beneath the stars.

Sleep came shallow.

Near dawn, a sudden chill cut through the camp. The horses shifted, muscles bunching beneath their saddles.

Clint's eyes snapped open.

The shadows stretched wrong—too long, too deep for the rising sun. The air shimmered. And beneath the thin wind, the whispers came again. Not voices. Not words. Grief given sound.

Slay was already on his feet, fingers twitching toward his rifle.

"Do you feel that?" he murmured.

Clint nodded. "We need to go. Now."

They mounted fast and rode hard as the light broke over the canyon.

The whispers followed. Not fading. Not forgotten.

Justice had not been served.

Ten miles out from Copper Creek, Clint spotted a single column of dark smoke rising into the sky. Without a word exchanged, he and Slay turned their horses off the trail and headed into the wilderness. The path was rocky and mean, but the horses were trained for worse.

The wind shifted. First came the smoke. Then the smell—char and death, thick on the air like spoiled meat.

They pushed hard through brittle mesquite and dry rock, the sun searing their backs. The wind howled like something grieving.

At the top of the ridge, they reined in.

Below them, by the bend of a narrow stream, lay a Paiute village, once a sprawl of tipis and cultivated gardens. Now, it was just a scar.

The shelters had been torn apart; most burned to nothing but ash rings. The only permanent structure, a supply cabin, was still burning, flames punching into the sky.

But it was the bodies that stopped Clint cold. Men. Women. Children. Some shot. Some slit. Some tied up before they died. Slay's jaw clenched. His knuckles went white around the reins.

From down among the embers came a sound—laughter.

Near the burning cabin, eight white men stood in a loose ring. One, a hulking red-haired brute, was fiddling with his belt buckle, chuckling wetly. A girl lay at their feet. Bloodied. Bare. Barely moving.

Clint didn't breathe.

Slay didn't wait. The Marshal dropped from the saddle in one practiced motion, Winchester in hand. He took three measured steps and racked the action—loud and final, like the crack of judgment.

The men froze. Guilt hit every face. Some fumbled for their guns, sluggish with surprise.

Clint dismounted, drawing his SpellShooter. The copper chamber pulsed faintly with runes, hungry for purpose.

The Marshal squared up. "I'm Marshal Michael Slay," he said, his voice carved from stone. "Drop your weapons. Now."

The red-haired man sneered as he yanked up his trousers. "You serious? What's your problem, lawman? They's just Injuns. Ain't people." His men laughed. Ugly, hollow sounds.

Clint stepped sideways, angling for a cleaner shot. The girl was clearer now, her limbs trembling, lips moving without sound, eyes too wide. Too open.

Something began to rise in him, something dark, something he hadn't felt since Kansas City.

Slay's voice deepened. "Last warning. Disarm and lie down. Or die where you stand."

One of them moved, going for his revolver.

Clint fired first. Anger and rage can make a spell hit harder, but can also make it more unpredictable. More dangerous. The rage that rose in Clint at the treatment the girl had received magnified the power of his shot, turned what might have been a simple knockdown into something lethal. The force beam hit center mass, crushing ribs with a wet, collapsing snap. Blood jetted from the man's mouth as he folded like damp cloth.

The rest drew, panicked and wild.

Slay didn't flinch. Seven shots—methodical, measured. He worked the lever between each with mechanical calm. Twice, shots from the men grazed him, once in the ribs, and once, a line drawn on his right cheek by a shot that was entirely too close. By the time the final round cracked, only one man was left.

The brute. He laughed as he raised his gun, yellow teeth glinting. Slay's rifle clicked dry.

The brute took aim—

And the girl screamed. Not a cry for help. Not a plea. *War.*

She moved like a thrown knife, knees landing hard on his chest. Reflex caused him to catch her, to hold her. Two blades flashed in her hands—bone-handled, blooded. No one saw where they came from. Maybe she'd hidden them. Maybe the dead had dropped them.

She drove them down.

The brute staggered, clawing at her. She stabbed him in the throat. Then the cheek. Then the eye. Repeatedly, faster than reason, deeper than rage.

Red sprayed in arcs. He dropped, gurgling. She didn't stop. Even when her arms began to tremble from effort. The thing that had once been a man slowly collapsed to lie in the dirt, where he belonged.

Only when she couldn't raise the blades again did she go still.

She sat atop his ruined chest, panting, soaked in someone else's lifeblood. Her hands shook. The knives slipped to the dirt.

Slay approached slowly. He pulled a blanket from his saddle, crouched, and draped it over her shoulders. "You did good," he said gently. "He's finished. They all are."

She didn't speak. But her eyes followed him slowly, wary.

Only then did Clint lower his shooter. It didn't occur to him that he'd been standing like a statue since his first shot, watching everything that had happened over the barrel of his shooter.

His stump throbbed, phantom pain, white-hot. He looked at the girl. And something inside him settled. Not pity. Not just anger. A vow, not yet spoken.

The sun had finally sunk below the horizon, leaving behind a smoldering streak of color over the western sky. The scorched remains of the Paiute village simmered in the cooling dusk, eerily silent. No insects. No birdsong. Just the crackle of fire and the distant whisper of wind through burned timber.

A few crows lingered, half a dozen perched on broken fenceposts, black silhouettes against the fire-kissed twilight. Watching. Always watching.

Clint sat at the edge of the stream, letting the cold water strip away the blood clinging to his forearm. His stump throbbed, raw, angry, but he left it wrapped and ignored it for now.

Across the fire, the girl sat wrapped in Slay's coat, unmoving. She hadn't spoken since the fight., hadn't looked at either of them. Just stared into the flames like they held answers no one else could see.

Slay crouched a few paces away, dabbing at the long line the bullet had carved across his cheek and ear. He didn't seem to mind the blood. If anything, he looked… satisfied. "Never been shot wearin' the badge," he said, not looking up.

Clint turned his head, blinking. "That sounds like something a crazy man would brag about."

Slay smirked faintly. "Crazy gets results. I stood still so they'd shoot first. Wanted to see what kind of men they really were."

Clint grimaced. "And what kind was that?"

Slay's voice darkened. "The dying kind."

A breeze stirred the ashes, lifting embers in slow spirals before snuffing them out. Clint picked up a stick, poking at the fire absently. "There's gotta be somewhere we can leave her. Someone who'll look after her."

Slay nodded. "Actually… there is." He tore off another piece of cloth, pressing it gently to his ear. "Copper Creek's got a Melville house. Run by a man named Cyrus. SpellCaster. Used to be Warden of the Nevada Territory before he stepped down."

Clint raised a brow. "You know him?"

"No. But I've heard the name. He takes in strays. Orphans. Runaways. Cases like this." Slay gestured toward the girl. "People say the ones he raises walk out different."

Clint studied the girl. Her eyes still hadn't moved from the fire. Her knives lay nearby, cleaned and gleaming. "She's not broken," Clint said. "Just... scorched."

"They all are," Slay murmured. "We all are."

Silence settled—not awkward, just still. As if even the fire was listening.

"You didn't flinch back there," Clint said finally. "When they opened fire."

Slay leaned back on his bedroll, gazing at the stars. "Didn't see the point. If I was gonna fall, I'd rather be remembered standing."

Clint shook his head slowly. "Every shot you took... it was like the Fist of God hit 'em."

"That's the law's job," Slay said. "Not just to kill. To warn the next man."

Clint watched the embers. "If I was gonna be a lawman, that's the way I would wanna be."

Slay's expression softened. "You're already on your way. You may not be a lawman in name, but you acted like one today. The Accorded protect humanity from the dark. I protect citizens from lawbreakers. The most important part is standing for what's right."

They didn't speak after that. The fire did all the talking. When Clint finally stretched out his bedroll, he noticed the air had changed. Something had been watching. And now... it wasn't.

He looked at the girl once more. Her face was slack, peaceful. No tears. No shaking. Just a girl carved into steel by fire and blood. He whispered, "Hang on, kid. Help's not far now."

Then the night folded around them—cool, heavy, waiting.

# Chapter Seven

Savannah pulled on her copper-wire gloves and drew a quiet breath.

At the tail end of a long day, her reserves were thin—but the last few tasks were simple ones. A string of fey lights for the Jensen farm. A modest heat field for their stove. Two hours at most. Then home.

The thought of the ride back twisted uneasily in her gut. The Jensen place sat five miles beyond the wards, and lately… the wilds had been wild. She had no interest in becoming coyote bait. Or something worse.

She selected a small crystal for the lights and gathered the ambient charge through the copper weave of her gloves, threading it gently into the stone. The magic responded like a well-tuned instrument—soft, obedient.

For just an instant, the glow in the crystal tinged a shade too deep. Too warm.
Savannah stilled, corrected the flow without thinking, and the light settled back into proper blue.

No one looking would have noticed the difference.

Melville House had saved her. She had known it from the moment she arrived eight years earlier.

Everything before that was mist and shadow—except for the Apache. That part never faded. Time dulled the horror, but not the shape of it. Some days she worried she could no longer remember her mother's face as it had been before the tomahawk.

Her baby brother, she still saw clearly—small, motionless, pinned to the earth by arrows too large for his body.

Secrets came easily after that.

The apprentices whispered about her sharp edges. About how fear slid off her where it clung to others. About the way she smiled at danger like it was a challenge instead of a warning.

Cyrus had seen through all of it. Once, he'd told her she had the makings of one of the greatest SpellCasters of their age. She'd believed him—not because it sounded grand, but because he had said it like a simple fact.

She finished affixing the last copper plate for the stove just as Mother Jensen entered with a basket.

"Savannah, dear, I gathered a few things for you to take back," she said. "Vegetables, potatoes... fresh bread."

Savannah's face lit. "Thank you, Mother Jensen. I promise it won't go to waste."

Mother Jensen laughed as she tested the plate. The heat field hummed to life, the metal glowing a dull red beneath her fingertips. "Perfect."

By the time Savannah mounted Emelda, dusk had begun to settle. Wind stirred across the road, carrying cold with it. She urged the mare faster.

Gunfire cracked in the distance. Not close—but close enough. Several shots. Then silence.

Savannah leaned low over the saddle and pushed Emelda to a gallop, every nerve taut until the first welcoming glow of Copper Creek's ward-lights rose ahead. Only then did she breathe again.

Cyrus was waiting when she entered Melville House. "Hello, Butterbean," he said gently. "How'd it go?"

"Mother Jensen loved the lights. Her husband mostly loved that he can work later now." She smirked faintly. "They promised us a goat."

Cyrus nodded. Then studied her more closely. "And the rest?"

She hesitated. "I heard shooting. Out past the wards."

His eyes sharpened. He said nothing.

"I didn't investigate," she added quietly.

A faint smile touched his mouth. "For now."

Later, fatigue finally caught her in the hall outside her room. She lingered, the words heavy and unfamiliar on her tongue. Cyrus had never asked for them. Never pressured. Only waited.

"I love you, Grandpa," she said suddenly. It felt strange. Overdue. Right. She fled before he could answer—but not before she saw the look on his face, startled and bright with something like wonder.

Cyrus remained where she left him long after she was gone, staring at the quiet ceiling, letting the weight of it settle at last.

The mine stank of suffering.

Savannah walked past rows of laborers—Paiute men and boys, thin, hollow-eyed, hands cracked and bleeding, skin loose over bones that should have held muscle. Their arms strained

72

beneath baskets of rock, heads bowed, movements dulled by exhaustion.

She had seen hardship before. Had seen war. Had seen her own people stand, fight, die for the right to exist.

The Paiute weren't warriors like the Apache. They were built to endure. And that was why they were here—because white men loved things that endured.

She saw one collapse. No one moved to help him. Savannah stopped. Crouched. Unhooked her canteen and pressed it to his lips. The man flinched, then drank in desperate, choking gulps. His hands shook as he clutched the bottle. He murmured something in Paiute.

She didn't need the words.

Behind her, Rusty shifted. "You're wastin' your time and your water, SpellCaster."

She didn't look up.

"He'll be dead by sunset."

Savannah stood—slowly.

When she slid on her copper gloves, the air changed. Even the overseers felt it. Heat shimmered overhead, bending light as though the desert itself had found its way underground.

Then the air moved.

Cool. Fresh. Sweeping through the tunnel, driving out the suffocating weight of sweat and stone. The workers sagged as they drew real breath.

Savannah lowered her hands. The airflow remained.

"Take me to the pump," she said. "I want to leave."

The repair was simple.

When it was finished, Savannah wiped her gloves once on a cloth and said, "I want to see Mister Riggs. Now."

Thomas Riggs lounged with his boots on his desk when she entered.

"You needed something?" he drawled.

"You owe me one dollar."

Riggs blinked, then laughed.

"I installed a ventilation spell without Melville authorization. Independent contractor rate. One dollar."

Amused, he flipped a coin across the desk. Savannah caught it.

"Anything else?" He asked lightly.

Savannah leaned forward a fraction. The air tightened. "Why are you keeping Paiute men in chains?"

Riggs snorted. "Indentured servants."

Savannah's voice remained calm. "If you do not begin taking better care of them, there will be consequences."

Riggs grinned. "Oh yeah? What're you gonna do—make a light?"

Savannah extended one finger and touched the edge of his desk.

The oak *detonated inward* with a sharp, concussive **crack**—not an explosion, but a violent pressure failure. The desk collapsed into a roaring spill of sawdust and splintered air, the sound like a shotgun fired inside a coffin.

Riggs stumbled back, choking on dust, face drained of color. The door burst open—Duda and a guard rushed in, weapons up.

Savannah straightened her coat.

"I can do much more," she said softly. "Take care that you don't learn exactly how."

She walked past Duda without a glance.

Duda looked from the ruined desk to the shaking man behind it.

"Hell," he muttered. "I'm glad she isn't mad."


The trek back to Melville House should've cooled her off. It didn't. Savannah's hands still trembled as she unlatched the ironbound gate.

Cyrus sat on the porch, a cooling mug of tea in one hand, a pipe in the other. He looked up. "You're late."

Savannah didn't answer. He studied her face. The tension. The rage that simmered just below the surface. A familiar gleam he hadn't seen in her eyes in years. *Oh, hell*, he thought. "What did Riggs do?"

She said nothing. Cyrus blew out a slow stream of smoke. "I should've fixed that pump myself." He sighed. "But I reckon you dug the grave just fine on your own. And if it comes to it, I'll be there with a spade."

She stopped just inside the threshold. "There are slaves in that mine, Cyrus."

"I know."

She turned to him sharply.

"I know," he said again. "The whole town knows. Most of 'em hate it. But fear and power make for stubborn bedfellows."

She closed her eyes. Breathed deeply. "They'll burn for this."

Cyrus nodded. "Not yet. But soon."

"I need to go for a walk, think about all of this." She looked at Cyrus and frowned. "I want to talk to you, but I need a few minutes."

Savannah disappeared upstairs to change. Cyrus sat on the porch a while longer, pipe forgotten.

# Chapter Eight

The town of Copper Creek fell away behind them as Clint Black and Marshal Slay rode the last stretch toward Melville House. Clint rode with the Paiute girl held carefully before him in the saddle. She didn't move, didn't speak, didn't weep. She simply sat, wrapped in a patched wool blanket, her small back straight, her face a blank stone mask. The child was bone-thin, silent as snowfall, and utterly still. Clint had carried wounded men across rivers with more struggle than this girl had shown.

As they passed the outskirts of town, Clint staggered in the saddle. The wards hit him like a wall—dense, compressed power meant to keep the supernatural out of ordinary lives. The ones around the dormitory were a masterclass. "Jesus," he muttered.

Slay arched a brow. "What, son?"

"The wards. Too strong. I've never felt anything like it. How?"

"Cyrus was Warden of the Nevada Territory," Slay said. "You think they handed that title to just anybody?"

Clint shook his head. "Didn't expect that kind of power in a backwater town."

They rode on. The closer they drew, the more the hair on Clint's neck prickled. Power lingered here like weather.

Melville House rose ahead—two stories of white stone capped with copper gutters and framed windows, its iron-banded door carved with protective sigils. One pulsed faint green above the archway, slow as a heartbeat.

Slay dismounted first and gestured Clint down. Clint eased the girl from the saddle. She stood without complaint. Just waited.

"You sure they'll take her?" Clint asked.

"They've taken worse," Slay said. Then he opened the door.

Inside, cool dry air carried the scent of copper, ink, and candlewax. A young apprentice looked up from his ledger—then straightened when he saw Slay.

"Marshal Michael Slay," Slay said. "We've got a survivor. Massacre. No kin. She needs a place."

The apprentice hesitated—then another voice cut in.

"I'll take her." Cyrus stepped from a side corridor, sleeves rolled, ink fresh on his hands. Older than Clint had expected. Worn—but honed.

He knelt before the girl. "What's your name?"

"Ahyoka," she whispered.

"You're safe here," Cyrus said. "Let's get you fed." He rose and glanced at the apprentice. "A quiet room. Not the dormitory. Then find Savannah."

As the girl was led away, the door opened again—and Savannah Melville entered. Gloves still warm from casting. Jaw set.

"Cyrus."

"Thought I'd see you by dinner."

"Riggs sent me to Tunnel Three. Said the water pump was down."

"And?"

"The pump was simple. But there were slaves. Ankles in irons. They were being whipped for drinking water."

Clint stiffened. Slay's voice went to iron. "Slaves?"

"Riggs called them debt labor," Savannah said. "Then he laughed."

Silence tightened.

The door creaked again. Sharon Steed stepped in, dust on her coat, hand resting near her pistol. "I saw horses. What's wrong?"

Savannah turned. "Riggs is keeping slaves."

"Did he admit it?"

"He didn't deny it."

"What did you do?"

Savannah replied evenly. "His desk no longer exists."

Steed studied her. "How long you been here?"

"A year."

"They teach that here?"

"No."

Cyrus hid a smile. "It was a very expensive desk."

"Now it's mulch," Savannah said.

The door opened once more.

Andrezj Duda entered like he belonged to doorways—coat open, hat low, eyes reading everything. His gaze passed Savannah, Clint, Slay—then paused.

He looked toward the stairwell.

Ahyoka stood on the first landing, wrapped in wool, watching him.

Neither flinched.

Something shifted. Too subtle for words.

Duda returned his attention to the room and smiled. "Looks like I'm late to the fireworks. I bring a message from Riggs," he said. "Miss Savannah won't be returning to the mine."

Cyrus leaned back. "Understood."

"They're still sweeping what's left of his desk out of the carpet." Duda looked at Savannah again. "You left an impression."

"It was intentional."

"Good work." Not praise. Recognition. Duda's gaze drifted back to the stairwell. "The girl up there. Where did she come from?"

Slay answered. "Sole survivor of a raid. Small Paiute settlement."

Duda nodded once. "If you ever go back to that mine," he said to Savannah, "let me know ahead of time. I might take the day off."

Not a threat. Not an offer. A line. He tipped his hat and left.

Savannah removed her gloves and set them neatly on the desk. "I'm not dangerous when I'm respected."

No one argued.

Slay followed Duda into the dusk.

And upstairs, alone in her quiet room, Ahyoka watched the path below where Duda had gone.

She didn't know why yet.

But she would remember him.

And he, in ways he didn't yet understand, would never forget her.

Duda had just stepped off the porch of Melville House when Slay caught up to him, the heavy door swinging shut behind with a muffled thump. The sun hung low on the horizon, casting Copper Creek in long streaks of gold and shadow, the sky a molten spill of copper and blood. Duda didn't turn when Slay called out, didn't slow immediately. He just kept walking, hat low, boots steady against the dust-packed road.

"You deliver many messages you don't agree with, Duda?" Slay's voice was quiet, but there was iron in it.

Duda adjusted the brim of his hat, still not stopping. "I deliver the ones I'm paid for," he said after a beat. "Doesn't mean I carve 'em in stone."

Slay lengthened his stride until he walked alongside the other man. Not too close. Just enough that the air between them suddenly felt charged, like lightning was waiting for a reason. "You weren't carrying your weapon high when you came in."

"Didn't feel like dying today," Duda replied, a thin smile tugging at his lips. The words were half-joke, but the tension underneath them was real.

"She wouldn't have killed you," Slay said. His tone was dry, but there was a flicker of something else there. Amusement, perhaps. Or warning.

Duda finally glanced over, just enough to catch Slay's eye. "That's a bold assumption. I didn't live this long by betting on kindness."

They fell into silence for a while, walking slowly past the livery, the saloon, the old blacksmith's shop now half-collapsed. Slay stopped beside a worn fence post and leaned back against it, boot hooked casually on the lower rail. "You think Riggs is afraid?"

"I know he is," Duda said flatly. "Didn't even finish his drink before sending me out. But he did take the time to change his britches." He didn't smile this time.

Slay's expression didn't change. "You afraid of her?"

Duda didn't hesitate. "No."

That earned him a long look. "Why not?"

Duda's smile faded a shade. "Because I don't underestimate people. She's got that look—the one the world carves into you when it takes everything and leaves you alive anyway. She's walkin' around with a debt to settle, and I ain't dumb enough to make myself part of that account."

Slay studied him. "You've seen that look before?"

Duda nodded once, slow. "In a mirror. And in graves."

Slay tilted his head slightly, as if trying to see the man beneath the words. "You don't like Riggs."

"Never said I did." Duda's face gave away nothing, but his tone turned clipped and dry. Slay thought there might be something interesting there.

"But you still work for him."

Duda flexed his fingers at his side, adjusting his coat like it itched. "I work for the contract. And the men I brought—thanks to a sloppy clause in that same contract—they work for me, not him. Riggs doesn't even know how badly he screwed himself."

Slay was quiet again. Watching. Measuring. "So why not walk?"

Duda looked up at the sky, still streaked with fire. "Because if I do, someone worse takes my place. Someone without limits. Without shame." His voice didn't rise, didn't break, but there was something in it—something cracked and old.

Silence stretched between them again.

Slay scratched lightly at the side of his face, where the wound still itched from the village. "You think you're a good man, Duda?"

Duda turned his gaze back to him. "Good?" he asked, voice flat. "No. I'm just necessary. Men like me, we get the job done. We don't flinch, we don't stall, and we don't lie to ourselves about what we are."

The words hung there a while, heavy in the cooling air.

Slay let out a breath. "If it comes down to it—between her and Riggs—where do you land?"

Duda didn't answer right away. He glanced back toward Melville House, toward one of the second-floor windows lit by pale blue glow. Then his eyes dropped, and his brow furrowed.

She was still standing there. The Paiute girl. Ahyoka. Wrapped in a too-large blanket, her frame small and worn down to the edge of survival. She was framed in the window, barely visible, but her eyes—those eyes—watched them both, unblinking. She didn't look afraid. She looked… present. Like she was waiting for something.

Duda felt something twist behind his ribs, something that hadn't stirred in years. He thought of the orders. Riggs' voice. The Bear and his men, dead now. He hadn't been there. He hadn't touched a blade or fired a shot. But he'd passed down the word. That was enough. He remembered the girl at the stairs, standing like a revenant under a blanket. And he knew.

He'd seen the aftermath of his orders before. Burnt buildings. Shattered men. That came with the job. But he'd never had to look it in the eyes. Never had it *look back*.

Slay waited, watching him. And finally, Duda looked away from the window and said, "If she ever goes back to that mine, Marshal, I'll be real slow gettin' in her way."

Slay nodded once. Not in approval. Not in agreement. Just acknowledgment.

Duda tipped his hat. "Evenin', Marshal."

"Duda."

The enforcer turned and walked off into the failing light, hands loose, gait easy—but Slay knew better. Something in that man had changed.

He didn't know what. But he suspected it had everything to do with a silent girl behind a sigil-marked window. And a long chain of sins that finally had a face.

# Chapter Nine

Slay stepped back into Melville House, the weight of his talk with Duda still clinging to him. The parlor hadn't quieted in his absence. If anything, the tension had thickened.

Steed stood near the window, arms folded. "It's spreading," she said without preamble. "Riggs fired the miners. Brought in 'contract workers.' Slaves, in everything but name. Homesteads on the outskirts are burning. His men are drinking in town every night and daring someone to stop them."

Slay nodded once. "And the town?"

"Angry," Steed said. "And scared. Which makes people stupid."

Slay glanced at Clint, then back to her. "If Jackson talks, are you going to interfere?"

Steed's jaw tightened. "My deputies swore oaths. Jackson has supporters. But slavery never took root here—not before the war, not after. This?" She shook her head. "This won't stand. Just don't expect applause."

"That's enough," Slay said.

She studied him a moment. "Riggs is the rot. Duda's the knife. I'd rather deal with the knife."

Slay exhaled softly. He didn't argue.

Her gaze shifted to Clint. "You're the one who brought Jackson in?"

Clint nodded. "Yes, ma'am."

"By yourself?"

"Yes, ma'am."

She looked him over again, slower this time. Clint lifted his left arm, just enough for the blood seeping through the bandage to speak for him.

"That answer your question?" he said quietly.

Steed let out a breath. "It does."

Silence settled. Not awkward. Respectful.

Slay broke it. "The girl."

Steed straightened. "She alive?"

"Yes."

"Then that's something," she said. "What happens now?"

Slay turned to Cyrus. "If we ride out again, we can't take her."

Cyrus nodded. "She stays here."

"She was assaulted," Slay added. "Badly."

Cyrus didn't flinch. "Then she needs walls. Time. Someone who understands fire."

Savannah, standing near the door, didn't look away.

"She Paiute?" Cyrus asked.

"We think so."

"Then eventually, we find her people," Cyrus said. "For now, Melville House." Steed nodded once. Decision made.

Slay rolled his shoulders. "We'll eat, clean up, and ride. Jackson's camp comes first."

Steed's mouth tightened. "Half the town thinks he's a hero."

"So did I," Slay said. "Until I saw what he left behind."

Clint spoke without heat. "He talks like he's righteous. But killing civilians to stop injustice is just evil with a better speech."

Steed snorted softly. "You'll learn. Sometimes it's still the only option."

Slay glanced at her. "Sometimes."

Clint shifted. "Marshal… the girl."

"She stays," Slay said. "We don't abandon survivors." That was that.

A beat later, Clint added, "Before we do any of that—can I get a bath? I smell like sulfur and bad decisions."

Steed huffed a laugh. "Saloon's got rooms. Watch the mine guards."

Slay's smile was thin. "We're good with difficult men."

Outside, twilight softened Copper Creek's edges. They walked a few paces in silence.

"Partner?" Clint said finally.

Slay paused. "You objecting?"

"No," Clint said. "Just surprised."

Slay nodded once. "Get used to it."

The saloon quieted when they entered. A table cleared. No one argued.

Clint sat, scanning the room. "So. The mine."

"One problem at a time," Slay said. "Jackson first."

Clint leaned back. "Feels like a rigged game."

Slay's eyes were steady. "Then we play honest and mean."

Clint nodded. "Let's play, then."

The lamps in the hall outside the infirmary burned low, casting long, syrupy shadows against the plaster walls. The air was cool—not cold—but it thrummed faintly with the aftermath of pain and power, like something enormous had exhaled and left its breath lingering in the quiet.

Savannah stood still just inside the threshold. Her hands were tucked into the sleeves of her robe. Her eyes were calm, but edged. There was controlled fire behind every blink. Her hair was tied back hastily, ink smudges on the side of her neck. She had not come to rest.

She had come because something had pulled her.

At the far side of the infirmary, sitting upright on one of the clean linen beds, was the girl. Small, but not fragile. Wrapped in a borrowed blanket, legs folded under her, posture straight as a blade. She had been bathed, her long black hair brushed until it shimmered in the lamplight, but her eyes were untouched by comfort. They were black glass. Still. Watching Savannah.

The two stared at one another in silence for several breaths.

Then the girl said, softly, "You're the one who burned them."

Savannah flinched. Not visibly. But behind her ribs, somewhere quiet and wounded, she felt the rip—fresh again. The ache that hadn't stopped since the firestorm. "I didn't mean to."

"I know." Another breath.

"You're safe now," Savannah said. And even as she said it, she knew it wasn't true. The girl knew it too. But the words had to be said. They were a bridge. A promise, if not yet a reality. The girl slid off the bed, bare feet whispering against the wood floor. She walked to within three paces of Savannah, never looking away. Up close, Savannah saw that her eyes were too old for her face. Not tired—ancient. Worn from the inside out.

"You have a name?" Savannah asked gently, crouching to meet her eyes.

The girl studied her a moment. Then, without hesitation, she said: "Ahyoka."

Savannah's breath caught in her throat. The name hit her like a blow to the sternum. She hadn't heard that name spoken in years—not since the day the soldiers came. Her best friend's voice had echoed through the canyon that day, laughter like wind in the stone. The only other girl who knew what it meant to feel the world speak.

Savannah rocked back, stunned. Her mouth was dry. "That... that was my friend's name. From when I was little."

"I know," Ahyoka said.

The way she said it—soft, certain, unquestioning—unnerved Savannah. Not because it was strange. Because it wasn't. There was no tremor in the air. No flash of magic. Just the kind of truth that doesn't need explanation.

Savannah didn't ask how she knew. Some answers don't belong to words. "I won't ask you about what happened," Savannah said quietly. "Not until you're ready. But I will tell you this: you are not broken. And you do not have to be alone."

Ahyoka didn't move, but her shoulders sank—just slightly. Just enough.

"You'll stay here, with us," Savannah said. "You'll find your healing. On your own time. And if you can't? We'll carry it with you."

Silence stretched. Then Ahyoka nodded. "I think I was waiting for you."

Savannah reached forward, gently brushing a strand of hair from the girl's forehead. Her fingers trembled. "I think... I was waiting for you too."

They stood together in the stillness for a long moment—two pieces of kindling that had survived the same fire.

Andrezj "Andy" Duda didn't shout. He didn't threaten. He didn't need to.

When he walked into a room, people stopped talking. Not because they feared a beating—but because they feared being noticed. Being seen by Andrezj Duda was like being pinned beneath the weight of a mountain—immovable, inescapable, inevitable.

This morning, the office was quiet. The kind of quiet that preceded bad news or bad weather. Duda sat in his worn and patched easy chair, staring at a grease-smeared report. Six indentured miners drowned in a tunnel after a failed pump allowed the area to fill with runoff. The miners were chained in place and couldn't even move out of the water. What a waste. The report included the usual bureaucratic nonsense—date stamps, foreman initials, maintenance requests never followed up on. Duda read it once. Then again. He closed the folder gently and placed it beside his custom Peacemaker, as if it were just another problem waiting to be solved with a single pull of the trigger.

"Hurley," he said without looking up.

The door opened immediately. Hurley, Duda's assistant, stepped in with the ease of a man long inoculated to danger. While the rest of the staff lived in a state of wary dread, Hurley alone moved through the blast radius without fear. Not just because Duda trusted him—but because he was useful. And because Duda never wasted ammunition on tools that still worked.

"Yes, boss?"

"I want the tunnel foreman in front of me," Duda said. "Now."

Hurley nodded and left. Exactly nine minutes later, Rusty Wallace was shown in.

The foreman had tried to clean up—scrubbed hands, slicked hair—but there was still dirt under his nails and panic behind his eyes. He stepped across the threshold like a man walking into a lion's den with pork chops strapped to his knees.

92

Duda didn't stand. He didn't even gesture. He just stared.

Rusty's confidence broke before he said a word.

"You know why you're here?" Duda asked softly, voice like worn leather.

"I—I read the report too, Mr. Duda," Rusty stammered. "There were... issues with the pump, I—"

"Did you fix it?"

"No, sir."

Duda nodded once. "And did you notify me directly?"

Rusty hesitated. "I filed the requests."

"Filing isn't the same as fixing," Duda said, rising smoothly to his full height. He moved around the desk like a shark circling a bleeding swimmer. He wasn't fast. He didn't need to be. Every step radiated inevitability. "I asked your father to send you here because he said you were dependable," Duda said. "He said you were smart. Said you could follow instructions."

He stopped just in front of the younger man, who had the decency to tremble. "I don't like being embarrassed," Duda continued, almost kindly. "But more than that, I don't like cleaning up someone else's dead." He punched Rusty once. A clean, professional shot to the face that dropped the foreman to the floor with a broken nose, like a sack of wet grain. The silence that followed was absolute.

Rusty coughed, tried to speak, then slowly pushed himself upright. Duda watched him rise with a flicker of interest, like a gambler watching dice roll. Blood streamed from Rusty's nose, but he didn't wipe it. Duda admired that. "I had to request a 'Caster," Duda said. "To fix what you didn't. You made me look like a fool to Riggs. That's unforgivable. I've killed men I knew better than you for less."

Rusty nodded once, slow, deliberate. Duda leaned in just enough to be in Rusty's breath. "Next time, don't make me choose between respect and reputation. I know which I value more."

He turned, already done with the conversation. "Hurley! Get an orderly in here. We've got cleanup." Hurley was already there.

"And Rusty," Duda said without looking back, "tell the rest of the foremen and guards. We hit the quota. No matter what it takes. Or who has to die." As Rusty left, staggering, Duda sat back down, hands folded in front of him.

He waited for the door to close. Then he frowned. He had forgotten for a minute that the Bear was dead. Riggs was going to want a follow-up mission to finish the work the Bear had started. And Duda was through using his own men for work like that. Bear and his 'men' were a bad choice, mercs who happened to be available in a hurry. Riggs had hired thugs who had no conscience. Let them get their hands dirty. Or themselves killed. Riggs, stupid son of a bitch that he was, would be next. He had no idea he was circling the one man who wouldn't hesitate.

Riggs thought the mine made him powerful. But power, real power, was knowing when to use violence—and when not to. Duda smiled, thin and cold, then picked up the next report.

# Chapter Ten

A large man, dark-skinned and road weary, rode a slow-moving horse along the dusty track into Copper Creek. His name was Kimari Jacobs, and though his coat was worn and his boots scuffed from hundreds of miles of hard travel, there was nothing tired in the way he held himself. His spine was straight, his gaze level, and the rhythm of his ride spoke of a man who had walked through hell without ever laying down his principles.

He paused at the crest of a shallow rise, the scattered town lying quiet beneath a low sky. The buildings were rough-hewn, some already sagging from bad wood and bad planning. Still, they stood. That meant someone here had hope.

Jacobs removed his wide-brimmed hat and wiped his forehead with a crisp blue handkerchief. The morning sun hadn't yet hit its stride, and already the heat pulsed up from the earth in waves. "Not even ten," he muttered to himself, voice like gravel wrapped in velvet. "Hot enough to burn truth out of a liar."

He checked the loads in his Colt Peacemaker, then slid his fingers across the warm barrel of his Winchester '88. She gleamed faintly with her coppered finish—Bessie, his oldest companion. She'd never failed him. He treated her like a holy relic. In many ways, she was. Certainly, she had fought enough evil.

The trail had been long from Kansas City. Jacobs hadn't planned to run, not again. But five dead men in a saloon meant five families grieving. He hadn't started that fight. But he'd finished it. And none of those men had been fully men anymore, not after what they'd become. But they'd looked human enough when they died.

Sometimes, God asked you to end things.

He nudged his horse forward, letting the hoofbeats echo into town.

As he passed the first weathered shacks, he found the street strangely still. One man stepped out of his path, looking down, then away. Jacobs didn't take offense. He understood the weight of his presence. He wasn't just a big man on a tired horse. He was black, he was armed, and he carried the scent of righteous fire, like judgment rode beside him.

Outside the farrier's shop, a man bent over an old mare's rear hooves. Jacobs dismounted, stretching slow and easy. He approached with a nod.

"Mornin'," he said, smiling faintly. "You got time to reshoe my horse? Tossed a back one yesterday."

The farrier looked up, took him in, then straightened. "Yep. Be a while, though. Gonna be late 'fore he's done."

Jacobs unbuckled his saddle. "Ain't in a rush. Been riding a long time. Name's Kimari Jacobs."

The farrier shook his hand—rough palm to rough palm. "Joe. I run the place."

"Appreciate it, Joe. Know anywhere a man can sleep a few nights?"

Joe hesitated, then said plainly, "Hotel don't take colored folk. Barn, maybe. Or someone kind enough to offer a cot."

Jacobs only nodded. "Slept in worse." He fished a twenty-dollar gold Eagle from his duster and passed it over. "This cover shoes and a few days' board?"

Joe bit the coin, gave a nod. "It does."

Jacobs set his gear down in the shop corner. Then he slung Bessie over his shoulder. She caught the sun and cast it back like fire. The look she got from townsfolk was worth more than gold. Folks didn't bother SpellSlingers—not even fake ones. The general store gave him no trouble. Another gold piece got him all he needed but bullets.

"You'll need Svensen for that," the shopkeeper said. "Gunsmith, just down the way. He don't smile much, and he don't care for anyone, but he's honest."

Jacobs tipped his hat. "Good to know."

By the time he reached the open-air kitchen, his stomach was protesting in earnest. Smoke rose from cook fires and the smell of salt pork and cornmeal choked the air. Miners of every color sat around scarred tables—white, Black, and Chinese, each man hunched over tin plates.

The cook behind the grill—white, stout, and sun-reddened—looked up as Jacobs approached. His eyes flicked to the rifle, then back to Kimari's face.

"Been on the trail?"

Jacobs nodded. "Three weeks. Hopin' you feed strangers."

"Ham, eggs, redeye gravy and sourdough?"

Jacobs laughed, a low, rolling sound. "That'll do just fine."

"Quarter. Coffee's free if you sit polite."

"I sit polite," Jacobs said, handing over the coin. "Even when I'm hungry."

The food was divine. He ate slow, listening. The mood in town was cracked. Miners were bitter—some dismissed, some displaced. Too many whispers about who was replacing them, not enough about why. No one looked at Jacobs twice once he sat down. Not after they saw how he sat. Still. Ready. Watchful.

Finally, he turned toward the gunsmith's shop—neat, meticulous, and quiet. Svensen met him with a cool gaze, tall as a chimney and twice as straight.

"Help you?"

"Need forty-five-seventy ammo. Bessie here likes to eat silver when the mood's right."

"You want custom?"

Jacobs reached into his saddlebag, produced a small, smooth ingot. "Silver slugs. No spell work. Just honest metal."

Svensen raised a brow but said nothing for a moment. Then, finally, "Bring me another Eagle. Two days."

Jacobs nodded once. "I'll be back."

When he stepped out onto the street, the sun had crested overhead. Copper Creek shimmered in heat and dust and the tension of something building just out of sight. Kimari Jacobs breathed it in, eyes sweeping the town. No, not home. Not yet. But he felt it in his bones. There was work here. Righteous work. And maybe—just maybe—that was enough.

Marshal Michael Slay and the SpellSlinger rode out early, dust trailing behind their mounts as the rising sun burned away the last traces of morning cool. Slay hadn't slept much. Today, he wanted answers—from Thomas Riggs, the mine superintendent. He didn't expect truth, but he'd settle for the tremor in a liar's voice.

The Copper Creek mine sprawled like a wound across the earth. Spoil piles, slurry pits, and rusting tailings stained the landscape. Hundreds of workers swarmed like ants, some hauling ore, others bent beneath sacks, guards with rifles pacing among them. From a distance, it was noise and motion; up close, it smelled like sweat, blood, and slow dying.

After a word with a stone-faced foreman, a guard escorted them toward one of two plank buildings that rose like scabs above the chaos. Inside, they found a man lounging in a threadbare velvet chair, one boot kicked over the armrest, a tumbler of amber liquor in hand. He was watching the mine through a cracked window.

He didn't rise at first. When he did, it was slow and theatrical, a man showing off. "Thomas Riggs," he said, holding out a damp hand toward the Marshal.

"Marshal Slay," Slay replied, taking it with the minimal grace of someone used to shaking hands with snakes.

Riggs didn't offer his hand to Clint, and Clint didn't mind. You don't reach into the gutter unless you're cleaning it.

Riggs motioned lazily to two mismatched chairs. "Please. Sit. Brandy?"

"It's a bit early," Slay said.

Riggs poured anyway. "Here, we work twenty-hour days. Time's a lie."

He took a sip, swirling the glass as he leaned back. "So, Marshal, what brings you to my humble operation? The government still want their copper? I'm just doing what needs doing."

Slay's face didn't change. "We need to talk about your labor policy."

Riggs's grin sharpened. "Since when is labor your business?"

"Since it turned into slavery. That's against the Constitution."

The grin faltered, just a little. "Indentured contracts. Legal as sunrise. The government gets its ore, I get work done. Everybody wins."

"No," Slay said flatly. "Not everybody."

Riggs barked a short laugh. "Let me guess—Sheriff Steed put you up to this. She's got her boots tangled up in morals, keeps sticking her nose where it don't belong."

Slay didn't blink. "Sheriff's busy cleaning up your men's damage. I'm here because of Jackson."

Riggs's tone changed. Just a shade. "Jackson's sore because I stopped hiring white miners and started using Native labor. Cheaper. Don't complain as much."

Clint shifted in his chair. "You mean, slaves."

Riggs shot him a look. "They owe debts. They work them off. It's all in writing."

Slay's voice cooled. "How many have worked off their debt?"

Riggs hesitated, then snorted. "None. Lazy bastards spend more time sick or hiding than working."

Slay and Clint exchanged a glance. That told them everything they needed. "We're done here," Slay said, rising.

And then the world exploded.

A blast tore through the air, so loud it seemed to pull the oxygen out of the room. The windows shattered inward in a storm of glass and wind. Riggs hit the ground, brandy flying. Clint shielded his face with his good arm, already moving. Slay didn't duck. He turned toward the door.

Outside, the sky boiled with black smoke. The guard barracks were gone—obliterated, reduced to flame, ash, and body parts. Charred debris littered the ground. Screaming echoed from the edge of the crater where survivors crawled, stumbled, or didn't move at all.

Clint's sharp eyes caught something—white fluttering on the ruined frame of Riggs's door. A paper, held with a single pin.

He plucked it loose and read it. Crude block letters, smeared in grease.

**FREE SLAVES OR YOU NEXT.**

He handed it to Slay, who read it in silence, jaw working.

Slay handed it to Riggs. "Looks like someone else has an opinion about your labor policy."

Riggs read it. His skin went pale. "There were twenty men in that barracks. Asleep."

"They're in hell now," Clint said quietly. "You should rethink your policy. Or at least upgrade your security."

As they turned to leave, a new voice thundered across the field. Duda.

The mine enforcer stormed out of the shaft, his coat dusty, his face unreadable. A soft-looking assistant struggled to keep up behind him. Duda's eyes swept over the burning crater, the wounded, the stunned crowd. His jaw clenched. He began barking orders at the guards, voice sharp as breaking glass.

Clint and Slay mounted up in silence, the air thick with ash, accusation, and the distant, vengeful echo of thunder.


Savannah arrived at the mine like a breath of clarity through the smoke and screaming. She dismounted quickly, her long coat snapping in the hot wind. Behind her, Cyrus slid down from his own mount, his older frame moving with surprising precision for a man his age. The two of them crossed the rubble-strewn yard without hesitation, spellbooks already in hand.

The makeshift triage was chaos. Miners, guards, and broken bodies lay scattered like discarded dolls. Some moaned. Some didn't. Savannah knelt beside the first man she reached—an indigenous worker with shrapnel across his chest. Her fingers glowed with subtle caster light as she steadied his pulse and began drawing the pain into herself with a quiet chant.

Cyrus moved like a surgeon of light, sharp and economical. His gestures spun diagnostic glyphs through the air. He barked precise orders to miners still able to move, directing them to fetch water, bandages, or makeshift stretchers. He treated three men before most had taken their next breath.

Riggs stood on the ruined office porch, watching. For once, he said nothing. Liquor forgotten. Eyes fixed on the calm in Savannah's movements and the crackling order in Cyrus's. Then, almost to himself, he muttered, "I'm leaving."

Duda turned his head, one brow raised. "Leaving?"

"So she can work," Riggs said, nodding toward Savannah. "I know better than to get in her way."

Duda blinked. It was the most honest thing Riggs had ever said in his presence.

"Didn't expect that outta' you," Duda said, voice low.

"You think I'm stupid?" Riggs snapped, but there was no fight behind it. "I've seen what she can do." He walked off without another word.

Duda watched him go, then turned back toward the smoking crater. His face, carved from granite, didn't move—but something behind his eyes tightened. "These were my men," he muttered to no one in particular. "My men." Then, without raising his voice, he began issuing orders. "Double the perimeter. I want a guard on every rise and rooftop before sundown. Nobody gets near this pit without clearance."

A chorus of "Yes, sir" followed as if by instinct. The remaining guards, many of them shell-shocked, straightened their shoulders and moved. Orders given by Duda were a lifeline in a world of chaos.

When the last survivor was stabilized and the worst of the dying eased into peace, Savannah staggered slightly. Cyrus caught her arm, murmuring something low and steady. The worst of the chaos was over—for now.

Duda moved through the rubble personally, not content to stand and delegate. He knelt beside the broken beams and twisted iron, brushing ash aside with a hand already blackened with soot.

Hurley appeared at his side, red-faced and winded. "Sir?"

"We're not done," Duda said. "There's something here. No way this was just a bomb and a message. Help me look." The two men moved deliberately through the wreckage, peeling back debris, checking the pattern of the blast, their quiet efficiency belying the weight of the moment.

Savannah worked over a guard whose leg had been nearly severed. Her eyes were hollow with fatigue, but her hands were steady. The magic flowing from her palm closed the worst of the wound. The guard would live. And walk again.

Workers began whispering around her, reverent. "That girl's no ordinary Caster," one muttered. "She's somethin' else."

"She saved my boy last month," said another. "Wasn't even asked. Just saw he was sick and helped."

Duda returned to the edge of the triage circle, boots crunching glass. "You saved lives today," he said. His voice was iron, but there was something else under it—respect.

Savannah nodded, eyes red. "Not enough."

"It never is," Duda said. His gaze flicked to the dark smoke still curling into the sky. "But it's a hell of a start." He didn't thank her. But he didn't need to. When their eyes met, the truth was clear. She had just earned the quiet loyalty of the roughest men in the territory—and the unspoken allegiance of the one man who held Copper Creek mine together by sheer force of will.

The sun was still low when Marshal Slay and Clint Black rode into the hills northeast of Copper Creek. The terrain was dry, dotted with scrub and wind-warped rock, and silent save for the soft clop of hooves and the occasional whirr of a distant bird. Slay led the way, guiding them from memory and instinct more than any map. Clint rode a little stiffly, his left arm bound just below the elbow, the wound still raw and aching beneath the bandages. Pain was a constant companion.

They crested a ridge and came upon it—a basin ringed by sandstone bluffs and streaked with the remains of a once-busy camp. Tents had stood here, maybe even for weeks. Now they were gone, leaving behind scorched outlines, broken stakes, and cold ash.

Slay swung down from his saddle, his face grim. "They were here. Recently."

Clint dismounted more slowly, wincing. "Camp like this, you don't build it overnight. But they pulled out fast. Left like they were being chased."

Tracks were everywhere. Deep ruts where wagons had been hastily loaded. Shovel marks, drag trails, even old boot prints. Clint stepped into the hollow of what had been a tent and kicked aside a half-buried crate. Copper ore spilled out—raw and unrefined.

Slay examined a burned scrap of parchment caught in the brush. Runes charred and faded, but he recognized the pattern. "Caster work. A masking ward. Cheap, fast, but clever."

Clint looked over, brow furrowed. "You thinking Jackson's got a real 'Caster?"

"I'm thinking someone bigger's helping him." Slay's tone was flat. "Someone who knew exactly how long to stay and when to vanish."

They found no bodies. No signs of a fight. Just signs of deliberate, thorough abandonment.

Near the bluff's edge, a crude lean-to had been set up as a lookout. Inside, Slay found a pack of partially burned ledgers. Most were ruined, but a few pages survived. Notations, copper weights, locations. One read:
**"Mule train ready. Creek crossing. Drop before second moon. All evidence destroyed."**

"Laundering," Clint muttered. "They're not just stealing copper. They're hiding where it's going."

Slay flipped the page, jaw clenched. "And none of this points back to Jackson. He's a front. Maybe a useful one. But someone's hiding behind him."

They stood quietly for a moment, the wind picking up dust in the clearing.

"Whoever they are," Clint said, his voice low, "they don't care who gets hurt. Or who dies."

Slay gave a short nod. "This isn't just greed. It's control. Of the territory, maybe more."

Clint looked out over the empty basin, his one good hand flexing unconsciously near his shooter.

"We need to find their next move," he said. "Before the next camp vanishes." He sounded tired, but his gaze was steady.

## Chapter Eleven

The moon was low and pale over Copper Creek, its light sifting through the bare trees like veiled warning. Mayor Dooley walked silently up the narrow path from his house, holding a small glass bottle and a rag. On the breeze, the faint scent of chloroform lingered—sharp and chemical, cutting through the late-night cool.

Inside the modest farmhouse, the Landshire home lay hushed. The little girl slept in her bed, entirely unaware. Dooley paused at her door, listening. At the next room over, the father stirred—a groan in his sleep—but didn't wake. Dooley pressed a gloved finger to his lips, shushing no one, and slipped inside.

The child's breath came soft and slow. Dooley moved with clinical calm. He saturated the rag and pressed it gently to her cheeks, holding it in place. She stirred once, eyelids fluttering, but didn't wake. The rag slipped down, weighted with ether. Within heartbeats, she drifted back into darkness.

Dooley murmured, then lifted her—still limp—into his arms. He carried her miles to his home, into the house, past the painting of his smiling family above the hearth and out the back door without a sound. Across the dark fields toward the barn where he kept his tools.

---

The barn's rough wooden walls smelled of old hay, dust, and rusting metal. A single low window spilled moonlight in pale stripes onto a straw-dusted floor. Dooley secured the gag and tightened the ropes around her tiny frame. He brushed a strand of hair from her face as she stirred, whispering something too quiet for her to register.

She woke with a muffled sob.

Tears glistened on her cheeks as she realized where she stood, naked, helpless, eyes wide with dread. Dooley held the hatchet loosely at his side, its blade catching streaks of moonlight.

He stepped closer, breathing slow and steady.

Her panic rose. A muffled scream tore from her throat. "*No! No!*"—but the gag silenced it. She pulled against the ropes, chest heaving. Her eyes begged the barn's shadowed corners for any hope.

Dooley paused, gaze level and unblinking.

The barn remained still for a heartbeat longer. Then the gurgle of tears, and the creek of a loose board overhead. The moonlight on his blade flashed once, ice-cold.

Outside, the wind stirred among the long grass. A tumbleweed rolled across the yard, skidding across the dirt as the world held its breath.

And then—silence.

Andrejz Duda was nearly certain one of his guards was stealing copperplate. That wasn't the real problem. Most of the guards probably skimmed a little—Duda wasn't naïve. The problem with Teddy O'Shea was that he was sloppy, careless...and now, he'd been noticed by Riggs. And Riggs didn't let things go.

The guard had just racked his rifle and was reaching for his hat when Duda caught him.

"Hey, Teddy? Need a word about shaft number three."

O'Shea straightened. "Sure thing, Mister Duda. Just so you know, that pump failure wasn't on me. I told the foreman before it went."

"I know, Teddy." Duda's voice was friendly. "Still need a few notes for the report. Come on back to my office."

"Yes, sir." If O'Shea was nervous, he didn't show it. That was his first mistake.

Inside the cramped office, Duda poured two short glasses of whiskey. "Drink?"

O'Shea blinked in surprise. "Thank you, Mister Duda."

Duda raised his glass, clinked it gently, then took a sip. "Teddy, how long have we known each other?"

The guard tilted his head while he thought. "Um..three or four years now, sir. Since Missouri."

"That's right. Three or four years." He sipped his whiskey, set it down. "So," he said mildly, "how long you been stealing from me?"

The stunned look that crossed O'Shea's face was all the confirmation Duda needed. When the guard half-rose from his chair, Duda's fist struck like a hammer to the gut. The whiskey came back up in a sour rush as O'Shea folded over himself and fell gasping to the floor.

"You really should've known better," Duda muttered.

O'Shea tried to speak. "Mister Duda, I—I'm sorry—"

Duda didn't wait for the end of the sentence. He slammed his knuckles into the man's jaw, then brought his boot down hard on O'Shea's knee. The joint cracked with a noise that would stay with them both. O'Shea screamed, high and sharp, then crumpled into a sobbing mess. A dark stain spread across his trousers.

Duda stepped back, breathing through his nose, watching the man writhe. "You're gonna be sorry, Teddy. That's a promise."

Later that evening, Duda knocked once and entered Riggs' office without waiting for an answer.

Riggs looked up from behind a cluttered desk. "Evening, Andy. How'd it go?"

Duda's face gave nothing away. "Fine. He had four pounds of copperplate under his coat. I took care of it. Crippled him and sent him on his way."

Riggs leaned back with satisfaction. "Good. Nobody steals from me. Nobody. I want him dead, though—once it won't point back to us."

Duda barely blinked. "Understood."

"Did he have family?"

"Wife. Son. They're in town."

Riggs didn't hesitate. "Them too."

Duda's voice cooled. "You want the wife and boy dead?"

Riggs looked up, eyes glittering. "I do. Sends a message. People need to *remember* what happens when you cross me."

Duda nodded once. "Yes, sir." *No, sir*, he thought.

Riggs shifted, brushing a fleck of dust from his cuff. "Anything on the bomb?"

108

Duda's jaw set. "Nothing solid. Found moccasin prints in the dirt, shallow ones. Could've been Paiute. There are two villages still in the area. Maybe one lost a family member. Still no sign of the Bear's crew. Pretty sure they are the ones the Marshal and his 'Slinger killed."

"Wouldn't shock me." He blew out a breath. "That Marshal seems like a tough nut."

"Maybe," Duda allowed. "Haven't had time to confirm. Been too busy shoveling bodies."

Riggs rose slowly, walked to the window, stared out at the smoke rising from the wreckage. "I want those villages gone. Both of them. Slaves if we can take 'em, but no survivors. Burn it down."

Duda's eyes narrowed just slightly. "You sure that's smart? There'll be talk. Maybe even retaliation."

Riggs turned. "I hired you because you weren't afraid of blood. You've done good work, Andy. You're richer now than you've ever been, because you do what I say. This is me saying it plain. I want them erased. Do it."

There was no room for debate. Not here.

Duda gave a single, clipped nod. "Understood. Gonna need to use your men, though."

Riggs frowned. "Why my men?"

Duda said, "Because I don't have men to send out, not and keep the mine guarded."

As he stepped out into the night, Duda didn't feel anger. Not yet. Just the same slow burn that had been building since the day he shook Thomas Riggs' hand. He had no intention of going after O'Shea's family. Getting fired now wouldn't be the worst thing. *One day,* he promised himself. *I am going to knock your dick in the dirt. Bet on it.*

The outer door creaked.

Steed looked up to see young Joseph Tompson—no more than ten, son of the general store owner—standing pale-faced in the doorway.

"Sheriff! There's a problem at the saloon! Miss Sal sent me—said some mine guards are making trouble!"

Steed sighed. She stood, buckled on her gun belt, and grabbed her short-barreled shotgun from the rack. She checked it was loaded, as always. "You never know," she said to herself as she reached for the door.

As she neared the saloon, the absence of noise was louder than music ever could've been. No laughter. No drunken piano. Just a heavy, expectant hush.

She approached slowly, peered through the window. At least thirty people inside, packed tight and tense. All eyes were turned toward the bar, where two drunken mine guards stood over a man in a ridiculous brocade waistcoat—fancy, terrified, and wet down one leg.

There were no deputies in sight. Of course there weren't.

Steed took a breath, pushed open the swinging doors, and stepped into the room with the kind of deliberate calm that made men think twice.

Heads turned. The tension shifted. Some of the townsfolk looked hopeful. Others—especially the guards—scowled.

The bigger of the two guards, clearly drunk and full of bluster, had a fistful of the gambler's shirt and was yelling in his face. "You son of a bitch! Give us our money back! You cheated us!"

The gambler shook his head frantically. "I didn't cheat no one! If you don't know how to play, don't sit at the table!"

The second guard, lean and red-faced, cracked the gambler across the mouth with his revolver. Teeth and blood hit the floor.

That was enough.

Steed stepped forward. The big one spun around, Colt already up, until he saw her.

He grinned, cruel and stupid. "Well, well. The bitch herself. You always come running when someone pisses in the sawdust?"

"Why don't you point that gun somewhere else before I arrest you for disorderly conduct?" Her voice was dry and even.

He sneered. "How 'bout you and me go upstairs, and we talk about your manners? You're a little long in the tooth, but you got a hell of a backside."

Behind the bar, Sal slowly slid her own shotgun into position. Rock salt, real low cut, just in case.

Steed grimaced. "Put your gun away. Now."

The guard grinned wider. "You ain't even got no deputy with ya."

Just then, the saloon doors creaked again.

Marshal Slay and Spellslinger Clint Black stepped in, both with holstered weapons, calm eyes, and the kind of presence that could turn the air heavy.

Clint looked around. "We were just here for a drink. Didn't know there was a show, too." His voice sounded cracked, strained, but he smiled.

Slay said, voice low but unyielding, "You heard the Sheriff. Drop it. Now."

The drunk turned toward them, and that's when Steed moved. In one fluid motion, she stepped inside his guard, swung the butt of her scattergun up in a brutal arc, and slammed it full into his chin. CRACK. His head snapped back, and he dropped like a sack of potatoes. His revolver clattered to the floor.

His buddy froze. Steed leveled the shotgun, one brow raised. "You got something to say?"

He holstered his weapon and backed up with both hands visible. "No, ma'am. Nothin' at all."

Slay gave her a look of quiet approval. Clint just grinned.

The townsfolk started breathing again.

Steed exhaled slowly. "Gentlemen," she said with a nod toward Clint, "your drinks are on me tonight. And Marshal?" She holstered the scattergun with practiced ease. "Appreciate the dramatic timing."


Kimari Jacobs sat atop a weather-worn slab of sandstone just north of town, his silhouette etched against a blanket of stars. The night sky, vast and unjudging, had always soothed something deep within him. Out here—away from noise, away from the mine, away from men—he could breathe. He could reach God.

He needed that reach more than most.

The rifle across his thighs was clean, oiled, and warm where it touched his palms. Its weight grounded him like scripture. For a man who had seen what men could do, such things were necessary.

Below, Copper Creek buzzed like a wound that refused to close. Even after ten o'clock, the mine lit up the dark like a fever dream—orange torchlight, flickers of fey lamps, and the low, rhythmic thunder of distant charges. *BOOM.* The sound was muffled by the ridges, but it traveled just the same.

"The government needs its copper," Kimari muttered, voice low and rasped by smoke and memory.

Stillness returned. He let it wrap around him. A couple hours in the dark could rinse the stain from most days, if he held still long enough.

But tonight... the stillness wasn't clean.

The air felt wrong, *tainted.* A soft tingle bloomed at the back of his neck, that whisper in the spine every fighter learns to trust. He shifted the rifle, slow and smooth, fingers brushing the trigger guard. Sitting outside at night, even inside the town wards, wasn't a thing most people would do. It was too dangerous. Too damn many things hid in the night, waiting.

He didn't move yet. Not because he wasn't ready—but because patience was still his strongest gift.

Being a free man had never made him safe. There was always someone who thought they could take from him, control him, own him. He'd endured. Grace first, always. But wrath? Wrath was still in the cellar, wrapped in oilcloth, waiting for reason.

He prayed nightly that he'd never need to open it again.

From his perch, he saw motion below—torches blooming like fireflies in reverse. A group of riders gathered near the mine entrance. Armed. Tense.

Not miners. Not drunks. They moved with purpose. And fear.

113

"Scared of the dark?" He whispered to no one. "Maybe they should be." But then, anyone with sense traveled at night with caution.

Even the fey lights down in town shimmered strangely, like fogged lanterns in the grip of some unspoken hush. The air had a taste now—copper, ash, and *cold*. Kimari watched until they vanished into the trees, shadows riding shadows.

Only then did he stand, bones creaking like old boards. He led himself quietly down the ridge and toward the stables, every step measured. That night, he slept lightly, his rifle propped against the bedframe, hand never far from its grip.

He had named the rifle Bessie. Not for a woman—but for the last good horse he lost in Mississippi.

Come morning, with coffee bitter on his tongue and the town stretching its limbs, Kimari heard the first whispers.

A child gone missing. Outskirts of town. No signs. No tracks. Just... gone.

And the day didn't feel any warmer for the sun rising.


The morning sun clawed its way up over the ridge like it didn't want to be there.

The light was weak, hazy. As if the air itself didn't want to carry warmth anymore. Copper Creek stirred with the sluggishness of a town that sensed, somewhere beneath the noise of hammers and wagons, that **something** was wrong.

Kimari Jacobs stood in the boarding house kitchen, the bitter steam of coffee curling around his face. He hadn't slept. Not really. He'd lain down, sure—rifle in reach, boots still on—but rest had never come.

114

Now, he sipped and listened.

And there it was.

A whisper, hushed. **"Another one."**

At first, the words came in pieces, carried in on wind and gossip like grit in the teeth.

A woman outside the bakery, whispering through pale lips. A ranch hand who swore he heard dogs howling in three different directions at once. A miner staring into his mug like the coffee held the answer. And then the words hit full:

Another child. Gone.

No scream. No break-in. No tracks in the dirt. Just a quiet house on the southern edge of town, a broken latch, and a father with a missing child.

Kimari felt it then—not fear, exactly, but recognition. The kind that burrows under your ribs and won't let go. The kind you *don't* pray away. He set his cup down slow.

The mine workers came and went. Wagons rolled. Boots hit boards. Life tried to pretend it hadn't changed. But the light was still wrong. And every breath tasted like something *old*.

Kimari tightened the sling on his rifle and stepped into the street. He didn't have a badge. Didn't need one. He was a man who had learned long ago that you don't wait to act when shadows start walking in daylight.

Mayor Dooley, meanwhile, remained oblivious to the horror taking root.

Behind town hall, hunched over a barrel of rainwater, he scrubbed blood from his fingers, muttering curses. The Landshire girl had fought, for a little girl. He bore the scratch down the side of his face as evidence.

He smiled into the water as the last flecks of crimson slipped away. He didn't hear the silence falling over the town. Didn't feel the cold creeping in. Didn't know the bad was coming.

Not yet.

Jacobs passed two miners who stopped talking the moment they saw him. They didn't nod. They didn't need to. The looks on their faces said it: They knew. Something out there was *taking*. By noon, nobody was calling it coincidence.

# Chapter Twelve

Sheriff Steed walked the town every morning before the day's work began. Today, she'd been up since just after five, combing the outskirts with volunteers and deputies, searching for the Landshire girl.

That search was still ongoing. If the girl was nearby, they'd find her. If not... Sharon didn't let herself finish that thought.

Dealing with the parent had been exactly as exhausting as expected. There was no mother. Died in childbirth. The father was tight-jawed and brittle, directing his fury at both of her deputies, as if grief were something he could beat back with impatience.

Three children. One month. No witnesses. No tracks. No answers. People had started to talk, and the talk was turning ugly.

So far, she had no suspects. No signs. Just shadows and questions, and a sick feeling building like storm pressure behind her eyes.

The walks served two purposes. They kept her grounded in the community, and they gave her a way to gather information without calling attention to it. Most mornings, that was enough. Today, it felt like trying to plug a damn dam with her bare hands.

School was already in session, though the Landshire girl's bench sat empty, the gap more painful than a grave.

How long before they stopped holding it for her?

On the schoolhouse steps, she spotted Ellie Clark, the new teacher, speaking quietly with Father O'Malley. He was in worn work clothes again, revolver on his belt, sleeves rolled and face ruddy. They were still building the new church—slow going, since only one SpellCaster in town could lift stone in bulk, and she was stretched thin already.

A large black crow watched her from the school roof. Unmoving. Its dark eyes locked on her. Steed frowned at it. Then moved on.

She made her way through Copper Creek, nodding to townsfolk along the way, her badge glinting just enough to remind folks who she was. Not everyone liked it. Some still called her *the widow* when they thought she couldn't hear. But most had learned she wasn't going anywhere.

The Thompsons were already busy at the general store. Young James loaded boxes into a wagon for Sam and Matilda Davis as Sharon passed. She paused, exchanged a few words. The pleasantries felt brittle in her mouth. She walked on.

Town Hall was already stirring—clerks, surveyors, officials milling about like ants in a kicked nest. The mine's recent boom had spiked the town's growth: copper first, then gold and silver. Every third man in town now claimed to be a prospector or a land agent. Most were just trouble waiting for a payday.

She was quietly glad she'd bought land early—five hundred acres abutting the mine. She never mentioned it. No need to. Folks would figure it out when it mattered.

She'd originally come to Copper Creek to start a café. Sal, her best friend, opened the saloon. That felt like another life now.

Herbert Steed, her late husband, had taught her everything he knew—riding, shooting, business. He'd died slow, worn down by the same shipping trade that made him wealthy. When he passed, she sold it all, packed up, and left with Sal.

Back then, Copper Creek looked like an opportunity.

Then Riggs showed up.

From the beginning, Thomas Riggs pushed the miners hard. Safety was a suggestion, not a requirement. The accidents were regular. Deaths, frequent. When a major copper pocket was hit, Riggs forced the crews into overdrive.

A tunnel collapse last year killed twelve men. The survivors walked out. Riggs replaced them with Native slaves.

The town nearly went up in flames.

Then Sheriff Blanton died. The "doctor" called it a heart attack. Mayor Dooley tried appointing his cousin, Daniel, as interim sheriff. Dan lasted a week—drunk, unreliable, and finally dead himself, neck snapped falling off his own horse after a long night at Sal's.

That's when Sal had pointed the finger at her.

"You can ride and shoot as well as any man," she'd said. "And Lord knows you need something to do."

Sharon had laughed. Then thought about it. Then marched into Dooley's office.

He'd laughed too. And that was all it took.


Her first official act had been to confront Riggs.

That meeting ended with her shooting one of his goons in the shoulder after Riggs tried to have her thrown out. She told him if he ever laid a hand on her, she'd kill him. He'd believed her. She saw it in his eyes. But he still treated her like a joke.

Maybe she should've shot to kill. Riggs, instead of the guard. Might have saved a bunch of folks some grief. She shook her head. She was in Copper Creek, standing up when it would have been far easier to sit down, because she valued the law, not there to take the law into her own hands. No matter how satisfying it might have been to dream.

This morning, the streets felt wrong. People talked quieter. Looked over their shoulders. The fey lamps flickered like they were tired of staying lit. The sky was a color it shouldn't be, and that damned crow was still watching her.

Something was out there. Or it was already here. And Copper Creek was running out of time.

Miles and Jessie, two of Sheriff Steed's deputies, were already in the office when she returned. They sat at the card table with Charley McFly, the jailer, who had one quiet guest sleeping off the night's bad decisions, the guard from Sal's.

She nodded to the three of them as she passed through. They responded with easy smiles—too easy. She'd overheard them more than once talking about how the badge might fit better on someone else.

That didn't bother her. She liked being Sheriff. And she'd done the job well enough that the *next* person who wanted it would have to earn it. But she'd never beg to keep it.

She stepped into her office and set to making coffee on her magic hotplate. The tin kettle hissed softly as it heated. A knock came just as she poured the water. Miles opened the door. "The Marshal's here. Asked if you've got a minute."

She nodded. "Send him in."

Marshal Slay stepped through with his usual quiet gravity. Tall, lean, sharp around the edges. The dark suit and open-collared shirt made him look half preacher, half gunslinger. The bandage on his cheek just highlighted how intact the rest of him was.

Steed fought the smile threatening to form into something *other than professional.* Damned man looked *yummy.*

"Morning, Marshal," she said, smoothing her tone.

He gave her a polite nod. "Sheriff."

"What can I do for you?" she asked, even as her mind conjured thoughts she hadn't entertained since Herbert died.

Slay's expression cooled a degree. "You can start by telling me how long you've been protecting Nate Jackson… and how long you've known he had a camp here."

Her smile died, sizzling off her face like water on a skillet.

"Few months," she admitted. "Since things got bad at the mine."

"You know you're compromising your job."

Her voice was even. "Not really. The official stance of the UA government is that slavery's illegal. Riggs not *calling* it slavery doesn't change what it is. But Mayor Dooley won't let me touch the mine. Not and risk killing the town's revenue."

"And the bribes?" Slay's tone was dry as dust.

"Yes," she corrected, "and the *bribes.*"

Slay's mouth tugged into a grim smile. "At least you still have a conscience."

"Marshal, I *always* will. I didn't take this badge because I wanted to have power—I took it because no one else would. Well, also because Mayor Dooley laughed at the idea. I do the job. I uphold the law. But I *can't* shut Riggs down. I *can't* stop the slavery. So I was helping General Jackson. That's the only way I can live with myself."

Slay studied her a moment. "I don't trust him."

"Jackson?"

"I think he's using the cause as cover. I visited one of his abandoned camps. Burned ledgers, stripped equipment. No sign of where the copper went. I think he's skimming off the top—and making himself rich."

Sharon frowned. "You should know—people in Copper Creek think he's a hero. He stood up to Riggs when no one else would. Everyone helped him—supplies, food, credit. Hell, even the Thompsons gave him an open ledger. That man counts buttons before he parts with a cent." She sighed. "This town's a powder keg. Miners are ready to riot. The townsfolk hate Riggs more than the Devil himself. And Riggs? He's sitting on more than a hundred armed men at the mine. If this blows, it's gonna blow *hard*."

Slay's face darkened. "I spoke to Riggs. Let's just say, he's not a man I'd trust with a lantern in a hayloft. Any idea who set off the explosives last week?"

"Take your pick," she said. "My bet's on the Paiute. Some of their villages were wiped out when the mine expanded. Survivors don't care who they hurt—white's white, and vengeance don't ask questions. The Army's got patrols in the hills. Outlying farms are losing livestock... and people."

Slay's jaw tightened.

Steed's voice lowered. "It's not just sabotage. We've had girls go missing. A dozen in the last year. Three in the last month."

122

Slay leaned forward slightly. "Common traits?"

She shook her head slowly. "Under twenty, mostly. Easy targets. Last night's girl—Landshire's daughter—is only eleven. Taken straight from her bedroom. Her father swears he heard nothing. But I thought I smelled ether in the room."

Slay's face turned unreadable. "Can you take me there?"

Sharon nodded once. "Let me get my coat."


The room was dark.

Not pitch—just the kind of dusk that settles in when no one bothers to light a lamp.

Duda sat at the table, coat off, holster still strapped tight. His boots were propped on an old crate. A bottle of whiskey rested within arm's reach—half-drunk and fully earned.

The knife he'd sharpened earlier lay across the table in front of him. Clean. Straight. Balanced.

He wasn't tired. That was the problem. When you weren't tired, the thinking crept in.

He stared at the blade. Not at the edge, but at the way it bent the light—just a little. Warped it. Twisted truth into something thinner, sharper. Something not quite honest.

"Don't fall for it, Andrezj," he muttered. He wasn't talking about the knife. Wasn't talking about Slay either. Or the spellcaster girl with the too-old eyes. Or the town, or the orphan girl, or the way Riggs smiled like nothing on earth could touch him.

He was talking about himself.

He'd seen too many men go soft at the wrong time. Seen them hesitate. Flinch. Try to do the right thing—and die with the thought half-finished.

That wouldn't be him.

And yet…

Slay hadn't flinched. Not once. Sheriff Steed? Holding the town together with stubborn grit and a sawed-off. And that girl, Savannah. That one *scared* Riggs.

Duda liked that.

Riggs. Christ. That man was a rot-sack in boots. You could smell it on him—sweat and wet copper and something worse underneath. Undeniably sick in the head. But he paid *very* well.

That was the trouble with money. It made bad things feel *reasonable*.

Duda had enough stashed away to disappear. Live like a king. Maybe even die in bed.

Instead, he was here. Still wearing the guns. Still pretending he gave a damn about the contract.

He looked back at the knife. There was a line in it—faint, nearly invisible. Not a crack. Not yet.

"Everyone breaks different," he said quietly. He poured another inch of whiskey into the tin cup. Drank it slow. Then he sat in the dark, with the quiet, and waited to see which way *he'd* break.

Soaring Eagle was nearly home. Ten days among the high places had left his joints aching, his breath short—but his heart light. His satchel was heavy with roots, blossoms, and herbs whispered of only in dreams, medicine for the children and his daughter's daughter, whose gift was awakening. She would be his legacy. He would teach her to speak to rivers, to listen to trees. He would pass the path to her and at last rest.

But the crows were wrong.

They swirled overhead in a black spiral, thousands of them, silent against the wind. No call, no cry. Just watching.

Soaring Eagle felt the wind shift. It carried the scent of ash and blood.

He ran. Seventy years gave him no speed, but the urgency in his bones gave him strength. He stumbled the last stretch over the bend, where the mountain opened to the valley—and stopped.

His world was gone.

The village was no more than a smear of charcoal and corpses. Smoke curled from the skeletal frames of what had been homes. Bodies lay in twisted heaps, blood dried to black crusts beneath them. His eyes found the center post where the sacred fire had once burned—and what was nailed to it.

Four women. Girls. Undressed. Bound. Throats open like butchered deer. Among them, his daughter. And her daughter.

The pain did not come like thunder. It came like ice. Like silence. Soaring Eagle dropped to his knees in the dirt, his satchel forgotten, the wind pulling tears from his eyes.

He did not scream. He did not wail. He just began to sing.

All through the night he sat and sang. The sun fell and the moon rose, and still he chanted—old words, older than the fire, older than the mountains. Words the white men had tried to forget. Words meant to wake the Earth.

At dawn, he left the circle of corpses and walked the length of the ruins, gathering what he could. Bits of flesh. Bone. Shards of hair, still warm with spirit. He took something from each of the dead, whispering their names, recalling moments from lives snuffed out too soon.

His daughter's daughter had once braided a rope from grass and made him a bracelet. He found it still on her wrist. He took it, pressed it to his heart, and kept walking.

Then came the fire.

He piled tools, blankets, trinkets—what little was left of the dead's possessions—on a flat stone and soaked it in blood, his own and theirs. The spirits had gathered. He could feel them. Watching. Waiting.

Then he danced.

Barefoot on the hot stone. Arms raised. Skin slashed in tribute. Blood painting his chest in sacred marks. The night came again and with it the storm of wings—thousands of crows filling the sky, circling above him. They screamed with one voice, a shriek like the sound of judgment.

At the peak of the dance, he fell to his knees and reached out—not to the gods, but to the Trickster.

And the Trickster came. In a place of no sky and stone that bled, the Coyote danced. It laughed. It whispered promises with teeth. "You want vengeance? Then become it."

Soaring Eagle accepted.

He woke under a sky the color of iron. The crows were still watching. But now they shifted, uneasy, as he rose, changed.

His body pulsed with power. Not warmth. Not life. Something else. Something deeper. Something hollowed out and filled with hunger. The spirits of the dead still sang to him, but their songs were twisted now, demanding blood.

The pain of his loss was gone. Only rage remained.

He stood, and his shadow stretched longer than it should have, curling like smoke. His skin cracked in places, hardened. His teeth were too many. His eyes glowed blue like frozen fire.

The Trickster's laughter echoed in his mind as the last threads of his humanity slipped away.

Soaring Eagle was no more. The Wendigo opened its eyes, turned to the horizon, and began to walk. The world had taken everything from him. Now he would return the favor.

Marshal Michael Slay leaned forward, speaking into the spiral horn of the Farspeak. "This is Marshal Slay of the Nevada Territorial Law Office. I need to speak with Acting Magistrate Tallman. Matter of urgency regarding Copper Creek."

The crystalline lenses buzzed with low blue light. A moment passed. Then another.

Finally, a dry voice crackled across. "Marshal. This is Agent Pershing. Magistrate Tallman is... unavailable."

Slay frowned. "Unfortunate. I need a warrant for Thomas Riggs. Slavery, sabotage, conspiracy to commit murder—"

"I'm afraid your request has been noted and denied pending further review."

"Further review?" Slay's jaw tightened. "What the hell does that mean?"

"It means, Marshal," said Pershing with a tone like glass over gravel, "that Copper Creek is of strategic economic interest to the governor's office. Disruptions—especially ones without hard evidence—are strongly discouraged."

A pause.

Then Slay asked, "Who authorized the denial?"

The line went silent. Long enough to be deliberate. Then: "The matter is closed, Marshal." The lenses dimmed. The light died. The conversation was over.

Slay sat still for a long time, the quiet pressing in like a weight. Then he rose, crossed the room, and pushed out into the street.

---

Steed was seated on the porch rail, a cup of bitter coffee in her hand. She raised an eyebrow as Slay stepped out and stood beside her, wordless.

"You look like someone just pissed in your cornmeal," she said.

Slay gave a tired chuckle. "They shut me down. Farspeak to Carson. I asked for a warrant. They said no."

"No?" Steed echoed, voice soft but sharp. "With what Riggs is doing?"

"They didn't say he didn't do it. Just that it's not the right time to ask questions." He looked out toward the darkened town. "Someone up the ladder is protecting him. And I don't think it's a someone I can arrest."

Steed sipped her coffee. "That's a problem."

"Yeah," Slay murmured.

They sat in silence for a time. The wind picked up again, carrying grit down the road in little hissing swirls. Somewhere, a shutter banged once, then fell still.

Steed spoke first. "You think this town's gonna survive what's coming?"

Slay didn't answer right away. When he did, his voice was low. "I think if it does, it won't be by the law. Not the way it's written."

Another pause.

Steed turned, studying him. "You always carry this much weight on your shoulders?"

Slay smiled, tired but sincere. "Used to it."

She laughed—just a little—and leaned back against the post. "Well. You ain't the only one here with a strong back." They didn't touch. Didn't speak more. But when Slay finally turned to go, she didn't stop him, and she didn't look away.

The shadows had come earlier than expected.

Outside Melville House, the copper-stained horizon gave way to a bruised violet sky. The crickets were late in their chorus. The wind, which usually whispered through the scrub with dry gossip, had fallen to an odd hush, like it too was listening for something. It was the sort of evening that didn't feel *wrong*, exactly—just not quite *right*.

Cyrus Melville noticed it first. He stood at the north-facing window of the common room, watching the stillness. His fingers drummed a slow rhythm against the sill. "Storm's coming," he said aloud, though there wasn't a cloud in sight.

Savannah looked up from her reading. "But not a weather kind, is it?"

Cyrus didn't answer. He didn't need to.

# Chapter Thirteen

They heard the knock at the door like it was louder than it was—three light taps, but they cut clean through the quiet. Apprentice Laurel started toward it, hesitated, then looked at Cyrus again. He nodded once.

She opened the door.

A tall woman stepped through, as if she had always belonged there and merely chose this moment to return. Her white braid gleamed against her dark traveling cloak. She moved with elegant purpose, eyes sharp, mouth still. The scar down her cheek was the only flaw in her otherwise ageless face—and even that seemed deliberate, like a seal placed by some divine forge.

She walked past Laurel without comment.

Her eyes settled first on Savannah.

"I am Glorious Dawn. You may call me Glory. You carry too much grief," she said softly. "It isn't weakness. But it will burn if you let it."

Savannah blinked. The words pierced deeper than they should have. She rose, nodded slightly. "Thank you. I—don't know how you knew that."

"I've known worse burdens," the woman replied. She offered nothing more.

Behind Savannah, Ahyoka stepped out of the hallway. She gripped her spear, gaze locked on the visitor like a predator recognizing another. Her hands were steady, but the spear's shaft groaned faintly under her grip.

The stranger's eyes met Ahyoka's and held them. A nod passed between them—uneasy kinship. And though Ahyoka did not relax, her stance no longer screamed challenge.

Cyrus cleared his throat. "Madam, you've the look of someone who travels by choice, not by need. I don't believe we've been introduced."

"You haven't," she said. "I am not here for you. I'm here for the Slinger."

Savannah blinked. "Clint?"

"Yes. His hand is waiting."

Upstairs, Clint Black lay wide awake, jaw clenched tight against the ache in his burned arm. He'd refused laudanum again. It dulled too much. The pain reminded him he was alive.

He heard the knock downstairs, faint through the walls. A moment later, the door opened behind him.

She didn't enter like someone stepping into a room—more like a change in temperature. A cool front. The room brightened without light.

He turned his head.

The white-haired woman stood with a slim, travel-worn satchel in her hands. She said nothing, but in her presence, the pain in his stump dulled—not from spell work, not from sympathy, but from... calm.

She opened the satchel and revealed the arm.

It wasn't just a prosthetic. Clint knew tools. This was something else. Copper, silver, gold inlays. Precision hinges. Stones set in the joints like miniature stars.

She handed it to him without flourish. "It was made for you, William Clinton Black. No one else."

He took it, his fingers trembling—not from fear, but from knowing this moment mattered in ways he couldn't define. He raised the prosthetic to his stump. It leapt into place. No latch. No straps. Just contact and... *lock*. A whisper of something ancient in the bones. The pain vanished. A slow exhale filled his chest, deeper than breath.

The woman stepped back. "The palm hums when your anger burns. You'll feel it. So will others, those responsible for your anger."

Clint stared at the hand. It flexed once, then again. Natural. Familiar. More his than his own ever had been.

He looked to the SpellShooter resting on the nightstand. For a heartbeat, he could have sworn it *noticed*. But the moment passed.

The woman turned. "Try to stay alive," she said over her shoulder, voice low but unwavering. "You have much still to do."

As she descended the stairs, Savannah stood waiting, Ahyoka beside her. Both watched the stranger with quiet reverence.

Cyrus, however, watched her with unease. "You are not a caster," he murmured. "Not a Concordium agent. And yet… you're something more."

The woman paused by the door, offered Cyrus a smile that was not quite a smile. "Even your archives don't know *everything..*"

133

She stepped into the night and vanished into the silence.

A few moments later, Savannah whispered, "Who was she?"

Cyrus didn't answer.

Outside, the stars blinked cold above the desert.

And far, far away, something stirred beneath the skin of the world—stretching, breathing, waiting.


Kimari Jacobs woke to bad news.

The Landshire girl was still missing.

It didn't sit right. Not with him. He may have drifted from town to town most of his life, but he believed in doing right by people when it counted. So, after a quick rinse and a check on Bessie, he joined one of the search groups.

He was the only Black man in the line, but nobody said a word. Not today.

They combed through brush, peered into dry wells, and checked crawlspaces. Nothing. Just a few droplets of blood near a fence line—maybe human, maybe not.

By midday, Kimari's stomach was rumbling, and so was his bank account. Custom ammunition wasn't cheap. He had enough coin for another week, maybe. No plans, no destination. But the Lord had always pointed his boots toward the road he was meant to walk. Today would be no different.

He hit the open-air kitchen with hope in his gut. Maybe a job. Maybe just a hot plate and a rumor.

The usual crowd of miners had gathered, hunched around a big, burly man with a red beard and louder voice—Rick Carter. Kimari bought food and coffee, settled nearby, and listened.

"Alright, boys," Carter said, holding up one thick hand. "I ain't waitin' on the mine to come back around. I got a claim two miles out on the creek. Prospectin' for gold. I need six men. Ten percent each of profits."

Mutters rippled through the crowd. Miners shifted on their stools.

"Rick," said an older man, "me and my boy Tuck'll go."

A few more hands went up. That made six.

Carter grinned. "Good. Grab your gear. We campin' out and working in shifts."

But no one moved.

"What's the problem?" Carter asked.

"Rick," said the older miner, voice low, "three farms burnt out last week. A couple bodies found half-eaten on the road. One man was ripped apart, and his rifle was empty—but there weren't no blood but his."

The crowd murmured uneasily.

Rick snorted. "Don't get your knickers twisted, Roy. I'll hire security." He looked around—and locked eyes on Kimari. "You! Hey, boy! You want a job?"

The word *boy* hung in the air like rot. Kimari stopped chewing. Set his tin mug down. Then stood. He was taller than Carter. Broader. And a hell of a lot quieter. "I ain't your boy," he said evenly, loud enough for every man there to hear.

Carter raised both hands, palms out. "I got you. No offense. I just need a gunman to keep the ladies safe."

Kimari let the tension hang, then said, "What're you offering?"

"Ten a day plus food."

Kimari smirked. "Look around. Twenty, plus food. And if you strike it rich, I want five percent."

Carter balked. "Twenty, fine. Beans n' biscuits, sure. But no cut of the claim."

Jacobs nodded once. "Deal. I'll get my gear."

Carter called after him. "We leave in an hour."

After collecting his custom ammo from the gunsmith—who beamed under Kimari's praise—he made a final stop at the saloon. A couple of drinks before disappearing into the hills was tradition by now.

The interior was cool and dim, thanks to preservation spells set into the beams. He took a seat at the bar and nodded to Sal.

"Two shots of whiskey."

She poured without comment. He'd already proven himself welcome here.

As he raised the first glass, a voice spoke from his elbow.

"Do many people mistake you for a Slinger?"

Jacobs turned to see the young man from the other day— the SpellSlinger. Tall, lean, quiet. He grinned.

136

"Enough that they usually leave me alone," Kimari said. "How'd you know I'm not?"

The Slinger chuckled. "Brass casings. SpellShells need copper to hold the magic. And your rifle… copper jacketed on the outside only."

"Copper don't make for a good barrel," Kimari said. "Warps under heat."

"Good to know," the Slinger said, and offered his hand. "Clint Black."

Jacobs raised an eyebrow—then took the hand. "Kimari Jacobs. Folks call me Kim." He did a double take. "Wait, weren't you missing an…arm?"

Clint gave him a grin. "Yeah. Got a replacement." He pulled off the work glove he was wearing over the apparatus, holding the hand up. Light gleamed off the metal surfaces and winked off the gemstones in the joints. Kimari was fascinated. He had never seen a magical replacement limb before. Clint continued, "And If you don't mind being named after a girl, why would I mind calling you that?" He tried to hide a grin.

Kimari almost bristled—then saw the mischief in Clint's eyes. He chuckled, finally relaxing. "Been a long fifteen years," he admitted.

"Orphan here," Clint said. "Fought for everything I ever had."

They were mid-sip when trouble entered: two trail-dusty cowboys stomping through the doors like they owned the boards under their boots.

They took the bar beside Kimari. Ordered whiskey. Then the bigger one wrinkled his nose.

"Blacks sit at the end of the bar," he growled. "Ain't tryin' to drink with the stink."

Kimari and Clint exchanged a look. "I sit where I damn well choose," Kimari said.

The cowboy squared up. Kimari stood. Same height. Not the same weight. "Back off," Kimari said, calm as a whisper.

The cowboy glanced at his buddy—and opened his mouth to retort—when the saloon doors creaked again.

Marshal Michael Slay entered like Judgment itself. He walked straight to the bar and nodded at Clint and Kimari. "Gentlemen," he said. Then he turned his gaze upon the cowboys, dead eyed, like twin gun barrels. The cowboys wilted under his scrutiny. He turned back to Clink and Kimari.

The cowboys bolted, bottle and glasses in hand.

Slay barely looked at them. "Clint, who's your friend?"

"Kimari Jacobs. Just met." Clint pulled the glove back on, then picked up his shot glass with that hand.

Slay extended a hand. "Mr. Jacobs. Marshal Slay. Pleasure."

"Marshal," Kimari said, surprised—and pleased. "Join us?"

Clint nodded to Sal. "Another glass. His drinks are on me."

Slay raised a hand. "Just sarsaparilla. I'm still on duty."

They moved to a table near the stage. The bottle, the glasses, the soda—quiet like a treaty signing.

"Where you from, Mister Jacobs?" Slay asked.

"Mississippi."

"You're a long way from home."

Kimari nodded. "War took my folks. Raised by my grandma. When she passed, I drifted."

"You need roots," Slay said.

Kimari shook his head. "Ain't found soil worth plantin' in yet."

"Well," Slay said, "I hope you do."

Kimari stood and shook their hands. "If I do, maybe it'll be here."

"What's next?" Clint asked.

"Just got hired to guard a bunch of miners out past the creek. They're spooked. Figures they need me and Bessie." He raised the rifle with a grin.

"Stay safe," Clint said.

"You too. Don't worry about me—me and Bessie been through worse. Besides, I'm right with the Lord. Everything is gonna' be jes' fine." He tipped his hat and left. Perhaps, if he and Clint knew they would never lay eyes on one another again, the goodbye might have been different.

Clint watched the door swing.

Slay said, "Just spoke with the Sheriff. Nothing on the girl."

Clint frowned. "Think we'll find her?"

Slay shook his head. "If anything on four legs had taken her, we would know more. Might have found a blood trail, or prints, or something. She was taken by a human, someone trying hard not to leave a trace. Unless we get luckier than we have any right to expect, she's gone."

"So, we wait for whoever did this to do it again?"

"Yep. And hope he makes a mistake." Slay's voice conveyed frustration, and more than a little anger.

"The Sheriff have anything else to say?"

"What do you mean?" Slay sounded baffled.

Clint smirked. "You two playin' nice now?"

Slay looked up. "What's that mean?"

"You know what I'm saying." His grin was getting wider. He was enjoying himself.

Slay grimaced, but Clint could just make out the slightest hint of a grin underneath it all. Slay said, "Kid, just say whatever smartass thing you got rollin' around behind yer eyes."

Clint leaned back, tipped the edge of his hat up, then grinned again. "She likes you, Marshal."

"She's a widow," Slay said, confused.

"So?" Clint grinned. "That mean's her husband died, not her. And from what I heard, it's been a few years. And, according to everybody I talked to, there's been nobody else since she moved to Copper Creek."

Slay huffed. "I haven't had time for that kind of thing. Not since I took up the badge."

Clint leaned forward, adjusted his hat. "Might be time to make some." When he looked over, he was almost certain the

Marshal was blushing. Good. Clint intended to have a little fun today.

# Chapter Fourteen

**Late afternoon. Mine outskirts.**

The Paiute boy lay crumpled in the dust, shirt torn, back laid open like a butcher's ledger.
Overseer Merrin—barrel-chested, face like boiled ham—reeled in the whip with methodical precision.

"Won't be warned again, boy," he muttered.

Crack.

The sound echoed off slag heaps and scaffold poles, sharp and final.

Not far off, Reverend O'Malley knelt beside a dying foreman, whispering the last rites. But the sound made him pause—then rise, slow and certain, the oil still fresh on his fingers.

He wore the collar like a man who'd earned it. Not born to it. Not bred for it. Chosen—after the blood, and because of it. Like most holy men west of the Divide, O'Malley carried a revolver. Worn grips. Clean barrel. Not for men, he always said. But sometimes, evil walks on two legs. He stepped forward. Boots crunching gravel. Voice clear and ringing like a chapel bell. "That's enough."

Merrin didn't stop.

"I said that's enough."

The overseer turned, jaw working, whip half raised. "You stupid, preacher?"

O'Malley's eyes narrowed, not with fear—but disbelief. That this man, in full view of God and copper and judgment, would raise a hand toward him. Toward a man anointed.

"I see a child being beaten half to death."

"You don't wanna see it, then you'd best look the other way."

O'Malley didn't move. "That boy's a child of God."

Merrin gave a snort and raised the whip again. "He's property. And you, best back off before you catch what's comin' to him." The whip came down toward O'Malley.

And was stopped. A hand like a wagon hitch caught it mid-swing. Merrin staggered, off balance. The man who held the whip's end wore a plain brown duster, with a copper badge glinting at his chest. One of Duda's men. Quiet. Big as a bear. Calm as judgment.

"I reckon you ought to reconsider your path," the man said evenly.

"You don't give me orders," Merrin snarled, tugging.

The guard didn't flinch. "You raise that hand again, you're not gonna like what happens next."

Merrin did. Tried, anyway.

Crack.
A headbutt, clean as a carpenter's swing. Merrin folded at the knees, blood gushing from his nose, too dazed to curse.

O'Malley stood where he was, unmoved. Not surprised by the violence—only the audacity.
The priest looked down at the whimpering boy, then up at the guard.

"You all right, Reverend?" the man asked.

"I am now," O'Malley said, quiet as prayer.

"Good," the man nodded, already turning away. "See to the boy. I'll see to mine."

The assistant was breathless. "One of Duda's men struck Overseer Merrin. In front of a priest. And half the shift saw it."

Riggs stood behind his desk, jaw tight, knuckles white on the blotter.

"I want that man broken. Dragged out in front of the men and made an example of. Strip his gun, toss him out the gate in pieces."

The door opened. Andrezj Duda stepped inside, calm as church marble.

Riggs rounded on him. "Your man laid hands on my supervisor. On *my* property."

Duda looked him in the eye. "Your man raised a whip on a priest and a boy. My man put a stop to it."

"That ain't his place—!"

"It's *exactly* his place. I gave my men orders: no harm to civilians. No beatings. No cruelty."

Riggs slammed his hand on the wall. "I want public discipline! Or your whole crew's finished!"

Duda's stare was granite. "No."

"You signed a contract!" Riggs' face was bright red, his voice rising, like a boiler about to blow.

144

"I wrote the contract. They work for me, not you." Duda was calm and cool, but only an idiot would have missed that his right hand was resting very comfortably on the handle of his favorite knife.

"You think you can just walk away from this?" Riggs was visibly trying to calm himself down, because he wasn't that big a fool, and he was, finally, starting to recognize the warning signs.

"I *know* I can." Duda turned. His man waited outside. Riggs watched them go, fury choking in his throat. And for the first time, Thomas Riggs looked like something he'd never allowed himself to feel before. Powerless.

Reverend O'Malley stood beneath the wooden cross, face gray with road dust, voice iron with conviction. He told them everything. The boy. The whip. The strike that never landed. The hand that stopped it. He named no names, but every listener knew.

By the time the church emptied, word had spread like brushfire in a canyon. The square filled. Fifty became a hundred. Then two. Then four. Men and women with rifles and revolvers. Miners with pickaxes and lanterns. Anyone who had had enough, they gathered. The town had not agreed to this uprising. It simply *happened.*

In the growing dusk, someone asked, "Where will the children go?" The people there looked to Sheriff Steed, flanked by Marshal Slay and SpellSlinger Black. She smiled. "I have asked the SpellCaster, Savannah Melville, to act as the children's guardian if anything should happen. I don't think anyone here would dispute that she can protect them, if it comes to that."

And just like that, it was settled.

Savannah stood on the schoolhouse steps, arms folded, eyes heavy with knowing. A dozen children gathered around her already.

145

She hated not being there to see Riggs go down, but she understood she had another duty now. Ahyoka stood beside her, stalwart figure in miniature, spear in hand. The message most of the townspeople got was a simple one. These two were going to keep the children safe, no matter what came knocking. And to every parent, when they passed over the most precious thing they had, she said, simply, "I've got them."

Joseph and Ludmilla Sanderson were preparing for bed. Their son, James, was already asleep in the loft, worn out from a full day's labor. Life as a farmer had never been easy, even in this age of enchanted plows and harvest charms. Sweat and soil were the daily currency of the Sandersons, and it left little energy for anything but food and sleep when the sun went down.

Outside, the dogs began to howl.

Not bark. Howl.

Joseph Sanderson, still in his long johns, frowned. "Damn coyotes," he muttered. The week before, a coyote had gotten into the henhouse and slaughtered four of his best layers before Joseph shot it. He pulled on his boots, grabbed his shotgun from its rack, and lit a lantern. The soft yellow glow did little to push back the dark.

As he stepped out onto the porch, a blast of frigid air hit him square in the chest and staggered him against the doorframe. He caught himself with a curse. That wind—unnatural and sharp as broken glass—bit through his clothes like they weren't even there.

His horses were shrieking, not whinnying or neighing, but full-throated screams of terror. They kicked and slammed against the walls of the barn. No coyote ever scared a horse like that.

Joseph's grip on the lantern tightened. His other hand thumbed the hammers back on the shotgun. He moved fast across

146

the yard, boots crunching on suddenly frosted earth. Cold settled around him like a second skin. Breath fogged thick and white.

A crash split the silence. It came from the henhouse.

Joseph lifted the lantern and swore. The front of the coop had been shredded. Not broken. Not opened. Shredded. Thick iron mesh twisted like old taffy. The wood was splintered inward. Something had gone in, not out. The hens were silent.

Inside the wrecked coop, something moved. Something big. In the swaying lantern light, Joseph glimpsed long limbs—too long—moving with a serpentine grace. He stepped forward, despite the icy dread crawling up his spine. He didn't speak, didn't call out.

He heard his son yell from the porch, "Father! What is it?"

Joseph didn't answer. He couldn't. His mouth was suddenly too dry, too cold to form words. He raised the shotgun, hands shaking, and leveled it at the thing inside.

The creature stepped from the shadows. It was at least seven feet tall, maybe more. Gaunt. All bone and sinew and gray, leathery skin. Its head was crowned with ragged antlers, blackened and broken, and its face—if it could be called that—was a ruin of fangs and glowing blue eyes that shimmered like frozen stars.

Joseph fired. Both barrels. The buckshot hit the Wendigo square in the chest—and did absolutely nothing.

The thing moved. It was on him in a blink, one clawed hand seizing his head with the force of a bear trap. Joseph's last thought was a prayer—half-formed, unfinished. The Wendigo ripped his head clean off, blood jetting halfway across the yard.

James saw it happen. He screamed in raw horror, grabbed the rifle by his bedside, and fired once. The bullet went wide. The Wendigo didn't stop. It flew across the yard like a nightmare given

147

wing, faster than any living thing should move. James barely had time to scream.

Ludmilla, still half-dressed, had begun to scream before her son's voice was cut short. The Wendigo didn't knock—it ripped the front door from its hinges, stepped through in a wave of frost and malice, and tore her limb from limb. She thrashed, fought, screamed until her voice broke, but the creature feasted before she had even died.

When it was done, it left the walls dripping with blood, a red spray painting a house that had once known only quiet, hard-earned peace.

Corporal Mineke's patrol was less than a mile away when they heard the double blast of a shotgun—then a shriek that stopped every man cold.

Private O'Shaunessy crossed himself instinctively. "Jesus, Mary, and Joseph—that sounded like the Devil hisself!"

"That's enough!" Mineke snapped. "Someone's in trouble!"

He spurred his horse into a gallop, saber bouncing at his side. The rest of the patrol followed.

None of them would ever be seen again.

Eleven o'clock struck, and the town square of Copper Creek pulsed with life and purpose. Men, women, old-timers, and youngsters too stubborn to be told no—all gathered beneath a sky weighed down by stars and silence. Anyone who had ever grumbled at Riggs over a drink, who had whispered doubts to a neighbor, or who had wept privately over the death of a loved one in that death trap mine—they were here. The quiet supporters stood beside the bold ones now, shoulder to shoulder, the line between silence and action erased by the sheer momentum of outrage.

Nearly every man was armed, and many of the women too. Rifles, scatterguns, pitchforks, hammers, kitchen knives—it didn't much matter. It was less about the weapon and more about the will. They weren't soldiers, not truly, but they had the same look in their eyes. That quiet certainty. That steel under sweat. That fire which had been stoked for too long.

The children had been placed in Savannah's care, safe within the fortified hush of the schoolhouse, wards humming faintly at the windows. Ahyoka stood beside her like a sentry, small but unflinching. Every adult in the square had passed by the school before assembling, some kneeling to kiss their little ones' foreheads, others just resting a callused hand on a sleeping brow. None lingered. No goodbyes. Only resolve.

Marshal Michael Slay stood near the front, his dark coat buttoned to the throat, his eyes sweeping the square like a field officer before a battle. To his left stood Sheriff Sharon Steed, short-barreled shotgun cradled in her arms, face set like river stone. And beside them, quiet and patient, stood Clint Black, SpellSlinger and newly anointed legend. His duster caught the lamplight, and the spellshooter at his side gleamed brightly, like something alive and waiting.

As more folks arrived, hands clapped backs, old grievances were forgotten, names spoken like benedictions. Hugs, nods, prayers. The moment didn't need speeches or banners. It had purpose, and that was enough.

And then, from somewhere near the back—a woman's voice, thin but strong—rose in song.

"Onward, Christian soldiers…" A beat passed. Then another voice joined. And another. And then a dozen. Then a hundred. Soon, the entire square was singing.

The old hymn rolled down the boardwalks and echoed off the buildings, weaving its way through the very bones of the town. It was the kind of sound that made hearts swell and knees tremble. It didn't come from the throat, but from someplace deeper—someplace forged in fire and bound by sorrow. The sound of a people who had remembered they were not alone.

Together, they began to march. Up the road. Toward the mine. Toward reckoning.

# Chapter Fifteen

"Holy smokes! Look at the size of that nugget!"

At the shout, Kimari Jacobs turned toward the speaker. One of the miners held a gleaming gold nugget in the firelight, its deep, rich yellow unmistakable even from where Jacobs stood. It looked nearly pure, heavy as a stone in the man's palm. Two or three ounces at least, Kimari reckoned. Not bad at all. The choice to set up camp miles upstream from the main mine, right along the banks of Copper Creek, was proving a sound one.

They'd been working steadily since early morning. Now, late into the evening, their collection bag was nearly three pounds heavier with nuggets and glittering flakes. At this rate, these men could buy a new life—if they lived long enough to get that gold to someplace civilized. Kimari allowed himself a quiet grunt of approval. It was honest work. But gold had a way of testing men's souls. And more than once in his life, he'd seen men break under the strain of sudden fortune.

He shifted his weight slightly against the wide oak he was leaning on, brushing at the bark with his shoulder. The tree stood sentinel near the roaring bonfire Carter had built, its warmth welcome against the cool night breeze. The forest beyond was alive with the usual nighttime murmurs—insects chattering, night birds calling, small animals rustling through the brush. Jacobs knew better than most to take comfort in those sounds. When the woods went silent, that was when the real danger began.

Tonight, he was on duty. He'd slept through most of the afternoon and taken the evening watch, preferring to be alert during the dark hours. It was quieter, but more dangerous too. He kept his long rifle, Bessie, close to hand, always propped against his boot or within easy reach. The others might rely on pickaxes and grit, but Kimari relied on experience—and faith.

The men were in high spirits. Haney had the coffee boiling, the aroma cutting through the pine-laced air. Carter and another miner were still sluicing gravel under the lanterns, eyes sharp for yellow glints. The rest were gathered near the fire, their tools set down, their hands warming on tin mugs. Laughter was easy, voices light. Carter was already talking about buying up more land along the creek. Jacobs didn't blame him.

Above, a heavy cloud began to drift across the face of the moon. The silver light dimmed, casting the forest in shadow, and the edge of unease touched Kimari's spine.

He turned and tossed two more thick logs onto the fire. Sparks lifted upward, momentarily banishing the encroaching darkness. In the flickering orange light, his features were hard and calm. His faith kept fear at bay, but vigilance was always his companion.

Jacobs checked Bessie again, slipping a round halfway out before sliding it back into the chamber. Seven .45-70 rounds, each hand-marked with a small cross cut into the soft lead. A personal touch. The round itself could drop a buffalo, and Jacobs figured that was enough for almost anything he'd encounter out here. But the cross? That was for his peace of mind.

He didn't believe in superstition. He believed in preparation. He believed in God.

The fire crackled. Carter handed him a cup of steaming coffee, and Jacobs accepted it with a nod.

"Much obliged."

"Ain't no thing," Carter said. "Figure it's gonna be a good night. Just look at what we've pulled out of this creek. Gonna be rich, boys."

Jacobs didn't answer right away. He stared into the flames, letting the warmth soak into his bones. "Maybe," he said finally. "Or maybe the creek ain't done testing us yet."

There were a few chuckles, but they sounded thinner than before.

He flexed his hand. The right one. Stiffness crept into the joints more often these days. Old injuries, old fights. He remembered the Marshal's advice: find a woman. Settle down. He'd smiled at the time. But now, with the firelight warm against his chest and the cold just a few feet beyond, he found himself wondering.

What would it be like to rest? To put down roots. To have a child that bore his name, his eyes. He didn't know. He'd always walked the edge of the world, between the living and the damned.

And something told him that edge was getting mighty narrow tonight.

Then they heard the shriek. It wasn't anything any of the miners had ever heard before—the bold, brazen call of something that walked the night without fear, without shame, and without challenge. It was the kind of sound that split the world in two—the time before you heard it, and the time after.

All the normal sounds of the forest stopped immediately. No birds. No crickets. Not even the wind stirred the trees. The world held its breath. The sound nagged at Kimari, sent a tiny shiver of worry down his spine. He was certain he had heard it before, somewhere long past, maybe in a nightmare he'd never quite remembered. The effect on the miners was instantaneous.

Carter exclaimed, "What in Hell was that?" His voice had lost all pretense of calm. It quivered, thin and stretched, and that fear began to leak into the others, cracking their nerves.

Haney grimaced. "I dunno', but it sounds mean, whatever it is. 'Least it was a ways off." His hand drifted down to the revolver he wore in a cross-draw rig, fingers brushing the grip like a charm to ward off evil.

Jacobs grunted. "I'm sure it's nothin'. Y'all just relax now. I'll check it out." He picked up one of the lanterns and walked a dozen or so yards out into the night. Cold had crept into the air—unseasonably so—and the change was fast. A breath ago, it had been crisp and pleasant. Now, it bit like autumn come early. Fog slithered in, pale and damp, seeping through the trees and pooling like smoke.

"Dang," he muttered. "I don't like this." He whispered a prayer under his breath and moved in a slow circle around the edge of the clearing, the lantern held high to push back the growing gloom. The light flickered across rough bark and tangled brush but showed nothing. Still, his skin crawled.

Then it shrieked again. This one was much closer—thirty, maybe forty yards. A stone's throw. Jacobs froze mid-step, his free hand going to Bessie's worn grip. He was sweating now, despite the cold that made his breath cloud the air. The fog deepened like a closing fist.

Back in the clearing, the miners were tense shadows. He could hear their curses, low and broken, like men half-drowning. They were armed but frightened in a way that weapons couldn't fix.

"It's me, comin' back. Don't shoot!" Jacobs called.

Despite the warning, several barrels tracked his approach until he stepped fully into the light. Then a third shriek rang out, right at the edge of the firelight. It was louder, more brazen...taunting.

A presence. Not just sound. It slithered through the air like a blade.

Dread thickened like syrup in their lungs. The cold pressed in. Every breath came sharp and slow, and even the fire's glow couldn't stop the feeling that something ancient had taken notice of them.

"This ain't natural!" Jacobs said. "Look sharp. I don't know what it is."

Their horses went mad—neighing, rearing, kicking at the air. Leather snapped as reins strained. They knew. Animals always did.

Jacobs' eyes scanned the trees. He could feel it now, not just hear it. A presence, malevolent and immense. Not just watching, judging. Weighing them like meat. The miners stood as close as they dared to the bonfire, eyes wide, sweat standing out on their brows despite the chill.

"We ain't alone," Jacobs muttered. "Something's out there."

The miners, except for Carter, were on the edge of a full-blown panic. Carter, older and a little wiser, kept his head. "Hang on, boys! Long as we stick together, we'll be fine!"

Haney was the first to lose his nerve. He grunted, said, "To Hell with this!" and bolted out into the fog, headed toward the horses.

Carter shouted, "Haney! Get back here!", just as Haney screamed and fired off a single shot from his revolver. The scream cut off abruptly, accompanied by what sounded like a loud SNAP of bone breaking. Silence reigned for almost a minute, before the night was split by another shriek, loud and obnoxious, from thirty or forty feet away. This time, it sounded, almost, mocking. The miners all huddled together, facing the direction where the horses were no longer neighing or whinnying. In fact, there was no sound coming from anywhere outside the circle of light from the bonfire. It was as if the entire world had shrunk to just what they could see, walled in by white and grey eddies of fog.

Then it all got worse as, with a wet thump, a naked skull, white, stripped of all meat, top broken open like a soft-boiled egg, landed just at their feet. Cries of fear erupted, sharp and panicked, as the miners broke ranks. The father and son duo ran out into the fog, cries of panic turning almost instantly to cries of pain. There were several shots fired, another of those shrieks, then nothing.

Jacobs imagined he saw a pair of bright blue points of light moving just at the edge of the fog, but they vanished as quickly as they appeared. Carter was holding a lantern in one hand, a Colt Peacemaker in the other, and had a look of grim determination on his face. "We gotta' get clear of this thing, whatever it is, and get back to town. We ain't gonna be safe otherwise."

Jacobs was thinking, connecting pieces in his mind, and then it clicked. "This is a Wendigo." His voice was firm, but the weight of the name made his heart thump harder.

Carter looked at Jacobs in surprise. "What the heck are you saying?"

"It's a Wendigo. I fought one years ago, when I was just barely a man. It's some kinda Native spirit—vengeance, hunger, maybe both. Like the Deer Woman."

Carter grimaced. "I don't know what that is. Look, are you saying you know how to kill this thing?"

Jacobs sighed. "I'm not sure. I think silver can hurt it but probably won't finish it off. Maybe fire? The one we killed, we used dynamite and kerosene. Didn't leave much. But we had a bunch of help with that one. And it was weak."

Carter scanned the fog. "Where the heck we gonna find silver?" He ignored everything else Jacobs said.

Jacobs said, slowly, "I have seven silver bullets in my pouch. I just had 'em made. For werewolves." He began digging in his pouch. "But it ain't gonna be enough."

One of the surviving miners laughed, a ragged sound that was more hysteria than humor. "There ain't no such thing as werewolves!"

"I wish that was true. I really do." Jacobs was ejecting shells from Bessie as quickly as he could, two clinking to the ground in his haste. He left them there, shoving silver bullets into Bessie's load gate as fast as possible. "Lead won't do much. Might hurt the Wendigo, maybe piss it off, but even silver might not kill it."

As the last round went in and Jacobs racked the rifle, another shriek came—from right outside the firelight. Carter and one of the miners fired in that direction, but there was no sign they hit anything. Carter's voice trembled. "What if we can't stop it? What if it gets us all?"

Jacobs looked him straight in the eye. "I would save those shots. Look, I'm gonna face this thing, try to draw it away from y'all. Between the three of you, someone has to make it back to Copper Creek, warn the town! If this thing gets there, it'll go through the whole place like a sickle through wheat. Tell them about silver, and about the fire. That's their only chance, if it gets past me."

Carter grimaced. "You sure? I can stay with you. Maybe help."

"Mister Carter, if I can't kill it, you sure won't. I appreciate you sayin' that. I do. But you hired me to guard y'all, and more than that, I got a calling. A duty given to me by the Lord. That thing—whatever it is—it's evil, and I can't let it reach those people. I ain't afraid to die. I'm right with God. Either I'll see you later, or I'll see y'all in Heaven. Get to town."

Jacobs pulled a large silver cross from beneath his shirt, kissed it once, then tucked it back under his collar. He gripped Bessie tightly. The rifle was cool in his hands, almost humming with purpose. "God is with me." He readied himself to move, breath even, muscles tight.

Carter's voice cracked. "What if it comes back? What if it gets us before we reach town?"

Jacobs grunted, yanked out his pistol and fired six shots, quick, about a foot apart, in an arc around where he intended to run. On the sixth shot, there was a different kind of shriek, full of pain and anger. Quickly, Jacobs snatched up one of the lanterns and hurled it out into the fog, targeting that shriek. The lantern hit a tree and cracked open, spilling kerosene everywhere. Fire blazed up, just for an instant, highlighting a tall, impossibly thin creature out in the fog.

Jacobs fired Bessie, just as the creature began to move. From the sound, a much deeper shriek, he'd scored a hit. That quickly, the monster was gone. Jacobs stepped out into the fog, staying near the light from the burning kerosene, before he realized it made him just as much of a target as the Wendigo had been a minute before. He quickly threw himself into a forward roll, moving a bare second before the Wendigo missed him, tearing a huge chunk of wood out of a nearby tree. He continued the roll, trying to stay away from the foul creature.

Up close, he could smell it, an awful odor of rotting meat and a wave of bitter cold assaulted him, almost stunning him in place. Jacobs forced himself to move, running forward into the fog, and he could hear a crashing and smashing from behind as the Wendigo gave chase. He could almost feel the thing getting closer, and he changed direction at the last second, haring off into the woods. Another shriek of frustration sounded as the Wendigo also changed direction, paralleling his course, and it seemed to be getting closer. For a few seconds, his feet pounded the ground as he struggled to try to gain ground on his pursuer.

With a start, Jacobs saw that he had reached the creek. Without a plan of any kind, he launched himself out into the water, landing waist deep. He forged forward onto the opposite bank, turning to look back as the Wendigo stepped out into view. He aimed and fired, again without thinking, scoring a hit in the thing's shoulder. It staggered back, mostly due to the impact of the silver, more than an ounce traveling at about twelve hundred feet per second.

A second shot and the Wendigo went to one knee, all breath driven from it by the bullet. Jacobs began to feel hope that he might just be able to finish the beast himself. Four bullets left, he thought. As he racked a new round, the Wendigo scrambled up and dashed away in the night and fog. As soon as the spirit was out of sight, he waded back across the stream, keeping Bessie well out of the water.

A glow in the wall of fog announced that the fire he had started with his lantern was growing, so he headed that way. He would need light to see the thing coming, or he would never have a chance. And the longer he kept the Wendigo busy, the greater the chances that the others would reach town. Luckily, it was mostly downhill to the mine and the town, so maybe they would be able to get there quickly.

As he neared the open fire, the fog was dissipating, driven back by the heat and lack of moisture in the air. A very brief whistling was all the warning he had before the next attack. Instinct drove him to the ground, and he felt the breeze as a claw tipped with razor-sharp talons just missed ripping his head from his body. He got off another shot, silver crashing through the damned beast's belly, then he was up and running while the shriek of pain almost blew out his eardrum.

The Wendigo was moving more slowly now, so he racked another round, turned, and fired again. His aim was true, guided, he imagined, by the will of God. As the Wendigo staggered back and fell, Jacobs blew out a breath he hadn't realized he was holding. God, give me strength, he thought, give me the strength to kill this thing! Then he opened the cellar door and unwrapped wrath.

The beast slowly rolled onto its back and stared up at the sky, breath coming in ragged gasps. As it lay there, Jacobs slowly approached, keeping what he imagined was a safe distance. The supernatural creature was holding the wounds made by Jacobs' bullets, staring down at the holes that still hadn't healed. It looked at Jacobs malevolently, with an accusatory light in its eyes. Jacobs smiled. "That's right. That's silver! Ain't like lead." He cocked his head sideways, looking down at the creature. "I bet that ITCHES!"

He laughed. "You just rest easy. It's all gonna be fine. I don't know what brought you here, but karma and God have a way of balancing the scales. Go back where you came from." He watched for a few seconds, then turned to walk away. A brief sound was all the warning he had. He whipped Bessie around and fired point blank into the creature that had jumped up and crossed the distance between them in an instant.

As the Wendigo staggered back, Jacobs ran up and jumped into the air, planting both booted feet in the creature's belly, driving it off its feet, directly into the fire behind it. Maddened bellows of pain followed as it struggled to pull itself from the fire. He fired his last silver bullet into the Wendigo at close range, driving it back and back, ever deeper into the blaze. Jacobs could feel the heat on his face and could smell burning hair as his eyebrows singed away.

Pride filled him, pride that he might have overcome such a dangerous opponent, in the service of God. *I am the Righteous Hand of God*, he thought. He pulled bullets from the bandoleer on his chest, replacing the rounds he'd fired, ordinary lead this time. He lost sight of the Wendigo in the flames and smoke, so he moved to get a better look.

From his new vantage point, he should have been able to see where the thing lay, but that spot was empty, save for a blow of ash and some fallen limbs. Damn, he thought, right before the claws ripped into his side. He gasped in pain as the claws clenched, ripping a large chunk of meat, and at least one rib, away from his body. He fell to the ground, rolling a bit away from the wound, and got off one more shot from good old Bessie. The lead bullet couldn't kill it, but he felt he needed to give it a hurt to match his own.

160

As the blackness closed in, his last view was of the Wendigo, standing over him. It opened its wide mouth, and said, in rasping and grating speech, "I bet that ITCHES!" Jacobs noted, almost clinically, the burns on the body, the bullet holes that still hadn't closed, black ichor running down like blood. I did that, he thought. He grinned with blood-stained teeth. "Go with God, bootlicker!" As the jaws closed over his head and violently ripped it from his body, his spirit was lifted up and away by an imagined host of angels.

Andrejz Duda was in his office, going over a few reports, when Hurley pounded on his door. Duda frowned. "This better be important. Come in!" He was a bit sharp. Neither of his groups of men were back yet, and he had had no information.

Hurley, his general right hand, was breathless from running. "Sir! There's a whole buncha' people coming this way from town, and it looks like most have guns!"

*Well, shit*, Duda thought. "Don't panic, Hurley. Round up as many men as you can, get 'em armed, and get 'em to the front gate. Now."

Hurley nodded and rushed out the door again, leaving it ajar, unable to speak. Duda took a moment to arm up, supplementing his usual pistol with a second, smaller revolver he kept in a holster in the small of his back, and a beautifully polished shotgun he'd gotten from the Pinkertons when they parted ways. Before he walked out, he checked his appearance in a small mirror by the door. As always, his white suit was immaculate, his very short hair perfect. He smiled at the mirror, the smile somehow predatory, then left the office.

As Duda strode through the mine yard, he could hear the alarm going up. Guards ran around him, racing to the front gate. All were armed. Hurley got that right, he thought. The lights were up in Riggs' office, so Duda knocked. "Yeah?" sounded from within, before Riggs opened the door. He appeared to have been napping, and he smelled like a distillery. Duda looked at Riggs without bothering to hide his disdain.

"There are people at the front gate for you from town. I think they want to lodge a complaint." He smiled mirthlessly before turning and walking away, toward the front gate.

Duda arrived at the front gate several minutes before the crowd, so he took time to set things up to his advantage. He had long expected something like this, so he had stacked the deck in his own favor. *A smart man leaves nothing to chance*, he thought.

When the crowd reached the gate, they had stopped singing. The mine was uphill from Copper Creek, and it took wind to make that climb. They found Duda standing by the entrance, shotgun in hand, laying back against his shoulder, relaxed, as if he were used to hostile crowds arriving late at night, all the time. He waited casually, watching as they couldn't decide what to do.

Finally, Mayor Dooley, unwilling to pass up a chance to impress the rabble, walked forward out of the crowd, flanked by Marshal Slay, Sheriff Steed, and Clint Black. "Duda!" The mayor pitched his voice so most of those present could hear him.

Duda nodded slightly. "Mister Dooley. What can I do for you?"

Dooley felt wrong footed, arriving at the head of a walking riot, expecting violence but being met with polite interest. Not usually at a loss for words, he said, "Um. We are here to free the natives!"

"Okay." Duda smiled. "Is there anything else?"

Dooley looked at the others, then said, "We want Thomas Riggs!" As he said that, Thomas Riggs all but skidded around the corner of his office, racing to the front gate.

162

Duda frowned. He started speaking just as Riggs arrived, panting. Riggs wasn't used to physical exertion. Duda said, "I don't care about the slaves, one way or another. They don't fall within the purview of my job, anyway. But keeping my client, Mister Riggs, healthy is definitely my job."

Riggs gobbled air. "Slaves? They can't have 'em!"

Duda stared at Riggs tolerantly, before turning back to face the crowd. "As I said, you are welcome to the Natives. But you can't have Riggs."

The crowd began to mutter. This was not going the way any of them had expected.

Duda turned and called out, "Hurley! I need the natives turned loose, right now! They are free. Got me?" Hightower was nodding his understanding as Riggs reached out to grab Duda's suit front.

Duda caught his wrist easily, turning a bit to keep the other man from touching him. Riggs shouted, almost directly into Duda's face, "Goddammit, Duda, you can't do that!"

Duda smiled and spoke quietly, just loud enough for Riggs to hear. "Asshole. Listen to me. We do not have enough men here, even if the groups I sent out were to come back right now, to stop these people. There is nothing I can do to stop them. But they also want you. Do you understand? It is my job to keep you safe. If they decide they want you badly enough, they will come get you. Now, kindly shut up and let me deal with this." Insultingly, he patted Riggs' cheek like a parent to a toddler.

Riggs looked like he wanted to explode, but, very wisely, did not speak. Clint placed a bet with himself that Riggs' head was going to pop like one of those rubber balloons.

Inside the mine, shouting and cursing could clearly be heard by the leaders of the riot. Riggs was looking wildly around as

163

the first of the natives came running out of the mine. They all looked malnourished and exhausted, and many bore marks of abuse. Riggs started getting some really ugly looks from people in the crowd. Duda was watching the crowd with one eye, Riggs with the other, waiting to see which would erupt first.

The natives that ran out first skirted the crowd and headed for the hills, not knowing that most no longer had homes to return to. Those that came after didn't have the strength to run. They were the last, the workers who had been in the depths of the mine and who had been working for many hours in the dark. Some were being carried by their fellows, unable to believe they were able to leave. As those unfortunates were carried out the front gates, the crowd closed around them, protecting them, and the muttering got darker.

Sheriff Steed was examining one of the natives who had flopped to the ground, unconscious. "Mike-Marshal!" She corrected herself immediately. "I need your help!"

Slay moved quickly, checking the native. After a hurried exam, he looked at her and shook his head. "He's gone." The man was probably in his fifties and weighed no more than ninety pounds. He was nothing but skin and bone. Steed's face hardened. The man had, literally, been worked to death. She and the Marshal exchanged a glance. Clint already had his SpellShooter out and was checking the load. Slay looked at Duda. "We want Riggs. He's going to answer to the law."

Duda looked chagrined. "Marshal. I understand what you want. And I sympathize. I do. But it isn't going to happen. Not tonight. You can come back with a warrant and we will comply. But you aren't going to get him now."

Slay opened his mouth to speak, but Duda cut him off. "Small victories, Marshal. Take what you can get."

Slay took a breath. "And if I insist?"

Duda considered and looked at Hurley. The men at the gate all racked rounds at the same time that three of his men moved crates to reveal a surplus Gatling gun. "Well, that might not go the way you think it will."

Clint reacted to that naked threat as any SpellSlinger would. He started to level his 'Shooter. Duda had been watching and snapped the shotgun down to point directly at Clint. "That would be a bad idea, SpellSlinger! I have this thing loaded with twenty silver dimes. I guarantee I can take you out before you can sling anything my way!" He paused, then said, in a slightly lower voice, "I don't bear any of you any ill will, but I will defend myself, this mine, and my client to the best of my ability! Got me?"

Clint wisely kept his 'shooter pointed downward. He nodded.

Slay conferred with Dooley and Steed. Finally, "Okay, Duda. We are going to do this your way. For now." He pointed at Riggs. "But if he leaves, I am going to hold you personally responsible."

Riggs had finally had enough. "That is BULLSHIT! You can't arrest me, you tinhorn excuse for a lawman! I don't recognize your authority, you hear me? I have too many friends in high places! You can't arrest me! I'll leave if I want, and you can't stop me!"

Duda cleared his throat. "I can. He has legal authority, and, as head of security, I must comply with his legal orders. The only reason you aren't in shackles right now is that he has to have a warrant to arrest you for constitutional matters. Unfortunately, there isn't any way around that."

Riggs' face darkened. "You'd just give me up? You coward! When I hired you, I made it clear that you would do whatever I ordered you to do!" He pounded his chest. "I made you rich!"

Duda's face showed no emotion. "Agreed. You did, and I did everything you asked me to do, no matter how unpleasant. Or illegal."

Riggs shouted, saliva spraying everywhere, "You Russian bastard! You God-damned coward!"

Duda smiled. Then, with no warning, he slung the butt of his shotgun sideways, butt stroking the side of Riggs' head with brutal force. As Riggs staggered back, Duda said, "You might want to watch your mouth, Riggs. While you still can."

Riggs barely managed to keep standing, blood streaming down his face from a cut on his left cheek. He struggled for several seconds before he was finally able to get words out. "You're fired!"

Duda laughed. "Are you sure, Suka?" Bitch.

Riggs face was purple where it wasn't white from the impact of the shotgun. "I said, you're fired!"

Duda's grin got huge. He leaned in, poked Riggs in the chest, and said, "Vashu mat!" Your mother. He turned to face Hurley. "That's it, boys! Pack it up! We are moving out!" The men all decocked rifles and started back into the mine yard.

Riggs was suddenly clear headed but perplexed. "What's happening?" The guards all ignored him, streaming past him to grab their belongings. Riggs slapped Duda's arm, or tried to. Duda moved with an economy of movement that was a wonder to watch. Riggs' hand missed him entirely. "You son of a bitch! What did you do?"

Duda turned, using the motion to backhand Riggs to the ground. The crowd had been getting restless, with some people breaking away to help carry ex-slaves to town. The call had gone out, and several younger men were running back to town to get wagons, and one man was running to Melville House to get the healer. Even then, there was only one 'The healer'.

When Riggs had cursed Duda, there were sharp intakes of breath all around. To call a man a son of a bitch was a deadly insult that almost no one was stupid enough to use, and many of them knew Duda's reputation. Riggs lay in the dust, unable to understand how his empire had crumbled so quickly.

Duda looked down at the man, laying there in the dirt, and began to laugh richly. Slay and Steed walked up to stand beside him, both also looking down at Riggs. Slay cleared his throat and said, "Care to let us in on the joke?"

Duda had the good grace to look embarrassed. "He gave me many orders I hated, but I did my job regardless. However, not long ago, I made myself a promise that, one day, I would knock his dick in the dirt." He looked quickly at Steed. "My apologies, ma'am, for my language. But as you see..." He motioned to Riggs and laughed again.

Slay grinned, Steed's cheeks heated a bit, and they both nodded. Duda said, "He's your problem now, Marshal. I have been relieved of my responsibilities, and my guards go with me." He turned without another word an, walking back to his office.

A half hour later, Duda had gathered his belongings and walked to the front gate. His men were already there, waiting. Riggs and the crowd were gone. Good, he thought.

Duda's men had done their jobs well. The mine was stripped of weapons, supplies, horses and wagons, everything they might need. Duda was carrying the important things, gold, silver, and copper that hadn't been shipped out the day before. It would take a very long time for the owners of the mine to piece together what had happened, and, by that time, Duda would be on another continent entirely. Hurley was just driving the last wagon through the gate, towing the gatling gun behind.

Duda pitched his voice so they would all hear. "Good job, boys! We are going down to town tonight. I will pay off anyone who wants, but I am going to Carson City from here. If you want to travel with me, I will extend your contracts until we get there, same rates!" There were mutters of agreement. Duda smiled. He knew their personal loyalty was to him, and he had been counting on that and their sense of greed to keep them together. Most of Duda's money was in a bank in Carson City, but, counting the money and ore he had just liberated from the mine, Duda had at least a hundred thousand dollars. So long as his men traveled with him, he had an escort and peace of mind.

# Chapter Sixteen

The woods had gone silent. Not just quiet, not merely still. Silent.

Even the wind seemed to hold its breath.

Flaherty sat on a wide, flat rock just beyond the ridge, overlooking the old trailhead like it was an altar to fate. The moonlight was dim and struggling to pierce the fog that curled like smoke through the trees. He placed one pistol on each knee, long-barreled, cavalry issue. Ivory grips, worn smooth by years of sweat and war. They glinted faintly with promise.

He was a big man once. Broad shouldered, heavy in the way old soldiers get from years of meat and hard liquor. But the war had taken some of him. The wilderness had taken more. Now he was all grit and angles, and the kind of resolve that only comes when you know your last sunrise has already passed.

From the tree line below, something moved. No noise. Just motion. And then it stopped.

Flaherty didn't rise. Didn't blink.

The Wendigo emerged slowly, as if it had all the time in the world. Which it did.

It was tall, lean in the grotesque way starvation is lean. Bones jutted at unnatural angles beneath gray skin stretched too tight, and the face—what little remained of a face—was a mess of raw muscle and bleached bone, a ruin of violence held together by will. Blue fire gleamed in its eyes, cold and ancient and utterly inhuman.

It studied him.

Flaherty breathed once, deep through his nose. The scent of pine sap and cordite clung to his mustache.

"Took your time," he said.

The Wendigo tilted its head. Then took a single, curious step forward.

Flaherty lifted the first pistol. Fired. Then the second. Both shots hit center mass, rocking the creature back on its heels.

It didn't fall.

It growled, a low, grinding sound that didn't belong to anything made by God.

Flaherty stood. He rolled his neck slowly, like a man rising from a nap. And fired five shots from each revolver. All hit, tribute to a life spent in war. His hands moved smoothly, breaking the spent cylinders, thumbing in new rounds with the same rhythm he'd once used to skin rabbits by the fire. No panic. Just ritual.

The Wendigo stepped closer.

"I seen the Devil at Shiloh," Flaherty said. "He had kinder eyes than you."

He raised both pistols and fired again. One, two, three, four. Smoke burst from the barrels. The Wendigo flinched once, then surged forward.

Flaherty dropped both pistols and pulled the blade from his boot.

170

They met in a savage crash of claw and bone and steel.

He fought like a man who had already died, silent and sure, carving long lines of blood into the beast's side. It slashed him across the ribs, but he didn't cry out. Another slash took him in the thigh, sending him to one knee. Still, he stabbed.

The knife sank deep into the creature's neck and the Wendigo shrieked.

It reached down, picked Flaherty up like a rag doll, and slammed him into the rock with bone-breaking force.

Flaherty coughed blood and laughed. "I hope I ruined your appetite, bastard."

Then the claws tore through his chest.

But when it was done—when the final breath left his broken body—the Wendigo didn't feed. It stood over him. Sniffed. Snarled. And stepped back. Maybe it sensed something sacred in the defiance. Maybe it recognized the taste of death that had no fear in it. Or maybe the old man had cut it deep enough that it needed to conserve its strength.

Whatever the reason, the Wendigo turned. It left Flaherty's corpse lying on the cold stone, arms outstretched, pistols beside him like offerings.

He had bought the others time. Not enough, but some.

Donaldson heard the shots.

All of them.

A flurry of sharp cracks from Flaherty's pistols. Then silence.

He didn't stop running. Couldn't. His legs burned, lungs raw from cold air and panic. Copper Creek shimmered ahead, barely visible in the predawn haze. The town — the mine — the lights. Safety.

He crested the last ridge and stumbled into the open. But the world had changed. The night wasn't just quiet now. It was wrong. The wind had teeth.

And behind him, he heard it. Not a growl. Not a shriek. Just... presence. Like a hand reaching down his spine. He turned. The Wendigo was there. Not twenty yards back. Walking. Slowly. It didn't need to run. It didn't have to.

Donaldson screamed. And ran.

Down the hill, toward the mine's outer path. He could see torchlight now — movement, maybe people. He screamed again, louder.

But his voice was already fading. He tripped, skidded into loose gravel. The last thing he saw was the light of Copper Creek — a promise he would not reach.

A shadow fell over him. No final words. No defiance. Just a flicker of horror in wide eyes before the Wendigo ended him with a whisper of motion — quick, brutal, final.

The fog swallowed the sound.


Rick Carter moved through the trees like a ghost. He didn't run. Didn't scream.

There was no point.

The others were gone. He'd heard the shrieks. Heard Flaherty's final stand. Then Donaldson's last cry — cut off sharp, like a snapped twig. That left him.

He followed the creek. Stumbled through thickets and shadow, boots soaked, heart hammering. The stream whispered beside him, cold and black, glinting under what little moonlight pierced the haze. He didn't look back. Not once.

At a bend in the water, he paused. Just long enough to slide off his coat and boots, teeth chattering from fear and cold. Then he stepped into the creek, the chill biting through him like knives.

*Let the current take me,* he thought.

That was the plan. Float downstream like driftwood, silent and low. If the Wendigo hunted heat, or sound, or motion — maybe this would fool it.

Maybe.

He drifted on his back, keeping his mouth just above the surface, every breath ragged and wet.

The current carried him slowly — too slowly — past stones and reeds, past trees that seemed to lean in to whisper secrets. His limbs were numb. His thoughts slowing.

But ahead, barely visible through the fog. he saw it. The low lights of Copper Creek Mine. Torches. Lanterns. Salvation. Ten more yards. Just ten more—

The water beneath him surged.

Something moved. He never saw it. Just felt the shadow fall.

The Wendigo landed on him with a splash like thunder. Razor claws drove into his shoulders, piercing bone and dragging him beneath the surface with inhuman force. The cold vanished in a burst of red-hot agony.

He thrashed once. Twice. Then everything went dark.

And his final thought, bubbling up through the pain, was one of despair: *If it found me... it means the others are gone. It means no one is coming.*

The water stilled.

Only the eddies swirled, red-streaked and silent, as the Wendigo rose from the stream and turned toward Copper Creek Mine.

Unchallenged. Unstoppable.


The night was too quiet. Not calm. Not peaceful. Just... still. Like the world was holding its breath. The children had all gone home, leaving Savannah and Ahyoka feeling...dissatisfied.

Savannah stood near the rear veranda of Melville House, watching the stars through the twisting shadows of the cottonwoods. Her gloves were off, hands resting on the railing, fingers twitching now and again — little nervous sparks of idle magic she hadn't noticed.

Behind her, the screen door creaked open.

Cyrus stepped out, coat draped over one shoulder, beard catching the moonlight. He didn't speak at first. Just joined her at the rail, sighing through his nose like the weight in his chest had been pressing down all day. "You're not asleep either," he said.

"Too much noise in my head," Savannah replied. "Not enough in the world."

Cyrus nodded. He pulled a small flask from his coat pocket, offered it. She declined. "Used to be I could sleep through anything," he said. "Gunfire. Spell riots. Three days straight in a Spell forge outside Monterrey. But lately…"

He trailed off. The wind rustled through the trees and died before it reached them.

"You feel it too?" she asked, quietly.

"I've been feeling it for days," he said. "The ley lines around the house don't sit right. Birds are flying wrong. Even my casting circle won't hold shape for more than a minute before something makes it twitch. And something has been prowling around the outside of the town wards."

Savannah turned toward him. "You think it's blood magic?"

Cyrus shook his head.

"No. This isn't like yours. This isn't rage or pain or memory. This is… something old. Something hungry."

She didn't answer. Just leaned closer.

"You're not afraid," he said.

"I am," she said. "But it's quieter now."

"Because you're stronger?"

"Because I finally know what I'd die to protect."

Cyrus smiled, proud and sad all at once. "You're not the little blood-soaked wild thing I found on the prairie anymore."

"Oh, she's still in there," Savannah said. "I don't think she will ever leave me."

"Good," he said. "You're going to need her."

Inside the doorway, Ahyoka crouched low, wrapped in a threadbare blanket, listening. Her eyes were wide, unblinking. Her spear was near at hand, though, taking shape as she worked her piece of obsidian glass. She started working on it the day after she'd arrived. Neither of the SpellCasters had objected.

They didn't see her. Neither of them.

"You've always stood taller than your shadow," Cyrus said. "But tomorrow, whenever this thing comes, you don't have to stand alone."

"I know," Savannah said. "But I might have to anyway."

They stood like that for a while, together in silence.

Cyrus reached over and squeezed her hand. She didn't pull away. "No matter what comes," he said softly, "you'll carry the light, Butterbean."

"Only because you lit it. I love you, Grampa. I always did, even if I never said it."

Cyrus smiled. "I know, Butterbean. I know."


The Lane brothers should've been in bed.

It was after eleven. The stars over Copper Creek burned sharp and still. Inside their small house on the north edge of town, their beds were neatly made and undisturbed. Their parents had no reason to check — they thought the boys were asleep, like always.

But Jason, fifteen, tall and lean and hungry for something more, was holding an oil lantern.
And Samuel, twelve, smaller and quicker and eager to be brave, carried an old potato sack.

They were in the mine. Trying to be clever. Trying to be useful.

"You think Duda's men left anything?" Samuel whispered.

"Maybe tools. Copper scraps," Jason said. "Stuff we can sell. We don't gotta tell Pa."

The tunnels were dark and still. The farther they walked, the heavier the air became. The copper had been stripped. The machines were silent. What was left behind was shadow and dust and creaking beams that sounded like whispers.

They turned past a split shaft. The lantern flickered.

Samuel froze. "Did you feel that?"

Jason turned. A sound. Wet. Dragging. Slow. Not like boots. Not like anything with rhythm or shape. Just… movement. The kind that doesn't belong.

Jason raised the lantern... and saw eyes. Not yellow. Blue. Icy. Unblinking. Floating in the dark like twin stars fallen from some wrong heaven. Watching them.

Samuel gasped.

Jason didn't speak. He dropped the lantern. The world went black.

And death came to Copper Creek.

Miss Eleanor Granger sat by lamplight, red pen tapping against her lip as she read over arithmetic sums with neat, childish handwriting. Her cat stirred restlessly at the window. She glanced up, irritated. "Not now, Clover."

The cat bolted.

That's when the door creaked open, unlocked.

She turned slowly. The flame flickered. Her breath caught.

In the doorway stood something hunched and tall, its shoulders brushing the frame. Its eyes glowed a brilliant blue, cold and evil.

She opened her mouth to scream, but it was already there.

The desk shattered and blood soaked the papers.


Laughter echoed down a darkened alley. Two men—one named Bill Travers, the other Andy Finch—slung arms around each other's shoulders, hiccupping from whiskey and a night full of dice and bad choices.

"Hey—what's that sound?" Andy said, voice thick with drink.

Bill squinted ahead. "Dog maybe?" Then the shadow moved. Fast. One flash of claws. One crunch. Bill tried to run, but his foot slid on something wet and heavy.

It was Andy's ribcage.


Father O'Malley was going over the ledger for the construction of the new church. It had been a long and emotional day, and he often sought comfort and solace in numbers. He spent hours every day reading the bible, and then would spend another hour or more going over those numbers. It kept him sane.

He heard a sound outside the rectory, a thump. He frowned. It was late, and there was no reason for anyone to be about. He strapped on his gun belt and stepped to the door. A minute or so of listening revealed nothing. He picked up the lantern he kept on the side table, adjusted the wick to provide more light, and opened the door. As he stepped out into the night, he heard a scuffling noise in the bushes along the side of the building.

Probably a raccoon, he thought. The scavengers had a tendency to haunt the buildings in Copper Creek, looking for scraps of food or other waste. He stepped over to the side of the building, intending to shake the bushes to drive them off. It was no raccoon. He had just enough time to register the size and the height of the creature there before it grasped him by his shoulder and waist and pulled in different directions. His body separated with a sodden ripping noise. There was no scream. He didn't have time.

Horace Kettle staggered out of the Copper Nugget with a bottle under one arm and a song in his throat. "I love a lass with ginger hair, who—hic—don't care what I ain't got—"

He tripped over a stone, laughed at the dirt, and never noticed the silent shape that stalked him from behind.

Later, all that remained of Horace was one torn boot and a leg bone gnawed clean to the marrow.

In a second-story bedroom, a woman lit a single candle and muttered a prayer. Her husband had died in the war; she hadn't spoken a word aloud since. Tonight, for reasons she didn't understand, she whispered to him.

"I feel... something, Charles. Like something awful's coming."

179

Downstairs, her dog growled once—then whimpered. She never heard the back window shatter.

They found her bed the next morning undisturbed. The blood pooled under it said otherwise.

This went on for hours, stragglers and groups of two or three, died without a chance to really fight, since word never came to Copper Creek. Entire families, wiped out in seconds. It was ugly and brutal. The Wendigo feasted, everywhere it went. The night was alive with the promise of death. But not everyone the wendigo visited, died.

# Chapter Seventeen

The bottle sat on the table, half-empty and untouched for hours.

Thomas Landshire had been there since sunset, unmoving save for the occasional twitch of his fingers against the walnut grip of his revolver. He hadn't cried. Not since the first day. That well had run dry. Now, he was hollowed out, a man-shaped void filled with grief too heavy to scream and rage too vast to act on.

The lantern on the wall guttered, the flame twitching like it too was afraid.

The revolver sat in front of him, gleaming faintly in the low light. Six rounds. All loaded. He'd checked five times. Maybe six. Just to be sure. His hand hovered over it every so often, then fell away. The courage to die, he thought, was different than the courage to live. And he had neither.

Then he heard it. A soft sound. A footstep. Not loud, not clumsy. Just present.

Thomas froze. Slowly, painfully, he turned his head.

It stood there. Inside the house. As if it had always been. The Wendigo. Massive. Gray. Wrong.

Its antlers scraped the ceiling. Its arms hung like twisted branches. Blue light burned in its eyes, colder than any winter he'd ever known. And it looked at him. Not like a predator. Not like a hunter. Like a judge.

Thomas felt it then, deep in his chest, a thing he couldn't explain. It was staring through him, past the grief and the fury, into something more fundamental. Something human.

His hand went to the revolver. The Wendigo didn't stop him. It just watched.

He picked it up. Slowly. His fingers curled around the grip, unsure. The Wendigo grabbed his arm, the one not holding the gun, then turned and began to walk. One massive hand gripped his forearm, gently at first, then with more insistence.

It was leading him. Thomas resisted, then realized walking was easier than being dragged. He stumbled at first, then kept pace, revolver still in hand. The night was silent. The fog crept along the ground like something alive. The Wendigo said nothing. It didn't need to. Its message was clear. Follow. They walked for two miles.

The trail ended at the edge of town. Mayor Dooley's home loomed in the darkness, smug and still.

The Wendigo let go. It stared at the door. Thomas looked at the house, then back at the creature. The front door was unlocked. He stepped inside.

Mayor Dooley sat at his table, surrounded by relics. Trinkets. Trophies. In his hands, he turned over a small necklace. A piece of string. With three colored beads. Thomas had made it with his daughter.

Dooley looked up. Smiled faintly. Then saw what was in Landshire's eyes. The door closed behind him.

The next day, the town awoke to a silence thicker than usual. The devastation of the Wendigo attacks became apparent, and the town turned to the mayor. Only one problem.

Mayor Dooley was missing.

When they found him, his body was hanging like a butchered hog in the rafters of his own barn. Drained. Gutted. Every bone in his arms and legs shattered like splinters.

There were no tracks. No witnesses. Only the wind. They blamed the Wendigo. They weren't wrong.

Andrezj Duda hadn't slept. The bed was too soft, the walls too quiet, and the wind outside carried a whisper that didn't belong. He told himself it was just the change in scenery—new town, new hotel, new ghosts—but he knew better. Men like him didn't get uneasy without reason.

After an hour of staring at the ceiling, he gave up. He dressed in silence, the leather of his boots creaking like old bones. The floorboards groaned under his weight as he stepped into the hallway, lit only by the flicker of a single oil lamp.

The hotel was full—ten rooms, two men to a room. Twenty of his best. Hardened men, loyal to the bone. He'd posted four guards: two on the ground floor, one upstairs, and one in the lobby. Routine. But tonight, the routine felt brittle.

Duda wasn't just a leader—he was a protector. His men ate first, slept warm, and got paid better than any outfit west of the Divide. They followed him not because they feared him, but because they trusted him. And because they knew he'd never send them into danger he wouldn't face himself.

Hurley had been with him the longest. Since the Pinkerton days, back when they still wore badges and pretended the law meant something. Hurley was no fighter—he was a scholar in a gunman's world. University-educated, fluent in four languages, and sharp as a Bowie knife. But Duda didn't need him to shoot. He needed him to think. Wars weren't always won with bullets. Sometimes, it was the man with the ledger who made the difference. And Hurley was the best damn clerk this side of the Rockies.

Duda stepped outside. The night was cold and dry, the kind of cold that crept into your bones and whispered that something was watching. He scanned the street. Empty. Too empty.

He went back to his room and armed up. Two knives—one for throwing, one for keeping. A six-shot Colt, worn smooth from use. And his shotgun: a presentation-quality heirloom, gifted to him when he left the Pinkertons. Walnut stock, engraved steel, and a brass plate etched with his name. Beautiful, but deadly. He'd loaded it with silver dimes—an old superstition, sure, but one he'd never stopped believing in. Silver had a way of settling things that lead couldn't. Finally, Andy was ready to play.

The back courtyard of the hotel was too quiet.

The wagons sat where they'd left them—tarps tied down, ore stacked neat, every supply crate intact. But there were no horses. No men. Just a long, wide swath of drying blood that soaked into the packed earth and cobblestones like something had painted with the bodies of his crew.

Hurley's shotgun lay in the dust near the fence. Unfired. Full. No struggle. No shouts.

Just blood.

Duda crouched low, examining the tracks. Not boot prints. Not hooves. Something bigger. Heavier. Like a bear, if a bear walked upright and hated the world. He drew his knife without thinking, his eyes scanning the dark. He'd seen death before. Plenty of it. But this felt… different. Not work. Not war. Something worse.

The stench rolled in before the noise, a wall of rot, bile, and something far older. Then it moved.

A shape detached from the shadows behind the stables—seven feet of twisted sinew and hunger. Pale flesh stretched over ribs like a drum. Its eyes burned cobalt. When it screamed, windows cracked.

Duda dove as claws scythed through the space his head had just occupied. He rolled, came up fast, slashing low. His blade opened meat across the beast's thigh. It stumbled, but only for a breath. Already the wound was sealing.

It charged.

He sidestepped the first lunge, slammed his boot into its chest, and drove his knife upward. The blade buried deep under its arm. It shrieked again, rage, not pain—and flung him across the courtyard like a doll.

Duda hit hard. Something cracked. He didn't stop.

The shotgun.

He lunged toward it, dragging himself, blood trailing in the dirt. The Wendigo followed, slower now, savoring the moment. Duda reached the shotgun. Rolled onto his side. Fired.

Both barrels roared, the silver dimes hitting center-mass. The beast reeled, smoke and ichor exploding from the impact. It staggered. Fell to one knee. Duda rose. He had time for one thought. *Best two bucks I ever spent.*

It came again, faster this time. Duda pulled his revolver, emptied six shots in two or three seconds. A man from another century would have said it wounded like a machinegun. The wounds were closing almost as they happened. Duda rushed forward, knives ready.

They collided near the crates. Teeth and steel. Claws ripped across his ribs. Duda grunted, drove his elbow into its throat. The creature slammed him into the wall, cracking brick. He headbutted it, stunned it, jammed the shotgun's muzzle under its chin and pulled the trigger.

Click. Empty. *Shit*, he thought. He swung it like a club, breaking off the stock across the creature's face. It flailed. He ducked under its swipe, jammed his blade into its ribs, twisted, then kicked off and rolled clear.

It wasn't enough.

The Wendigo barreled into him, claws like sickles punching through his coat and into flesh. His leg gave out. It hoisted him by the chest, slammed him down, then again, hard enough to break wood beneath him.

He didn't scream, didn't beg, just kept stabbing. His hands were slick with blood—his and its. The world shrank to breath, to pain, to motion. And still he fought.

It shrieked again, a deafening cry that cracked glass and silenced the world.

That's when the rest of his men arrived. Rifles barked. Dozens of shots. The Wendigo jerked, twitched, reeled. Duda slumped to the ground, slick with blood, barely breathing.

The creature didn't fall. But it fled, screaming, leaking black ichor across the stone as it vanished into the dark.

The courtyard was silent, save for Duda's breath. Shallow. Sharp. He looked up at his men—eyes clear, jaw tight. They rushed to him, hauling him up, dragging him toward the hotel doors as blood pooled behind him. Thirty seconds later, the SpellSlinger and the Marshal arrived at the back door, summoned from their rooms by the boom of Duda's shotgun. After one of Duda's men filled them in, they took up defensive positions by the door. Neither man was aware of the devastation that had fallen upon Copper Creek.

Duda's men called for a healer. Sent riders for Melville House. Offered anything. Because every man there knew: Andrezj Duda had just stared down death and made it bleed.

The sun hadn't yet crested the rooftops when Savannah arrived at the Silver Queen Hotel, her coat flapping open over a nightdress, copper casting gloves buckled tight to bare hands. Her hair was unbrushed, eyes hollow with exhaustion, but alight with something deeper, something that made every man standing guard straighten as she stepped past them.

The hotel courtyard was a shrine to butchery.

Shattered glass and cratered stone. Black scorches across pale walls. Blood pooled in every crack. And at its heart lay Andrezj Duda's broken shotgun.

The runner had told her they had Duda in the lobby, and they were waiting. Inside, Duda was laying on a couch, barely breathing, his skin pale, blood leaking from beneath a torn coat and fraying bandages. His men stood around him, grim and still, like sentries at a king's tomb.

As Savannah stepped through the lobby doors, the wall of men parted, not because they knew her, but because something in her walk said they *should*.

"Miss—he fought it alone—held it off till we came—"
"Didn't run. Not a step."
"He saved us. We owe him."

Their voices tangled over each other in urgency and guilt and awe.

She raised her hand. "Quiet." Silence. Twenty grown men, killers and mercenaries to the last, shut their mouths and stepped back like schoolboys scolded by a stern mother.

Cyrus stood by the fireplace, silent until now. As he stood, Clint walked quickly down the hallway and entered the room. He stopped short, standing by Cyrus, but didn't speak.

Cyrus moved to stand by Savannah. "You can't fix a wound like that, Savannah. Not without a cost. Not without calling something back with it."

She passed him without looking. "Then I'll make sure it doesn't stay."

Duda lay sprawled on the ruined chaise, shirt peeled back, his midsection soaked with blood. The skin around the cut was graying. Dried. Dead. That he was still breathing at all was a testament to just how tough a son of a bitch he was. Savannah knelt beside him and pressed one palm to his chest, one to his belly.

The first spell came gently, runes of healing, golden and green, danced in the air. The marks of Melville House. Controlled, regulated. Taught.

But they weren't enough.

She could feel it—the cold creeping up through his blood, the failure of tissue beneath her touch. She closed her eyes. The runes flickered. Changed. The golden lines deepened to red—old red. Not painted. Not inked. The kind of red that meant life. And price.

The room grew warm. Then hot.

Savannah's breath quickened, and her hands trembled as the power coiled through her like fire through copper wire. Somewhere, deep in her chest, she felt the magic pulling—not from the world, but from herself. From her blood.

Cyrus took a step forward. Watching. Watching her eyes. Waiting for them to go black. The glow around her flickered, and for a moment the light in her pupils turned as dark as obsidian—as dark as memory.

The room tensed. None of the men understood what was happening, but every one of them felt it. And men like that have one rection when they don't know what's happening. They all reached for weapons. They didn't know for sure what kind of threat they were reacting to, but they were ready.

They all felt the edge of something bigger, older, sacrificial. Savannah whispered words not spoken in centuries. And then the magic collapsed into Duda like a wave. He arched, shuddered, and breathed.

Cyrus exhaled like a man surfacing from deep water. She turned to him. Her eyes were blue. Clear. Beautiful. Savannah's eyes.

And in that moment, every man in that room realized they'd been holding their breath, waiting for something they couldn't name. And they let it go. Quietly. Wordlessly.

Savannah stood, slowly, her knees wobbling from the effort. She didn't speak. She didn't need to. She had done what none of them could do. She had pulled Andrezj Duda back from the edge. Not with coin. Not with guns. But with her soul.

And as the silence settled around the room, no one said a word. Not yet. But word would spread. It would travel from lip to lip, whispered with reverence and warning: *"She saved Duda."*

*"She burned something inside her to do it."*

*"She stared into death—and told it 'Not today.'"*

The wind was rising again. Low and hot, not enough to move the trees, just enough to lift the dust and make the corners of the town taste like ash.


**Dawn**

The sun never rose over Copper Creek. It merely bled into a sky of ash.

By morning, more than three hundred residents were unaccounted for—missing or dead. Blood soaked into dry earth. Houses sat open, doors splintered. No alarms had been raised. No one had heard more than half a dozen screams.

It moved silently. Efficiently.

In yards and alleys, inside parlors and along the far edge of the mill, the survivors found bones. Bones stacked in eerie neatness or scattered like splintered kindling. Every one of them gnawed clean. As if something had *feasted*.

The sheriff's deputies walked the streets at dawn with pistols drawn, their faces pale, their hands shaking. The townsfolk who remained said nothing. Couldn't. Not with the silence pressing in.

All anyone could hear... was the wind.

Marshal Michael Slay stood on the back porch of Melville House, coat off, arms resting on the rail. The sun was low, finally beneath the cloud cover, throwing gold across the rooftops of Copper Creek. It would've been beautiful, if not for the silence.

Behind him, Cyrus lit a pipe with hands that didn't shake, but only because they were too damn tired to try.

Slay looked far more relaxed than he felt. "I tried to call for help. Old Harold, the telegraph operator, was killed in his bed last night. Telegraph wasn't damaged, but nobody left alive knows Morse. Farspeak isn't workin' either. Don't know why, but nothin' is sending, and we aren't getting anything back."

Cyrus grunted. "If this thig is that powerful, it's presence is going to disrupt magical communications. Don't know why, but it always does. That's part of why hunting creatures like this down is so hard. Can't coordinate, and it picks people off one by one."

"Well, I guess we wait."

Cyrus grunted again. "Not dead yet. We still have a few tricks to pull. I'm worried about Savannah. What she did for Duda...she shouldn't have been able to do it. Not alone. It was too much."

"She's stronger than she knows," Slay said, not looking back.

"Stronger than *anyone* knows," Cyrus answered around the stem. "That's what scares me."

Slay nodded slowly. "You think she's a danger?"

"No. Not yet." A pause. A drag on the pipe. "But she's not built for what she's carrying. None of us are. Magic's like fire—you can light a hearth with it or burn your house down."

Slay tilted his head. "And she's the house?"

"She's the match. She always was."

They stood in silence, watching the streets, empty but not abandoned. Somewhere, a door slammed. A child laughed. Then quiet again.

"She saved Duda," Slay said.

"Yeah."

"But it cost her something."

"Yeah." Cyrus took another long pull. His eyes were on the horizon but Slay knew he wasn't seeing the sky. He was seeing Savannah—barefoot, bleeding magic, whispering spells older than the hills.

"I raised her to be kind," Cyrus said finally. "To be smart. To think for herself. Not to save the world." His tone was flat, grim.

"Maybe she's doing all three."

"And maybe she's burning alive and doesn't know it yet."

Slay turned. Leaned against the post. Ran a hand through his hair, then looked at the older man. "I want to evacuate the town," he said. "Take everyone I can, head for Carson City. Get the kids out. The ones that are left."

Cyrus raised an eyebrow. "You think this thing's gonna stop at Copper Creek? We don't know what it's after, but I wouldn't bet on it. You can't run far enough or fast enough."

"I think I don't know what the hell it *is*." Slay's jaw worked. "And that's the problem." More silence. More smoke. Then, quieter than he meant to say it: "You think it's after Riggs? He ordered the massacres."

Cyrus didn't move. "Don't know."

"What if... we put him out there? Tied to a post. Called it justice. Let the thing take him and leave the rest of us be?"

Cyrus finally looked at him. Not with shock. Not with judgment. Just tired eyes, as if Slay had finally said what he'd been trying not to think.

"And what if it doesn't leave?"

Slay exhaled slowly. "Make it a trap, then. Dynamite, kerosene, whatever we can find. When it goes for Riggs, set it off."

Cyrus grunted. "You know that might not kill it? Many things of the night cannot be killed with normal weapons at all."

"Then I suppose we'll know exactly what we're up against."

"Im going to set up a web of detection wards, separate from the defensive wards we set up before. Anchor them to myself. I should be able to know when and where it's coming. Once we know that we can fight. And maybe I can cast a few wards to control which way it goes, hurt it a bit if it strays. But again, its gonna have to be anchored to me, so once the fighting starts, I won't be able to move much. Else everything will collapse."

Slay grunted." Anything will help."

The light kept fading.

And somewhere, far beyond the edge of town, something breathed in the shadows and waited.

# Chapter Eighteen

The half-built church stood quiet beneath the midday sun, its frame casting jagged shadows across the hard-packed dirt. The sound of hammering had long since faded. The children had been taken home for the afternoon—fed, bathed, tucked into familiar blankets by hands that trembled a little less now.

Ahyoka sat cross-legged on the stone foundation, idly watching ants crawl over a scrap of bread. She said nothing. She rarely did.

Savannah stood nearby, arms folded, jaw tight, eyes fixed on the northern horizon where the hills knotted into mist. The air had changed—too still, too quiet. She felt it again.

The cold. The pressure. The waiting.

She didn't flinch when the footsteps approached behind her. "Clint," she said.

"How'd you know it was me?"

"You walk like you're trying not to be heard but still want someone to notice."

He stopped a few feet behind her, hat loose in hand, SpellShooter over his shoulder. "You're starting to sound like Cyrus."

"Maybe I'm starting to understand him."

They shared the silence, the breeze refusing to touch the church.

Clint shifted. "Folks are talkin'."

"I know."

"They're not sure what to make of you."

"Neither am I."

"You here to ask if I'm still human?" she added.

"No," he said. "I'm here to say it doesn't matter."

She blinked. "Is that supposed to be comforting?"

"You saved Duda. I saw twenty hard bastards freeze because you told 'em to. I saw power. I also saw control."

"That control didn't come easy."

"I didn't figure it did."

She studied him. "You afraid of me, Clint?"

He gave a small, tired smile. "I don't got room for fear anymore."

"You and me," he added, "we're standing in the breach now."

"You're a damn fool, Clint Black."

"Probably."

"But maybe you're my kind of fool."

He stepped beside her.

The wind finally moved.

———

Parents came one by one to drop off their children at the half-built church. None spoke much. They knelt, whispered prayers, tucked ribbons and tokens into small hands. Before leaving, they looked at Savannah—not with fear, but not with ease either. She was something between guardian and storm.

Ahyoka eased beside Savannah with a strip of dried meat. "I remember the first time you killed a rabbit."

Savannah turned. "I never told you that."

"You didn't. I don't remember it. I see it."

Savannah looked away first.

—

Across town, Andrezj Duda stood despite fresh bandages. His men were everywhere—on balconies, roofs, alleys. At the telegraph, Morgan Haley clicked SOS over and over, the only message he knew.

In Carson City, the confused operator repeated it to Warden Rusk.

Rusk muttered, "That's where Marshal Slay and Clint Black were headed... Find a skyship, anyone willing to take an emergency contract. I don't care who. Just find somebody. Offer whatever you have to. let me know." The operator nodded as Rusk left the room.

The dormitory was partially empty. Most of the 'Slingers stationed there were out on assignment or patrol. Most of those left were there for disciplinary reasons, or for rest.

Within minutes, he had a dozen SpellSlingers standing at attention, most drunk.

"Anyone willing to work for free?"

Every man stood.

SpellCasters arrived moments later, led by Frederick Melville. The group moved into the bar area as if they were coming home.

Fred smiled. Hey, Rusk. heard you might need some help."

Rusk smiled. "Hey, Fred! You know you and your boys are welcome at any party I'm puttin' on." Rusk was interrupted by the operator.

"Sir, the only ship I could get to respond was... *The Grand Empress*. Captain..."

"Tillman." Rusk groaned. "This just became an interesting night."

—

The hotel courtyard felt like a held breath. Duda chambered a shell.

"If it comes here," he muttered, "we feed it lead until it chokes or runs."

Everyone understood: there was no better plan.

—

Riggs sat chained at the center of the pit—ten feet wide, six feet deep, packed with dynamite and kerosene beneath a thin crust of earth. He wasn't told, but he knew. Everyone knew.

Cyrus knelt in the dirt, drawing old wards made of chalk, salt, memory, desperation. They pulsed faintly when he finished.

—

By sundown, fourteen townsfolk had slipped away into the hills.

As the last orange light died, a long howl drifted across the plains.

The waiting was over.

# Chapter Nineteen

The Wendigo approached Copper Creek slowly, arrogantly, certain nothing could harm it. The homes on the outskirts were mostly empty—its work from the night before. But not all.

The Wendigo never saw him coming.

Something thudded into the dust at its feet. A fuse sparked.

Then the world flipped sideways in a blast of heat.

When the ringing cleared, it looked up.

Elias stood on the roof of his cabin, Civil War coat open, grinning with half his remaining teeth. He drew back another stick of dynamite.

"Hey, you freak!" Perfect throw. Perfect explosion.

"Son of a bitch can throw," someone whispered behind a barricade.

"Son of a bitch *is* throwin'," another answered.

Elias kept going—each toss impossibly precise, each blast forcing the Wendigo back.

For two whole minutes, it was man versus monster. And the man was winning. Elias's grin got wider.

Finally the Wendigo bounded toward him.

Elias waited at the peak, holding a bundle of dynamite with hissing fuse. "Up yours, goat fornicator!"

He dropped it through the trapdoor.

The cabin detonated in a single thunderclap.

When smoke cleared, the Wendigo crawled from the wreckage—burned, limping, very much alive, very much pissed.

Somewhere in the human part of it, a thought surfaced: *They're all crazy.*

On the ridge, Clint had watched everything. At the biggest blast, he muttered, "Damn. I'd fight for a town like that."

Just after midnight, the alarm wards screamed.

The first scream came far off. Then another, closer. Then silence. Then more screams.

A woman staggered into the square, coated in blood to the wrists.

She managed one word: "Teeth." She died before midnight.

Screams echoed from alleys, homes, the mill. Some swore they saw the Wendigo at the ward line—still, watching.

Shots cracked uselessly.

It vanished, leaving a scorched mark shaped like three crossing claws.

"It's learning," one of Duda's men muttered.

From the hotel balcony, Duda grunted, broken shotgun in hand.

"Damn right it is. I taught it pain." He didn't smile. He kept watching the dark.

# Chapter Twenty

The mooring deck creaked as Warden Rusk and the gathered SpellSlinger and SpellCaster volunteers approached *the Grand Empress*.

The ship loomed above them—patchwork hull, scorched seams, rivets stained with things they didn't want to name. By the looks of it, She should've fallen from the sky years ago.

Instead, she hovered steady, humming like a held breath.

At the top of the ramp stood Captain Jack Tillman.

Scarred jaw. Burnt coat. One pale eye, one too-dark eye. One hand resting casually on a thick pipe that used to be a rifle barrel.

"You're gonna be late," he rasped. "Flying into a forty-mile headwind."

"We weren't expected at all," Rusk said.

Tillman nodded like that pleased him. "Good. I don't like surprises."

Behind Rusk, a young SpellSlinger whispered, "Is that the Tillman? With the talking shooter?"

Tillman heard. He turned to the boy with a grin that didn't belong on a sane man. "It doesn't talk anymore. Not to me." He tapped his skull. "We reached... an understanding."

Silence.

"Get aboard," he said. "The ship doesn't bite. Much."

A Caster flinched when a glyph on the hull blinked like an eye. Tillman chuckled without joy.

Inside, *the Grand Empress* was a contradiction—gleaming bolts, reinforced braces, war wood, spell-cabled helm. A wolf in patchwork wool.

Tillman guided them through it like a preacher through a graveyard.

Finally he stopped at the forward war deck.

Rusk crossed his arms. "You sure this thing's safe?"

"No," Tillman said. "But it's loyal."

"To whom?"

Tillman met his eyes with sudden clarity. "To whoever bleeds for the right reasons." He turned and opened the hatch.

# Chapter Twenty-One

The sky had turned that color between black and gray, the kind that meant the moon was close but not quite ready to rise. Fog clung to the buildings, low and cold, curling like breath from the mouths of ghosts. The fires around the town square had burned low, and volunteers raced around to feed them.

Most of the town was awake. They were too afraid to sleep, too keyed up to even try.

Clint Black stood near the barricades, behind a stack of crates and a half-burned wagon turned on its side. His spellshooter was loaded—ruby-core chambered, copper casing flawless, polished for focus. He'd only brought three of the fire bursts with him to Copper Creek. Now, he had one left after this.

His hands were steady; his eyes weren't blinking. He wasn't afraid.

The silence broke. A lantern on the far side of the square hissed out, as if snuffed by invisible fingers.

Every rifle rose. Every breath caught. The fog shifted, and they saw it— It came again just before midnight.

Just for a second. The Wendigo.

Thirty yards out. On top of the old mercantile roof. Blue eyes flaring like twin stars in a corpse's face, its elongated limbs splayed wide, its skin steaming in the cold. Bone and sinew and hunger, wrapped in something that mocked the shape of man.

It didn't move; it simply stared.

Clint fired. The ruby burst tore through the fog like a comet—white-hot flame erupting across the space between them. The impact struck the roofline in a flash of fire and steam. But the Wendigo was gone, vanished before the fire could touch it. Only the echo of its snarl remained, rattling the bones of every man and woman still standing.

Clint didn't move. Didn't lower his shooter. Smoke rose from the barrel. His heart pounded behind his ribs like a judge's gavel.

Behind him, someone whispered, "Did he hit it?"

Another voice, lower, "I didn't even see it move."

Duda and his crew scanned the streets below, hunting shadows. The Wendigo had vanished, but they knew it wasn't gone. Not really. That's why the faint crunch behind them—a whisper of mortar surrendering under something ancient and heavy—snapped every head around.

It rose over the edge of the roof like a curse made flesh. Gaunt. Towering. Eyes pale and endless. It stood, steam rising off its hide, and faced them.

Duda didn't blink. He drew his knives, one in each hand, and spread his arms—not in challenge, but in welcome. Like he'd been waiting. Like he was welcoming a friend back from Hell.

The gun crew scrambled, dragging the Gatling around. *Scree. Scree. Scree.* Metal shrieked. Breath held.

The Wendigo scanned the rooftop, slow and deliberate. Then its gaze locked on Duda. And held. Something flickered in its eyes. Not rage. Not hunger. *Memory.*

It tilted its head, the way a predator does when it's not sure if the prey is worth the wound. A moment passed. Then another.

And then, it stepped back. One pace. Then another. Still watching Duda. It turned. Dropped soundlessly over the edge. Gone.

Silence.

One of the crew let out a breath. "Sumbitch remembered," he muttered. "Didn't want to pay that price again."



And then—screams. From the far end of town. Shouting. A burst of gunfire. The sound of someone begging. Then nothing. The fire hadn't stopped it. The wards hadn't kept it back. And now, the defenders were shaking.

A man dropped his rifle. Just let it fall into the dirt and walked away without a word. A woman sitting behind a crate burst into quiet sobs. Another crossed himself and turned away from the square, vanishing down an alley without even taking his weapon.

No one stopped them, because no one had the strength.

Clint holstered his spellshooter slowly. His jaw clenched, his knuckles white. He looked toward the half-finished church. Toward the dome. Toward Savannah.

"Didn't miss," he muttered, talking mostly to himself. "It just wasn't there anymore." And for the first time since the ambush in the canyon—since the boy he had been almost died—Clint felt doubt curl cold fingers around his spine.

The monster wasn't just killing now, it was playing.

# Chapter Twenty-Two

Three hours into flight, the *Grand Empress* soared above a jagged sea of ridgelines, her battered envelope cutting sharp against the deepening dark. The volunteers had taken up loose stations— some resting, others maintaining their gear in silence, a few simply pacing the gun decks with nerves twitching like bowstrings.

Warden Rusk stood near the fore observation blister, arms folded, watching the terrain blur below. The ship was fast—faster than it looked—but not fast enough. Not in that headwind.

A voice rasped behind him. "You're frowning like a man who knows what the math looks like."

Rusk turned. Tillman stood there, backlit by the flicker of helm runes, pipe still clutched in one hand. No coat now—just an old harness over black-stained linen. His smile was lazy, but his eyes… too alert.

"I just checked our speed," Rusk said. "At this pace, we're not making Copper Creek before dawn."

"True."

"Which means we're no help at all."

"Also true."

Rusk exhaled. "You have a suggestion?"

"I do," Tillman said. "You're not going to like it."

"Try me."

The captain stepped closer, tone dropping to something quieter, heavier. "There are two sealed canisters mounted just forward of the rear turbine cluster. Naphtha rockets. Meant for emergency thrust—old Concordium tech. Never rated for crewed airships, but back when I was young and full of bad ideas..." he trailed off. "They work. Kind of."

Rusk stared at him. "Kind of."

"Look, I'm not promising finesse. What I *am* promising is altitude loss, turbulent crosswinds, and a brief period where this old lady tries to tear her own guts out through the stern." He leaned in, too close. "But we'll be over Copper Creek by three a.m."

"That's still an hour too late."

"Better than the alternative," Tillman murmured. "Something is happening down there. You feel it too."

Rusk didn't answer.

Tillman stepped back and lifted a brow. "You're the ranking Warden here. Say the word, and I'll keep sailing slow and proud like a parade balloon."

The silence stretched. Crewmen looked up from their stations. Volunteers paused at what they were doing.

Rusk looked at the deck, then back at the captain. "Do it."

Tillman's smile widened—no joy in it. Just sharp teeth and momentum. "Very good." He turned and strode across the bridge with purpose, shouting over his shoulder. "Chief Kallis! Prep the infernal twins!"

From a hatch near the aft platform, a lean woman with burn scars and soot-streaked goggles stuck her head out. "Sir, say again?"

"I said—ignite the damn naphtha rockets!"

She blinked. Then grinned. "Aye, sir. You're all mad."

"Better mad than late."

Below the deck, a deep groan rumbled through the keel. Somewhere inside the engine housings, something hissed. Then another hiss, longer, sharper. Warning klaxons—not magical, but mechanical—chirped three times.

And all across the ship, the crew strapped in.

One of the volunteer Casters gulped. "What's happening?"

Another muttered, "I thought this was the safe ride."

The gunnery officer whispered, "There *is* no safe ride with Tillman."

From his place at the helm, Tillman barked one last command: "Hold on to something. If you love your teeth, clench 'em. If you believe in anything, now's the time to start praying." Then, under his breath—just loud enough for Rusk to hear: "Let's show them what the *Grand Empress* can still do."

Outside, the night rippled. The mountains below screamed past. And the stars began to blur as the ship surged forward, reckless and roaring, into the jaws of fire.


The dome shimmered in the dark like frost in moonlight.

Its glow was faint now—blue-gray and pulsing softly above the unfinished church where Savannah stood. She hadn't moved in hours. Not since the last spell, not since the moment she'd added the final layered weave of shielding around the children.

They slept.

All twelve of them, bundled into blankets, heads tucked under arms, curled against each other like puppies in a storm. Ahyoka was the only one awake, sitting beside Savannah's knee, eyes wide and unblinking.

Outside, the wind had stopped. The town held its breath.

The ward lines Cyrus had drawn still hummed beneath the streets, but they were growing weaker—Savannah could feel it in her bones. Magic had weight. It had memory. And it was tired.

She was tired. The last hour had brought no fresh screams. No gunfire. Only silence. That was worse.

That was *hunting* silence.

She stood barefoot on the timbers, copper gloves forgotten behind her. Her fingertips brushed the dome. The weave trembled slightly at her touch. Her skin prickled with cold and something deeper, a knowing.

It was close.

She reached back, feeling for the next thread of magic, already knowing what it would cost her.

Ahyoka touched her sleeve. "You're not alone," the girl whispered.

Savannah didn't answer. Because she wasn't sure it was true.

When the wards sang, everyone in earshot froze.

Everyone except Riggs.

Jenkins, one of Steed's oldest men, pressed a lantern into Riggs' hands. "Nobody should meet death on anything other than his own terms," Jenkins said.

Slay didn't argue, just gave Riggs a long, level look.

Riggs chuckled low. "Guess this is mine, then."

The pit beneath his boots was a killing ground—dynamite, blasting powder, kerosene, and every scrap of hell they could scrape together. All he had to do was wait.

The Wendigo's silhouette appeared in the dark, stalking forward with that unnatural, loping gait. Riggs raised the lantern high, letting the beast see him plain. "Over here, goat-fornicator!" he bellowed. "I've been savin' you a seat in hell!"

The creature hissed, circling warily, the earth shuddering beneath its steps. Riggs kept talking, taunting, and cussing it in ways that would have made Elias proud. "Elias danced you around with dynamite—me, I'm gonna bury you in it."

It closed in, drawn by the noise, the light, the heartbeat it could almost taste. In seconds, it was at the edge of the pit. Riggs' grin turned into something sharper, almost a sneer. "Alright," he said, voice low but carrying. "Let's see if you can take this with you."

He dropped the lantern.

For a heartbeat, the world went silent. Then the pit erupted in a white-hot roar—earth, flame, and splinters of the street exploding upward in a shockwave that rattled windows for blocks.

When the smoke cleared, the Wendigo staggered out of the crater—burned, bleeding, but still moving. It moved away into the darkness before anyone could fire more than a few shots.

And Riggs was gone. In death, Thomas Riggs gave the town one thing he never had in life: a moment of courage.

# Chapter Twenty-three

Marshal Michael Slay stood alone at the far edge of the detonation site. Smoke still curled from the shattered crater, rising in thin gray ribbons that twisted like remorse into the night sky. The flames had long since guttered out, and nothing of Riggs remained, no body, no bones, not even a piece of clothing. Just scorched rock, churned earth, and the faint metallic scent of burned powder and old blood.

He had expected to feel satisfaction. Maybe relief. Instead, he felt hollow.

Riggs hadn't hesitated—not long, anyway. Just a flicker, a pause before the fire. Riggs had been a monster, sure. He had brought misery and cruelty to the mine and everyone under its sway. Slay had come to Copper Creek convinced the man was a parasite, a wart on the soul of the territory. But in those final minutes, watching Riggs face the Wendigo without flinching, something had shifted.

Riggs had known what was coming. He hadn't begged. Hadn't screamed. He had cursed the Wendigo like a man who knew exactly what he deserved. And when he dropped the lantern, they had all heard the laughter.

The words haunted him now. Not because of what they were, but because of how they were said. There had been no anger. No spite. Just grim acceptance. And maybe—just maybe—a sliver of something like redemption.

Slay hated the thought.

Men like Riggs weren't supposed to get redemption. They weren't supposed to find courage at the end. But he had. And that, more than anything, unsettled Slay. It made things murky. Complicated. Human.

He crouched at the edge of the crater and ran his gloved fingers through the soot. It crumbled between them, gritty and still warm. Somewhere in that black dust were the last fragments of a man who had enslaved others, profited off pain, and turned men into tools—but who, when the moment came, had chosen to die standing.

Slay closed his fist, holding the ash a moment longer before letting it fall.

He could not speak of this to the others. Not the way it truly happened. They would remember Riggs as the tyrant who got what was coming to him, and that was fine. That was how it should be. But Slay knew the truth now. The bastard in the pit had gone out like a man—defiant, proud, and alone.

And that truth would live quietly in the Marshal's heart, where it would fester. Because now, in the deep hours of the night, Slay couldn't help but wonder: if Riggs could find courage at the end, then what excuse did he have?


*Time: 2:12 A.M.*
*Altitude: 5,000 feet and dropping fast*

The *Grand Empress* screamed through the night like a comet bleeding brass and canvas. The hull rattled. The struts groaned in protest. One of the older volunteers, a SpellCaster who'd seen the Siege of Wichita, muttered quiet prayers between clenched teeth. Another retched into a bucket and swore he'd rather fight demons on the ground than trust airships ever again.

And then came the sound.

**A shriek.** Metal on metal. Pressure valves blowing in sequence. And then—
**BOOM.**

A blast rocked the aft quarter, hurling two crewmen into the port rail. A plume of fire shot back from the rear turbine, spiraling into the sky like a dying star. A thunderclap of twisted magic and failing metal rolled across the deck.

"ROCKET TWO'S GONE!" someone shouted. "FAILURE IN THE CLAMP—SHE BLEW HERSELF LOOSE!"

Sparks lit the sky in a sweeping arc as half the rigging cables from the port side snapped free and lashed across the top deck like steel whips. The ship bucked hard. Screamed again.

Tillman didn't blink.

"Trim the envelope. Kill the second rocket. Drop ballast from midships and steer into the yaw!" he barked, already at the wheel, yanking it against screaming resistance.

"But we'll lose altitude!"

"We're already losing altitude!" he snapped. "You've still got a ship, don't you? Fly it like you stole it! Just make sure we don't lose the whole damn ship!"

Rusk staggered to the fore blister and looked out. They were descending hard—fast—but the nose was holding steady. The explosion hadn't crippled them. But it had delayed them.

# Chapter Twenty-Four

It didn't come like a monster. It came like a calamity.

The Wendigo burst into the town square just past 3 a.m.—a streak of bone-white muscle and shrieking, bloody hunger. It vaulted from the courthouse rooftop, its claws carving stone as it landed, hurling dust and shards across the defenders' line.

Everything exploded.

Clint Black fired the first shot—his spellshooter roaring with a viridian burst of force. The spell smashed into the Wendigo's path, tearing up stone and wood, but the creature blurred left, slipped behind a wagon, then leapt over it like a beast with wings.

Slay stepped into its path, firing twice. Silver-jacketed rounds slammed into its flank—one burst in a hiss of light, searing flesh. It howled, lunged, and swept an entire barricade aside with one blow.

"On it!" Slay barked. "Circle up! On me!"

Then the monster was among them.

Gunfire split the night—defenders falling back, blood spraying into the dirt. A man screamed as he was lifted clean off his feet and torn in half before he hit the ground.

Sheriff Sharon Steed stood firm at the edge of the alley, her scattergun braced tight against her shoulder, jaw set like iron. Behind her, the last of the townsfolk staggered through smoke and shadow—women sobbing, children clutching for any hand they could find, bloodied survivors limping or crawling into the uncertain dark. Every step she took steadied the line between salvation and slaughter. When the Wendigo's bone-rattling shriek echoed through the corridor, she didn't flinch.

She fired once, smoke curling off the creature's chest, pumped, fired again. The recoil slammed into her shoulder, but she held fast. A massive claw slashed through the mist, aimed for her heart. She dove sideways, steel raking her ribs in a blossom of fire. She rolled hard against a wall, came up bleeding, and fired a third time. The impact made the beast rear back with a shriek that turned blood to ice. Her revolver was already in hand—six shots straight into its chest. It barely noticed.

Then came Slay's voice, sharp over the chaos. "Sharon, get back!" His rifle barked seven times as he moved forward, shots striking the Wendigo's spine. It turned. Slay didn't hesitate. He lunged forward, dragging Sharon into a crouch with him just as the beast swung again.

The blow landed square. Bone split. Slay was lifted and flung like a ragdoll, blood trailing in the air before he hit the ground hard and didn't rise. Sharon scrambled to him, grabbing at the ruin of his coat, pressing useless hands to wounds she knew she couldn't close. His eyes met hers—dim, barely focused—but they found her. He saw her. Knew her. Knew what was between them. Then nothing.

Clint Black entered the alley like judgment incarnate, his copper arm catching moonlight in sharp lines. He took in the sight—Sharon hunched over Slay's broken form, tears soaking into his shirt—and didn't speak. Didn't cry out. He turned toward the thing that had taken his friend.

The Wendigo rushed him, jaws wet with blood. Clint stepped forward without a word, the street going silent as something deep inside him uncoiled.

The creature struck. Talons like knives, full of rage. Clint didn't move. But his arm did.

The copper prosthetic snapped out like a striking snake, catching the Wendigo's claw mid-swing. The buzz that followed wasn't mechanical. It was alive—like a storm trapped in brass, like

214

fury made metal. The Wendigo shrieked and pulled, but it couldn't break free. That hand held on with something more than muscle. Clint hadn't told it to move. Hadn't even thought to.

It didn't matter. His SpellShooter was already in his other hand. He didn't remember drawing it, but the moment it touched his palm, it roared to life. He shoved the barrel into the creature's belly and fired.

Once.

Twice.

A third time.

Each spell hit harder than the last. Sparks chased bullets up the creature's chest, splitting open fur and flesh, snapping bone. The last shot, the fifth, he let go as he said, in a whisper, "Die, you son of a bitch!" That fifth round—a comet forged in grief and wrath—slammed into its jaw like the will of Heaven and sent the beast flying. It crashed into the stone wall behind it, then flipped backward into the wide pit Andrezj Duda had prepared hours before, the same one where Riggs had met his end. The Wendigo hit the bottom hard.

It didn't rise, not immediately.

Across the square, on the hotel's second-floor balcony, Duda stood in the shadows, long rifle steady in his hands. His voice tore across the square. "Turn it! It's in the open—now!" His men moved like a machine, the Gatling gun swinging around on makeshift braces. The crank turned. The barrels spun into a blur. Then fire, a foot long, erupted from the barrels.

Hundreds of rounds slammed into the pit in seconds. The Wendigo twitched. Then stirred. Then stood.

Not dead.  Not even truly wounded.  But rattled.  It turned its head toward the rooftop team, then bolted toward the dark, trailing blood and rage.

Clint didn't follow.  He stood where he'd been, his SpellShooter still warm in his hand, the copper filigreed arm slowly uncurling, steam ghosting from the joints.  He looked down at the hand.  Felt the hum beneath the surface.  "We're not done," he said softly.  And somewhere inside the metal, something answered.  Agreed.

The Wendigo slowed—not from pain, not from injury, but from certainty.  It had found what it was looking for.  Its head turned, smooth and slow as ice over glass, until its eyes locked on the faint, shimmering glow radiating from the half-built church.  The dome pulsed, dim and resolute beneath the broken rafters.

The creature stopped killing.  It stopped chasing and shrieking.  It simply started walking—straight toward the church.  Not fast.  Not urgent.  Just moving.  Deliberate.  Hungry.  Certain.

Duda saw it first, and something in his gut twisted.  "Oh, hell…"

Clint Black was already loading fresh rounds into his shooter, movements precise despite the burn of fatigue.  His voice was low, urgent.  "Savannah."

He checked his belt—four rounds left.  None were inferno-class.  Nothing he had would stop what was coming.  Still, he ran.

The Wendigo passed through gunfire like it was mist.  Duda's men opened fire from rooftops, alleys, second-story windows—but nothing slowed it.  It didn't look at them.  Didn't acknowledge the bodies it left behind.

And when a dozen defenders, too brave or too desperate to let the thing pass unchallenged, charged it with knives, with shovels, even with their bare hands, it cut through them like wheat.  Until

216

one, desperate and strong, swung a pickaxe, with a full windup, into the wendigo's back. Then, it screamed! For an instant, host and spirit were in step, shocked by the incredible pain and unable to move. Then, without thinking at all, the beast turned and smashed the man into and through a brick wall. The stuff that ended up on the other side didn't look much like a man anymore. The rest died a few seconds later. And yet, the host beneath the spirit felt... a touch of admiration? Then it was gone, buried under a new wave of anger and desire for revenge.

The beast hadn't been hunting the dozen; it wanted the girl. It only saw her.

# Chapter Twenty-Five

Inside the dome, Savannah Melville stood barefoot on ash-streaked stone. Her gloves were gone. Her dress torn. Her skin smudged with copper soot. And still she didn't move—not when the Wendigo stopped at the barrier, not when its claw touched the surface and made the air sing.

The shimmer lit up white, then cracked with veins of silver lightning. A ripple passed through the dome. Children stirred. Ahyoka opened her eyes.

The Wendigo leaned in, pressed its forehead to the barrier, and screamed. Not in rage. In joy. It had found its match.

It raised both claws high, spread wide, and struck.

The sound wasn't thunder. It was judgment. The force split the air, blew banners from poles, turned ash into whirlwinds. The outermost layer of the dome shattered, a luminous shatter-wave rippling outward. The Wendigo reeled, talons digging into the ground to brace itself.

Savannah didn't move.

It came forward again, slower now, savoring it. It pressed a claw to the dome again, and this time it didn't test—it struck.

The second layer shattered in a cascade of blue light, the sound like bells dropped into water. Wind blasted the square. Crates skidded across cobblestone. Cyrus, watching from a distant alley, winced.

"That one was mine," he muttered. "Best I ever built."

The Wendigo smiled, a jagged, wrong thing. Then brought down its claws a third time.

The golden-orange layer ruptured in a molten cascade, fragments hovering like fireflies before winking out. Nearby buildings cracked. The square shook. The defenders paused, stunned by the impossible sight.

Cyrus dropped to one knee. "No," he breathed. "No no no—" His hands trembled. Not from fear. From futility.

Inside the dome, Savannah opened her eyes. They were glowing—bright blue, like white-hot steel before the forge takes it.

She breathed in. The magic came willingly.

The air around her shimmered. Sparks jumped from her skin. Her hair floated upward. The church groaned beneath the pressure. She didn't use gloves. Didn't use symbols. She cast from instinct, building a new layer. Then another. Under the ones collapsing, she built more. Not as walls—but as ribs. Bones.

The Wendigo screamed and struck again.

The fourth blow exploded, a violet layer, in a tremor that cracked the cobbles and fractured stone foundations. Defenders were thrown down like dolls. Savannah wove faster, pulling from ley-lines, from the air, from herself. It hurt. Every breath a fire in her chest.

Cyrus stumbled forward. "She's rebuilding faster than it can tear down…" Then he stopped. "No—too fast. Savannah, you're not ready—"

The fifth strike came like a curse.

A sick-green weave—woven from tangled roots and bitter truths—imploded, sucking all sound and warmth away. The wind reversed. Ash swirled inward. Even moonlight bent toward the dome.

The Wendigo doubled its attack, claws hammering down. Each blow cracked a layer. Savannah dug in harder. Sweat beaded her brow. Her arms shook. Her lips moved, but no words came. Only magic.

Cyrus stared in horror. "She's direct casting," he whispered. "She's not just weaving—she's drawing ambient raw…"

The dome flickered.

The defenders saw it. Not spell work. Not control. Just need. And force of will. Savannah was no longer building to protect. She was building to survive.

The Wendigo struck again—harder and faster. The sixth blow sent a spiderweb of energy flashing across the dome's surface. Savannah staggered. Blood streamed from her nose and eyes. Still, she cast, burning something of herself in her haste. Pain began to throb behind her eyes, and a buzzing filled her ears, an old friend from the first time she ever manifested magic.

Her eyes were blue—but fading. Flickering.

Behind her, the children were silent. Ahyoka stood with her, spear in hand, stone-faced. Ready.

Savannah inhaled magic like air, like life, and forced it outward. Deep inside her, the blood magic stirred.

And then, Clint stepped from the shadows. He fired one last shot—an overloaded flare, straight into the Wendigo's back.

It hit. It fizzled. No damage, but enough to annoy the monster. The Wendigo turned and swiped. Clint flew backward, crashed to the ground, and didn't rise. His arm twisted beneath him, mangled, his body still.

Savannah's throat clenched with a scream that never escaped.

Cyrus stepped forward. No gloves. No cloak. Just light. "You want her?", he asked. "Come through me." He didn't wait. He raised his hands and cast. *Nailstorm.* Typically, SpellCasters don't use offensive spells. But people being people, sitting around, drinking beer, they would, invariably, start talking about spells that could be...repurposed. *Nailstorm* was such a spell, normally used to drive nails for construction. This was different. Deadly, not something spoken of outside the bar.

A storm of iron nails screamed into being—dozens, hundreds, flying from nowhere. The Wendigo shrieked, torn open. Then turned. Moving as a blur, it ended him. One claw. Cyrus folded like parchment, blood spraying across the stones.

Savannah watched him fall, and something inside her broke.

She pulled. Not from the ground. Not from the ley-lines. From the dome itself, a giant static reservoir of magical energy. Every weave, every strand, every shell she had built—she pulled it inward. Into herself. Into her soul. And she reached for her old friend, the blood magic.

The blood magic surged, roaring in delight, a happy puppy getting attention. Not a whisper this time. Not a voice, a roar.

She glowed—blue rimmed in deep, ancient red, too bright, too THERE for anyone to bear witness.

She raised her hands, and let it go.

It wasn't a spell. It was an event, a cataclysm. A detonation of light and fury. Red and gold and screaming white. The unfinished church became the eye of a sunburst. The Wendigo was caught full-on, lifted from the earth, and hurled—screaming—into the night sky. Not slain, even then, but gone.

And the dome was no more. Only silence and fire remained. And a girl on her knees, breathing smoke. A girl who slowly collapsed to the ground, like a balloon losing its air.

The town broke. Buildings shattered, walls caved in, and glass exploded outward like shards of fallen stars. The ground cracked and trembled beneath the force of the blast. Men and women were flung across streets like leaves caught in a gale—and some would never rise again. Overhead, a pillar of flame shot into the sky, so bright that it turned night into day for a full thirty seconds and so hot it burned the shape of Savannah's rage into stone.

The stars above seemed impossibly bright in the frozen air. And then, all at once, the world changed.

**At 3:34 a.m., the sky lit up.**

Far to the west—perhaps fifteen miles—something erupted in the darkness. A bloom of fire. A swelling pillar of light and heat and raw, impossible energy. **A mushroom cloud,** colored in gold and hell-red, roared up from the horizon, tearing the sky in half. The cloud lifted, churned, and then stilled—**silent** from this distance, but visible like a sunrise that had come early just to watch something die.

No one spoke.

The volunteers leaned over the rails. The crew could only stare, witness to the light of destruction.. And even Tillman went quiet, one hand on the helm, eyes locked on the rising column.

Rusk stepped forward. His voice was low. Grim. "Copper Creek."

Tillman didn't nod. Didn't curse. He just tightened both hands on the wheel. "I saw something like that once," he murmured. "When a rogue Concordium artificer tried to contain a fire god in a wine cask. Didn't end well."

Rusk turned. "Can we still reach them?"

"We'll be over the ridge before four," Tillman said. "If the engines hold."

"And if they don't?"

Tillman grinned, and this time the gleam in his eye was something more than crazy. "Then we jump."

# Chapter Twenty-Six

**Time: 3:44 A.M.**
**Altitude: 4,300 feet. Descending fast.**

*The Grand Empress* banked around the final ridgeline like a wounded hawk, smoke trailing from her aft, her silhouette glowing in the distant light of a world just burned.

Copper Creek was gone.

Not entirely—not yet—but the damage was done. Entire blocks lay flattened. Timber, stone, and shattered metal had been blasted outward from the epicenter like matchsticks. Fires still licked at what few walls stood, embers swirling in the wind like fireflies with a taste for grief.

At the center of it all: a ring of soot.

Twelve children stood in a perfect circle, motionless. Faces blank. Eyes wide. Silent.

At their center lay a young blond woman, unmoving. Her skin was blackened at the edges, like parchment singed in a stove. Her copper gloves were gone. Her dress in tatters. Her hair matted with soot and blood.

A young girl in native clothing stood over her, spear in hand, daring the world to come closer.

Clint Black stirred on the far edge of the blast zone. Pain knifed through him as he rolled onto his good arm. His prosthetic burned like molten iron. Still, he dragged himself upright.

"Savannah…"

She lay curled on scorched earth, her breath shallow. Around her, the twelve children did not move, as if the blast had frozen them in place. Ahyoka stood at Savannah's head, barefoot and steady, a sentinel carved out of the end of the world.

Clint limped toward them, eyes sweeping the devastation. No one approached. No one dared. The survivors watched the girl who had saved them all with awe, fear, and disbelief—none sure whether they had just witnessed salvation or a calamity wearing human skin.

Above the ruin, *the Grand Empress* circled once, its shadow falling over the crater like a shroud.

And the world, for a long breath, held still.


The sky had gone white for a heartbeat. Then red. Then black with smoke.

Hundreds of miles west, the crew of the *Skyward Mercy* saw the flash ripple across the night. Magic like that did not happen quietly. Captain Helena Ward stood rigid at the observation deck, arms clasped behind her back, as the afterglow burned on the low clouds.

She didn't wait for confirmation.
"Signal every skyship within reach," she ordered. "Call for medevacs, relays, reinforcements. Prep every medic onboard. We're going in."

Communications Officer Arik Vell paled as a farspeak directive crackled into being—Concordium authority code crimson, demanding the *Mercy* land and detain whoever had triggered the magical catastrophe.

"Captain," Vell said, brittle, "they're ordering full containment. Immediate seizure of—"

225

"Tell them I've got casualties on the ground," Ward snapped. "And they can damn well wait their turn."

"Ma'am, that's a—"

"Not debating it."

She turned to her officers.
"Commander Denz—get every medic into parachute harnesses. Gunnery Chief Thorne—I want the spellcannon warm and watching. If something crawls out of that crater and looks unfriendly, we erase it."

"Aye, Captain."

*The Skyward Mercy* dropped into a dive, engines screaming as the ship knifed toward the smoke.

As they descended, a shadow drifted into their path—a battered, familiar silhouette. Captain Ward narrowed her eyes at the broken-gilded hull.

"*The Grand Empress,*" she muttered. "Tillman… you crazy bastard."

No time to worry about him.

Below, Copper Creek smoldered—ruined buildings, broken streets, ash drifting like gray snow. At the epicenter lay a girl, surrounded by twelve silent children, guarded by a SpellSlinger who looked half-dead and wholly unwilling to take a single step back.

Gunnery Chief Thorne whispered, "By the gods…"

Ward didn't blink.
"Drop medical," she ordered. "No weapons unless fired upon. We help first. If justice comes, it comes later."

Medics leapt from the sky, parachutes blooming like white flowers against the smoke.

And the *Mercy* descended into hell.

# Chapter Twenty-Seven

By dawn, a fleet hovered over Copper Creek.

Two UAN vessels—*Star of Texas* and *Resolute*—anchored above the smoke. SpellCaster research ships arrived next, then SpellSlinger auxiliaries, private airships, Concordium vessels in full regalia. Hundreds of medics, engineers, artificers, and first responders parachuted in the moment anchors set.

But no one approached Savannah Melville.

Not until Clint allowed it.

He sat beside her on the blasted stones, his splinted arm strapped tight, his copper prosthetic humming like a wounded engine. His face was carved with grief—fresh and raw and beyond words. He did not look up when they asked questions. He did not acknowledge titles, ranks, or badges.

He stayed with her. Breathing. Bleeding. Watching.

Two Weavers and two Coppers formed a quiet ring around him—not ordered, not commanded, just present. An honor guard built out of respect and fear of the man who had stood, broken, against a thing from nightmares.

Ahyoka kept her spear in hand. None challenged her right.

When Cyrus Melville's death was confirmed and transmitted through farspeaker, the magical world shuddered. His students came. His colleagues. His rivals. By morning, a thousand Accorded had gathered—SpellCasters in mourning cloaks, Slingers in dust-streaked dusters, shamans and healers and quiet watchers from every corner of the Territories.

They formed a perimeter around the crater. Not to imprison Savannah, but to protect her.

From the world. From the Concordium. From whatever came next.

Clint barely heard them. His mind replayed the moment Slay fell, the way the Wendigo turned, the weight of a friend dying in his arms. Something in him had cracked in that alley. Something that would not heal clean.

He looked at Savannah—burned, unconscious, glowing faintly with the remnants of impossible magic.

And he whispered, "I'm here. I'm not leaving."

No one tried to move him.

At the far edge of the gathering, a message changed hands—from Concordium scouts to senior agents to the frail, iron-willed Director Vellum himself, present but cloaked, not officially part of the scene.

A single sentence, whispered quiet enough to be ignored by most:

**"She survived."**

And the world tilted.

That afternoon, the wind shifted. The sky darkened again. The crowd in the square simmered like a powder keg.

Ash still hung in the air, drifting down in flakes from the fractured sky. The wreckage of the Wendigo battle surrounded them—burned buildings, shattered stone, crumpled bodies draped under makeshift tarps. Yet in the heart of the square was Savannah Melville, unconscious and guarded by a ring of warriors, mages, and survivors. At her head, Clint Black stood still as a statue. Beside her, Ahyoka held her spear as if it had grown from her bones.

When the warship *Oculus Directive* dropped anchor high above the smoldering ruins of Copper Creek, its arrival carried the weight of inevitability. A calm, clipped voice crackled over the farspeaker: "Captain Ward, this is Command Overseer Renneth. By Concordium Directive, *Skyward Mercy* is relieved of station. You are to depart immediately."

Captain Ward paused, cool and measured. "Overseer," she replied, her tone polite yet unyielding, "*Skyward Mercy* is conducting a humanitarian mission. We will not be relieved by Concordium order."

There was a moment of static before Renneth's voice tightened: "Repeat—depart now, or we will take further action."

Ward raised an eyebrow and, with innocently clipped precision, called over her shoulder to the gunnery officer: "If these idiots persist, put a spellshell directly through their command deck." The words carried well, just loud enough to penetrate the *Oculus'* comms system.

Renneth wasn't quite ready to escalate into all-out war. The *Oculus* backed off to a safer distance, its hull drifting into moonlit distance. Seconds later, a dozen enforcers descended in silent formation, their boots thudding onto blackened stone below. They moved with confident purpose, eyes cold behind polished helms bearing the Concordium sigil. Their single objective: seize Savannah Melville. As they snapped into formation, the eerie silence of the ruined town square hung heavy.

A sudden hush fell across the courtyard as the twelve Concordium enforcers marched into view, all gleaming armor and mirrored helmets, rigid and pristine against the soot-streaked ruin of

Copper Creek. At their front was Enforcer Third Class Horatio Blander, whose robes had never seen a wrinkle and whose posture suggested he'd spent the better part of his life browbeating furniture into standing at attention.

He didn't announce himself with humility. Or grace. He announced himself like a man who thought his title granted him dominion over the weather.

"Citizens of Copper Creek," Blander called, voice resonating with magically amplified authority. "Under Statute Forty-Seven, Section Eight, Sub-Clause Eleven of the Concordium Accord, we are hereby authorized to extract any individual responsible for extraordinary magical displacement for questioning and arcane debriefing."

Several hundred fists tightened. A ripple moved through the Accorded like the prelude to a tsunami.

Blander, oblivious to the coiling violence around him, continued. "This extraction is temporary. The subject, designated Savannah Melville, will be provided every courtesy during containment, including a Class-Three comfort cell, scheduled nutritional maintenance, and access to authorized non-volatile spell literature."

A stone hit the ground somewhere in the back. Someone coughed the word, "Jackass."

Blander pressed on. "Furthermore, due to the scale of recent events, we reserve the right to memory-wipe select witnesses under Emergency Directive Forty-One, which clearly delineates the importance of magical discretion in emergent civic disasters—"

Clint Black cleared his throat. "You done?"

Blander paused, looked toward the figure standing near Savannah. "You are not authorized to speak."

231

Clint blinked once. Then said anyway, "You do remember we're all supposed to be on the same side, right? Just keep that in mind before you dig this hole any deeper."

Blander sneered. "You are in violation of no less than—"

*Clang.*

Rufus, Clint's SpellShooter, snapped into his prosthetic with a sound that made a dozen enforcers flinch, like steel to a magnet. The crowd went still. Nobody breathed. All, save Blander, stared at the darksteel surface of the shooter, copper glyphs glowing brightly.

"You're going to want to stop talking now," Clint said. His voice was mild. Patient. Like a man offering a coyote one last chance to un-bite the hand it was chewing.

Blander puffed his chest. "What do you imagine you can do? Concordium enforcer armor is proof against every form of known assault magic. Even your kind's crude alchemic spell work can't—"

**BLAM.**

The Gutbuster hit center mass. Developed initially as a prank round, a thing to do to people you don't like very much for laughs, it had evolved into a dueling round. It was the ultimate way to put paid to the other duelist's ticket without killing them. It was the perfect response in this case.

For a second, nothing happened. Then Blander's knees buckled and a noise escaped him, something between a startled walrus and a broken accordion. His staff clattered to the cobbles. He dropped to all fours like a man praying to a furious god.

The crowd leaned in.

One of the enforcers, horrified, whispered, "Sir?"

Blander burbled. Gasped. And then the **smell** hit.

The first wave sent a third of the enforcers into full retreat. The second swept the front line of casters. A healer gagged audibly. A fire mage staggered, wheezing, "Sweet stars, that is *criminal*."

A woman with a silver badge muttered, "Jesus Christ! That's awful!!"

Somewhere in the back: "Momma, is he dying?"
"No, sweetheart," she replied, deadpan. "He just *wants* to."

A nearby SpellCaster, fanning her sleeve, added, "Those rounds use a humor magnifier in the matrix."

The man beside her blinked. "A what?"

"The funnier we think it is," she said, nodding gravely, "the worse it gets."

Blander convulsed again, face red, eyes watering, dignity circling the drain. Close at hand, someone dry-heaved. The stench expanded in concentric rings, measured by the crowd's expressions of disgust. And laughter.

Then came the *third* wave.

The stench hit like a wet hand to the face. Even the toughest Slingers recoiled. A veteran combat mage who'd once survived a downworld breach stumbled back, pale, muttering, "That's worse than infernal hex rot."

Behind him, a chaplain whispered, "By the Lady's mercy… it's worse than a rotting corpse!."

Blander moaned. It sounded... apologetic.

The crowd scattered like rats from a drowning ship. The remaining enforcers took one look at Clint Black, still holding his spellshooter, and started backing up.

Very slowly.

Clint holstered his weapon, gave the pitiful heap one last glance, and muttered just loud enough for those nearby to hear:

"I gave him a chance. Not my fault he was a fool." He looked up at the enforcers, who were trying to decide the best way to get Blander back to the ship *without actually touching him*, and said, "Anybody else want one?"

They declined. Twelve Concordium enforcers became six. Then three. Then gone.

All that was left was Clint standing over Savannah like the last sane man in a world on fire. Ahyoka stepped closer, looked up at him, and nodded once. Clint reloaded. The casing of the gutbuster clicked onto the cobblestone with a soft metallic *plonk*. All he had left was a screamer shell, a prank noisemaker. But if it came to that, he would find a way to use it offensively.

"Gonna be hell to get that smell out of the square," someone muttered.

Clint looked down at his twitching prosthetic, lips pressed in a tight line. The air reeked of fear and failure. And worse. He didn't seem to notice. "I'm just glad nobody died," he muttered. Then he turned slightly, eyes scanning the crowd, what was left of it, Accorded of both stripes, civilians, all keeping their distance now. His voice dropped, low and even:

"I swore to protect her. And I don't give a damn what colors they wear or what title's on their badge. If they come for her again..." The mechanical limb gave a soft click. He looked at it. Grinned. "They better bring more than diapers."

A moment passed. Then boots scuffed against the stone. An older Copper stepped forward—gray at the temples, coat sun-bleached and patched with long use. Hands up, slow, respectful. No threat. He stopped a few feet from Clint. Gestured toward Rufus with a tilt of the chin. "Caliber?"

Clint blinked, caught off guard. ".45 long."

The man nodded, then reached into his bandolier pouch. Pulled out a small roll of cloth, unwrapped it, and handed over five shells. The copper gleamed dully in the light—each round marked with deep-etched runes, cores dark with lethal intent.

"For later," the man said. "Just in case."

Clint accepted the shells silently, tucking them away without breaking eye contact.

Another Copper approached, Rusk, quiet, composed, sleeves still singed from the earlier fight. He stopped beside the older man, paused, and asked, "You need anything else from us to fulfill your contract?"

Clint looked between them. Saw the steadiness in their faces, the weight behind the question. His voice, when it came, was quiet. Honest. "Sir... you already gave me everything I needed." And it was clear he wasn't talking about bullets.

# Chapter Twenty-Eight

Ahyoka curled beside Savannah's unconscious form, fitting into the hollow of her body like a shadow finally come to rest. The scorched air of Copper Creek hung thick and unmoving, heavy with the smell of ash and the weight of the day's violence. Clint Black stood nearby like a statue carved from iron, one hand resting on his SpellShooter, his eyes unblinking. Sleep came to Ahyoka not gently but like a tether snapping—sudden, sharp, and absolute.

Darkness swallowed her.

She found herself standing in a vast black void beneath a velvet sky, no stars above, no sound around her but the soft beat of her own heart. A lantern flickered to life in her hand, its flame warm but not burning, pulsing like it breathed. Around her was a ring of stone etched with living symbols, their lines glowing faintly with breathless rhythm.

Out of the dark stepped Monster Killer, towering and still. His mask was carved from wood the color of dried blood, and across his shoulders rested a copper-barreled firearm older than time. When he spoke, the words didn't pass through her ears, they settled into her bones.

"You stand between what burns and what watches."

He lifted one hand and pointed beyond the ring. Savannah stood at the mouth of a wide, black cave, her body lit only by flickering candlelight. Inside the cave, something stirred. It shifted shape—a man, a beast, something between. The Skinwalker. Its eyes wept black and followed her even here.

Monster Killer stepped forward, his form towering in the dream-space, carved from smoke and memory. The cedar mask caught the lantern's flicker, expression unreadable, yet heavy with meaning. From beneath his cloak, he drew something ancient and reverent—a spearhead, black as a starless sky, veined with threads of molten gold that pulsed gently, like they remembered the heart of the earth.

It wasn't just black. Its polished surface drank the dim light of the dream, but deep within, veins of gold shimmered softly—like fire beneath ice, or lightning caught in volcanic glass. The glow was subtle, reverent. Meant only for the one destined to see it.

Monster Killer stood at the edge of darkness in her dream, and spoke, his voice a low whisper carried on wind that didn't move. "Toi Na Vudah," he said. "Blade of the Water People."

Ahyoka stared at it, her breath shallow. The name stirred something ancient in her, something rooted deeper than blood or tribe—something that spoke of duty, and choice.

He didn't place it in her hand. She took it. And when her fingers closed around the obsidian, the gold veining pulsed once—bright, alive. The spearhead wasn't warm, but it knew her. It welcomed her. It had waited.

She turned it slowly, feeling the balance, the silent strength coiled within. This was not a weapon of anger. It was a promise. A line drawn in shadow.

Monster Killer faded into smoke, his voice the last to go.

"You chose fire. Now choose who you will burn for. If you stand beside her," the voice warned, "you will carry fire. But fire draws smoke. The Skinwalker sees. It doesn't just want her. It waits for those who guard her."

The spear hummed in her grasp. She felt warmth run up her arm, not heat, but power, sharpened and old. Behind her, she sensed movement and turned. Two figures stood beyond the circle's edge.

The first was Clint, calm and watchful, a sentinel of the boundary between order and ruin.

The second was Duda.

But not as the world saw him. Not even as he presented himself. This Duda stood with his shoulders square and his chin lifted. No swagger. No bravado. Only resolve. A man made of steel and silence, not pride. A man not trying to be a hero—but trying, finally, to do something right. To protect someone who needed him.

Monster Killer stepped back into the dark.

"You will move faster. See further. Strike harder. That is the gift," the voice said. "But the strength has always been yours. Given by the wolf. Forged by the path."

A whisper brushed against her mind—Savannah's voice, soft but certain. "Watch the children."

The cave pulsed. Inside, the darkness crept closer. She stepped forward, her grip tightening on the spear. Not hesitating. Not flinching.

Monster Killer touched the obsidian to her brow. "You will walk into fire. You will feel fear. But you will not flee."

The world shattered in white.

She woke with a sharp breath, heartbeat steady, muscles coiled. The dream was already fading, but the weight of the spearhead lingered in her palms, and her limbs thrummed with new power. She moved with purpose, testing the reach of her body. She was faster now. Sharper. Stronger. And she had chosen it. Not because someone asked. Because it was time.

In the dim quiet of the tent, a figure stood just beyond the edge of the lanternlight. Duda.

He didn't speak. Didn't nod. Just looked at her, not like a creature, or a relic, or a ghost of the land.

He looked at her like a person. And that, more than the dream, told her something important had changed.

Clint stood a few paces away, silent and unmoving. His arms were crossed, one boot resting against a chunk of broken stone, his eyes scanning the horizon but shifting the moment Ahyoka stirred. He didn't speak. Just watched, like he'd been doing for hours.

Ahyoka sat up with fluid grace, her body responding before her mind had fully settled into waking. She didn't look at Clint. She didn't need to. Something tugged at her—just under the surface of memory, but deeper than instinct. Without hesitation, she stood and walked to a patch of scorched ground about thirty paces from the fire. Her bare feet made no sound. She dropped to one knee, fingers brushing away ash and soil with slow reverence.

Clint cocked his head slightly, curious. He didn't move. Just watched.

She dug with her hands, quick and sure, until her fingers found it: cold, humming with hidden life. The obsidian spearhead emerged from the ground like it had been waiting for her all along. A single black triangle of polished stone, veined with something unnatural—like light trapped in glass.

She held it up to the dawn, let the firelight catch in its edge, then wiped it clean with a bit of worn cloth pulled from her satchel. No ceremony. No flourish. Just certainty. She returned to where her broken spear shaft lay and, without speaking, seated the blade into the wood with a snug twist. It held. Of course it held. It had always belonged there. "Vudah." She said, low and reverently.

Still, Clint said nothing. But the faintest glimmer of a smile touched the edge of his mouth—bemused, thoughtful. Like a man

239

watching a thunderhead gather, knowing it will break eventually, and respecting the storm for taking its time.

Ahyoka tested the balance of the spear. It felt like part of her arm now—natural, inevitable.

She didn't speak either.

They just stood there, guardian and watcher, weapon and will.

And the morning began.


She rose slowly, moving with a grace that felt unfamiliar and earned. She didn't run drills. She didn't draw attention. She *watched.*

Andrezj Duda was the first to notice. At first, it was small—the way she mirrored his stance when he paused near a doorway, the way she scanned the terrain with the same rhythm he did. Then came the way she walked, where she placed her feet, how she measured people with her eyes before they spoke.

She wasn't just copying him. She was *committing him to memory.*

Duda, who had lived a life steeped in blood and silence, had never imagined legacy. Never dreamed of leaving anything behind but scars and rumors. But now he saw it—stalking him quietly, wearing a girl's face and carrying a weapon that looked older than sin.

She didn't ask to be taught. She *absorbed.* She watched him train. Then she trained herself.

When he caught her the next evening, working through a sequence of blocks and footwork he hadn't shared with anyone in decades, he didn't yell. He didn't ask why. He simply stepped up beside her, adjusted her elbow, and told her to do it again.

From that moment, Ahyoka wasn't a stray kid underfoot. She was his student. And more than a student. Duda had never had children. Never thought the opportunity would arise. Now, watching her move through firelight like a blade brought to life, he saw something he'd never allowed himself to want: a legacy. Not in name. But in *impact*. And maybe, just maybe, the world could survive what he had made of himself—because she would be what came *after*.

Savannah drifted in sleep the way a leaf drifts on a still pond: not by choice, but by gentle inevitability. The flicker of dying embers from the fire outside her window danced against the dark walls, and that glowing warmth carried her mind beyond the boundaries of the physical world.

The earth beneath Savannah's feet felt both solid and forgotten, like a place lost to time. Crimson sand whispered in spirals around her bare ankles, and above her, the sky rippled like the surface of a drum—sunless, endless, and strangely alive. She stood alone in a vast canyon painted with ancient handprints and constellations rendered in white ash.

From the horizon came a low hum, rising like the first note of a sacred song. The world seemed to still. Then she saw them: three figures stepping from the shimmer at the edge of vision— White Painted Woman, flanked by the Twins, who walked always in balance.

The Painted Woman moved like wind over wheat, silent, ageless. Her gaze met Savannah's, and in it was a weight that felt older than the mountains.

"You carry echoes not meant for your time," the Painted Woman said.

The Twins circled behind Savannah, one laughing like a child at play, the other whispering something in a tongue Savannah did not know but somehow understood: *You opened a door... and what stepped through was watching before the latch fell.*

Savannah's breath caught in her throat. "I don't understand."

"You will," said the Painted Woman. "Power does not care for understanding. Only for shape. And now it wears yours."

Without motion, without cause, the canyon around her became something else—molten, burning with impossible light. High above, she glimpsed a sphere—floating, sealed, glowing from within. Something inside pulsed once, and the world dimmed in response.

"What is that?" Savannah asked, shielding her eyes. But the Painted Woman only raised a finger to her lips.

"It is not for now. But it has known your name since long before you were born."

The canyon blinked away, and they stood in a meadow of wild sage. The wind whispered through the stalks, carrying the scents of blood and starlight. The Painted Woman stepped close.

"Your soul has grown sharp," she said. "Too sharp for its sheath. You see differently now, don't you?"

Savannah hesitated. "Things shimmer. I can feel them— threads between people, choices, places I haven't walked."

"Good," the Woman said. "But be wary. Sight is a gift and a curse. You may not always like what you see."

One of the Twins crouched beside her and drew a circle in the dirt. Inside it, he etched a flame. The other etched a cage. Then they pressed their hands flat to the ground, and the circle vanished into dust.

"When fire burns too long," one said, "the air forgets how to breathe."

"When cages break," said the other, "some things do not wish to be free."

Savannah didn't know if they were warning her or preparing her. She didn't know if there was a difference.

The Painted Woman touched Savannah's chest, over her heart.

"You have changed," she whispered. "And the world has taken notice. Carry your strength. But do not forget your sorrow. One without the other is a blade without balance."

The Twins vanished into smoke. The canyon crumbled into stars.

As Savannah fell back into waking, the Painted Woman's voice echoed once more, distant and strange. "A fire waits beneath the mountain. Not all that shines is salvation."

Savannah woke with her hands clenched and her heart racing. Something had shifted. She could feel the ley lines of the world like threads on her skin.

She didn't understand the vision.

But deep in her bones, she knew: something had seen her. And it was not finished.

# Interlude

## Internal Concordium Memorandum – Eyes Only

**To:** High Inquisitor Vellum Arkwright
**From:** Enforcement Officer Third-Class Horatio Blander
**Date:** 3rd Day of the Ember Crescent, Year of Binding 112
**Subject:** *Formal Complaint and Request for Disciplinary Action Against One Clint Black (alias: "The Wall")*

**High Inquisitor Arkwright,**

I write to you today in a state of considerable discomfort—both physical and professional—following an encounter at the Copper Creek engagement site which, I must be blunt, has brought *personal shame, public disgrace,* and a highly persistent stench upon not only myself, but by extension the Concordium's authority.

The individual known as William Clinton Black, a registered SpellSlinger operating under questionable status, did grievously insult and incapacitate me during the attempted pacification of the Copper Creek remains. While executing standard post-cataclysm containment protocol, I issued lawful instructions for the containment and retrieval of a suspected blood mage (the girl, Melville ward, unconscious at the time).

Mr. Black, in a clear act of premeditated mockery, fired a dueling-class spellShell, designation "GUTBUSTER," directly at my person.

Let me be clear, Inquisitor: this is not a metaphor.

The spell functioned precisely as its crude name implies. I was seized by *sudden and violent digestive distress*—simultaneous from *both ends*—rendering me unable to speak, stand, or even breathe without substantial loss of composure. My regulation armor, a Class

244

Four Enforcer's Harness with spell-channeling lattice and reinforced cowl, was not rated for this kind of internal sabotage.

I was vomiting inside the helmet, sir. Do you understand? I had to be *unscrewed* from it.

There were witnesses. Dozens. Perhaps hundreds. SpellCasters, Slingers, volunteers, civilians. At least one skyship captain who had the gall to sketch the aftermath. The drawing has *spread*, Vellum. They're calling it "The Siege of Both Ends."

I am now an object of *derision* within the enforcement barracks. Just last evening someone cast a minor auditory loop that played "squelching" noises every time I entered the mess hall. I have reason to believe my boots have been charmed to emit the scent of cooked cabbage. My *boots*, Inquisitor.

Therefore, I submit this formal petition for **disciplinary sanctions** to be levied against Mr. Black, including (but not limited to):

- Immediate revocation of SpellSlinger license and travel permissions

- Detainment and trial for *sorcerous indecency*

- Lifetime ban from sanctioned duels involving *digestive-class hexes*

Additionally, while I am not prone to hyperbole, I urge you to recognize the threat posed by Clint Black to the **dignity of Concordium enforcers** everywhere. If left unchecked, we may soon find ourselves mocked as the very punchline of frontier justice.

*He didn't even use a lethal spell, sir. That's what haunts me.*

With deep personal offense,
**Officer Horatio Blander**

245

Third-Class Enforcement Officer
Concordium West-North Quadrant

**Office of the High Inquisitor**
**Internal Correspondence — Concordium Eyes Only**
**Vault Stamp: Ember Crescent, Year of Binding 112**
**Subject: Re: "Formal Complaint and Request for Disciplinary**
**Action Against One Clint Black"**

To: Enforcement Officer Horatio Blander, Third-Class
Stationed: Western Front, Copper Creek Expanse

Officer Blander,

Your complaint, dated three days past, regarding your encounter with SpellSlinger Clint Black has been received, reviewed, and recorded for posterity in Vault File #77B– "Non-lethal Magical Incidents Causing Disruption of Uniform Protocol."

Allow me to begin by stating that your health and safety are important to this office. The Concordium does not take lightly any incident resulting in harm, however self-inflicted, comical, or gastrointestinal in nature.

That said, I must express my profound disappointment in the *tone*, *content*, and *overall fragility* exhibited in your report.

It is true that Mr. Black's spell—classified, amusingly enough, as a **Defensive Ritual of Maximum Nonlethal Humiliation (Class 3-Humor Variant)**—successfully incapacitated you in front of witnesses. It is also true that his actions fell within the letter of the Accords, given the circumstances and your own regrettable choice to "assert dominance" on sovereign, post-trauma territory without first establishing rapport or consent from local SpellCasters.

This was, in short, a duel of egos. You lost. Violently. From both ends.

Your focus on the "cabbage aroma" and "public disgrace" has been noted. Extensively. And archived. Possibly in the Concordium's next internal ethics training module, under *"How Not to Handle a Volatile Magical Situation with a Living Legend Present."*

Furthermore, I remind you that Clint Black—yes, **the Clint Black**, also known as *The Wall*, also known as *The Man Who Gave Quarter at Carrion Ridge*, also known (regrettably) as *The Gutbuster General*—remains a registered and active SpellSlinger in good standing. Whatever your personal vendetta, Officer, it is not the policy of this office to pursue vendettas rooted in embarrassment.

You have not been grievously wounded. You have not been magically compromised. You were not, to my knowledge, permanently fused to your undergarments. You were, however, publicly humbled. Consider this... instructive.

Now. Unless you have a legitimate accusation of magical misconduct—or sustained injury requiring a healer and/or therapist—you are hereby instructed to:

1.      Cease filing petty grievances.

2.      Retract your informal campaign to have Mr. Black's SpellSlinger status reviewed.

3.      Put on your big boy pants.

And for the love of the Spiral Sun, **quit whining and get back to work.**

Sternly,
**Vellum Arkwright**
High Inquisitor
West-North Concordium Office
Seventh Seat, Adjudicator's Circle

# Chapter Twenty-Nine

At the edge of the clearing, the townsfolk and Cyrus's supporters and friends stood watching.

Some lowered their eyes when Savannah looked their way. A few bowed their heads. Most stared, not with judgment, not with hatred, but with something colder. Fear.

Not because they hated her. But because she had done something no one should have survived, let alone wielded.

Savannah didn't blame them. Not yet.

A shadow stepped into view, then. Clint Black, one arm wrapped tight in a fresh sling, shirt torn, face bruised, eyes calm. He didn't flinch. Didn't hesitate. Didn't look away.

He walked to her, past the children, past Ahyoka, through the haze and ash, and crouched.

He didn't offer comfort. He didn't make excuses. He just looked her in the eye. "You gave it everything," he said quietly. "And you're still here."

She swallowed. "He's not," she whispered.

Clint nodded. Then offered his hand. "You think Cyrus would've let himself die unless it mattered?"

Savannah didn't answer. She didn't need to. She took his hand. He pulled her gently to her feet.

They stood together in the ruin, amid survivors who couldn't speak, children who wouldn't leave, and the ghost of a man who had given everything to keep her burning just a little longer.

And Clint, steady as stone beside her—not afraid. Not anymore.


Savannah sat on a crate just outside the remains of the church, a blanket draped over her shoulders. Her fingers were wrapped around a cup of tea someone had thrust into her hands, though it had long gone cold. She hadn't sipped it. Hadn't moved much at all since they sat her down.

The silence around her was a strange one. Not tense. Not reverent. Just... waiting.

Clint Black stood nearby, his sling tight against his chest, one boot resting on the edge of a broken wagon. He watched her the way only he could—steady, unjudging, waiting for her to say she was ready.

She didn't. So he spoke. "You were out three days."

She blinked. Three?

"You slept like the dead," he added, softer. "But you weren't. We... made sure."

Savannah glanced toward the burned clearing. The children were still there. Still twelve. Still silent.

They hadn't spoken much since the blast. Not even to one another. They moved in strange synchrony—too in tune for children their age. They reacted to things no one else noticed. Heard sounds no one else reacted to.

Ahyoka always remained closest to Savannah. She hadn't left the edge of her shadow, her spear always within reach. It was more than loyalty. It felt like a kind of... bond.

Savannah looked back to Clint. "Are they... alright?"

He didn't answer right away. Just shifted his jaw. "Different," he said finally. "Not hurt. But... not kids, not anymore."

Savannah shivered.

Clint glanced up at the sky, then back down. "That spell. Whatever you did. It wasn't just a blast. You cracked the world, Savannah. That much magic in one place... it leaves a mark. On things. On people."

He turned his palm upward. The broken arm.

At first, she thought it was a burn. Then she saw it— faint metallic thread, etched just beneath the skin, like copper fused into flesh. Barely visible, unless the light hit it just so. Her breath caught.

Clint gave a tired shrug. "Doesn't hurt. Yet. But I've felt... different. Like I'm carrying something I wasn't before." Then he held up the prosthetic. It looked different, somehow more real. "And this won't come off anymore. But here's the thing that worries me. When that thing killed Slay and was going to kill Steed, I stepped up to shoot it. When it swung an arm at me, this-" he gestured with the metallic arm, "-moved by itself and grabbed the claw it tried to hit me with and stopped the swing. I didn't do it, IT did. I'm different." He didn't sound afraid. Just thoughtful.

"We all are, I think. Everybody who stood here. Even the ones that ran."

He nodded toward the children. "But them most of all. They were inside it. With you."

Savannah's gaze drifted back to Ahyoka, who now stood sentinel beside a half-crumbled column, watching the world with eyes that felt far too old. The girl met her gaze. She didn't smile, didn't blink. Just nodded—like someone who had seen too much and chosen to remember anyway. Savannah looked down at her tea. Still cold. "What else?" she asked.

Clint's voice dropped. "Cyrus."

She didn't answer. She didn't need to.

"He bought us time. He made sure you had enough to finish it."

Her knuckles whitened around the cup. "The town?"

"Some of it's still standing. Some… ain't. Duda's boys are rebuilding the wall. Steed's organizing the rest. Got lots of help." He gestured again, to the sky, then all around. There were a dozen airships still anchored above the town, and more than a thousand people moving about in the ruins.

She looked up, eyes tired and hollow. "Why?"

Clint didn't blink. "Because whether you like it or not, Savannah… you're the center of it now. Whatever comes next—it's gonna come through you."


Ash still clung to the eaves of Copper Creek like old regrets. The air was dry and taut with silence, a hush that wrapped around the scorched bones of the town. Here and there, survivors moved like sleepwalkers—rebuilding walls, clearing wreckage, saying little. The wendigo's rampage had not ended with the creature's retreat. It lingered in the sounds that no longer echoed, in the scent of fire that would not fade.

Clint Black stood near the edge of the square, one gloved hand resting on the rail of a shattered porch. He watched a child—barefoot, grimy, too quiet—help her father replant fence posts where a home had once stood. The prosthetic at Clint's left side flexed slowly, an unconscious mirroring of his thoughts. He didn't notice it anymore. Not in idle moments. It had become... familiar.

The morning broke into motion with the clatter of hooves.

A rider approached down the dusty road—a man dressed too cleanly, in a black coat with silver buttons that caught the light like polished bone. His face was smooth, ageless, and held a calmness that felt slightly out of tune. His horse was unsweated, unscuffed. Too perfect.

He reined in by the edge of town, surveyed the ruin without visible emotion, and then swung down from the saddle with a fluid grace that made Savannah, watching from the church porch, narrow her eyes. Steed approached him, gun on her hip and tension in her shoulders.

"Can I help you?"

The man removed a sealed tube from a saddlebag and held it out like it was a holy relic. "Message for William Clinton Black," he said, voice soft and wrong. "From the Concordium. I was told to place it in his hands."

Clint stepped forward. The man turned toward him, and for just a moment, just a flicker, something passed between them. Not a smile. Not recognition. But… intent.

Clint took the scroll.

The messenger gave a stiff nod and returned to his horse. No food, no water, no words to the other townsfolk. Within moments, he was riding back the way he came. Ahyoka watched from the corner of the square, standing half-shadowed behind the blackened remnants of the saloon's sign. Her grip tightened on the shaft of her spear until her knuckles whitened. She did not look away.

Clint opened the scroll. Savannah and Steed leaned in as his eyes moved across the page. The message was written in fluid, elegant hand, sealed with the Concordium's cipher.

"To William Clinton Black,

Word has reached us that the threat you faced may not be vanquished. A presence stirs beneath the depths of Lake Tahoe— its essence still intact. We believe it to be the Wendigo, wounded but not destroyed.

In the western hills, under the ruins of Fort Callahan, lies a vault constructed during the early purges. Within it, should rumors be true, is a weapon called the Sunshell. It predates most known SpellTech, and its deployment should not be taken lightly.

If the creature rises again, this may be your only recourse. But understand—its power could level a city.

This advice comes from a friend of Cyrus Melville. I admired the man. I admire your tenacity.

Use caution. And use the Sunshell only if you must.

—E.C., Concordium Senior Advisor."

Savannah's face darkened. "You ever hear of this 'E.C.?'"

Steed shook her head. "No. But Cyrus knew a lot of people. Maybe someone he dealt with privately."

Clint didn't respond immediately. His fingers gripped the edge of the scroll like it might bite. "Too convenient."

"Someone knew exactly what to send and when," Savannah agreed.

254

Steed blew out a slow breath. "Feels like we're being pushed toward something."

"Or into something," Savannah said.

Across the square, Ahyoka finally moved. She stepped into the full light of morning, gaze still fixed on the road where the messenger had disappeared. Something in her posture had stiffened—not with fear, but alertness.

She said nothing. Not yet.

The council of war was held in what remained of the schoolhouse—a scorched frame that had once echoed with the hopeful clamor of children. It was cooler there, despite the ruin, and someone had cleared enough ash from the floor to make room for a large table and a half-dozen chairs. The survivors who mattered most had gathered: Savannah, Steed, Clint, Duda, and three of the older townsfolk who had taken up leadership in the vacuum left by death.

The scroll lay open on the table like a loaded weapon.

"Fort Callahan," Duda said, eyes narrowing. "That's not a place people go looking for things. The original garrison reported strange stuff—men waking up with their teeth missing, all their dreams the same. By the time the Fort was sealed, most of its records had vanished along with its last commanding officer. Officially, it's marked as unstable ground. Unofficially?" He shook his head. "It's cursed. That's the only word that fits."

"Every mining party that's tried digging there has vanished or come back touched," Steed added. "Last group returned after just two days. Sunburnt, half-mad, and one of them shot himself before we could even question him."

"Touched how?" Savannah asked.

"Nightmares," Steed said. "Compulsions. One woman tried to cut her eyes out. Said there were things in the stone watching through her."

"And this is where the Sunshell is?" Clint asked quietly.

Savannah crossed her arms. "None of this makes sense. How would anyone know the Wendigo wasn't dead? No caster could reach that deep—too much interference. Unless someone already knew where it was hiding."

"You think this letter is a setup," Duda said.

"I think someone wanted us to know. And they were smart enough to dress it up like a warning from the Concordium."

"Then the question is," Steed said, "who would want us to find the Sunshell?"

"No one who has our best interests at heart," Savannah answered.

Duda leaned back in his chair. "The Sunshell's a god-killer, in theory. But it's not meant to be handled by people. There are stories going back generations. If it exists, it was made to wipe out something that couldn't be killed by force or spell. Detonate it in the wrong place, and you could erase a city. Maybe more."

"And still," Clint said, softly, "it might be the only way to stop this."

No one spoke for a moment.

Then Duda added, "You understand what kind of bait this is, don't you? You go into Callahan, there's no backup. No way out if things go bad. And if this is a trap, you're walking straight into it."

"I know that. I'm still goin'." Clint said.

Savannah started to speak, but he shook his head.

"I'll go. I've seen what the Wendigo can do. And if the Sunshell's real, I'll find it. If it's not, then I'll improvise."

Steed looked ready to argue, but Duda beat her to it. "You're not going alone. If you go dark in there, someone has to make sure your sacrifice means something. I'll see to that."

Clint gave him a nod. "Appreciate it."

Savannah, oddly, said nothing. Her hand had dropped to rest on the map, and her gaze was elsewhere. Focused. Burning.

Only Ahyoka, standing by the doorway, remained still. She wasn't watching the table, or the scroll, or the men preparing for a suicide run. She was watching the tree line beyond the shattered glass.

There was something moving in the dark. She couldn't see it. She could feel it, though.

But it saw them. And it was waiting.

# Chapter Thirty

The ruins of Fort Callahan loomed above them, jagged and brooding, half-consumed by earth and time. What had once been proud sandstone walls now lay in collapsed tiers, swallowed by brush and bramble. Storm clouds had gathered by late afternoon, turning the daylight to iron gray. Clint paused at the arching remnants of a collapsed gate. The wind bit colder here. It smelled faintly of ozone and buried things.

They stepped carefully over shattered stone, boots scraping against the past. Savannah walked beside Clint, her gaze everywhere. Duda followed close behind, his repaired shotgun slung over one shoulder, his machete loose at his hip. His eyes didn't miss much. They never had.

"It's wrong here," Duda muttered, voice low. "Like a cellar full of bodies."

"You sure you weren't a poet in a past life?" Clint asked.

Duda didn't smile. "Not unless he was buried face-down."

The team moved deeper, ducking through a broken arch that led into the old supply house. The interior was black with shadow, the walls cracked by root and water. Savannah murmured a soft cantrip and a ball of warm light lifted from her palm, revealing a heavy iron trapdoor in the center of the floor, rusted and locked with chain.

Cyrus would've said something clever here. But Cyrus was gone. Clint looked at the lock—no spell work, just stubborn metal. Duda knelt, examining the rust, then pulled a curved blade from his coat and drove it into the hasp. With a snap, the chain came loose.

The trapdoor opened on a scream of hinges.

Below, stairs descended into darkness.

Ahyoka lingered at the top, her eyes drawn downward, jaw tight. She didn't speak. She didn't have to.

They went down single file. Clint first. Savannah next. Then Duda, who moved like a wolf, every sense attuned. The walls wept moisture. The stone was cold. At the bottom, the hallway opened into a chamber far older than the fort above.

The air was thick here, not just with dust and time—but power.

At the far end of the chamber stood the vault: black iron, domed like a reliquary, its surface inscribed with ancient runes and strange spiraling motifs. Savannah whispered something in a language older than the continent. The vault pulsed faintly, as if it recognized her voice.

"Think that's it?" Clint asked.

Duda didn't answer. He was watching the shadows. Every muscle coiled.

Savannah approached the vault. "The wards are sleeping," she said. "But something's been feeding them. They're not decayed."

She pressed her hand to the sigils. Light bloomed. Runes flared, then dimmed. The vault unlocked with a sigh—one that sounded almost relieved.

Inside, nestled on a stone pedestal, lay a single object: the Sunshell. It didn't glow. It didn't whisper. But everyone in that chamber felt its presence like a nail through the soul.

Duda stepped forward, his voice quiet. "We shouldn't be touching that."

Clint looked at him.

Duda's gaze didn't waver. "Weapons like that don't get made without a price."

"No," Savannah agreed. "They don't."

Ahyoka stood in the archway, arms crossed, eyes not on the weapon—but on the walls. Something had watched them come down. Something was still watching.

"Let's get out of here," she said flatly. None of them argued.

Clint wrapped the Sunshell in his duster and turned toward the stairs. It pulsed once—just once—like a heartbeat trying to match his own.

They climbed out of the dark with a treasure meant to kill gods.

And something else followed them up.

The road back from Fort Callahan felt longer than the journey out.

The Sunshell—cradled in thick canvas and nested between runed steel and blessed cedar—rode in the center of the lead wagon like a holy relic. No one talked near it. Even the horses stepped lighter when they passed close, as if some primal instinct warned them against the thing inside.

Clint rode point, one hand loose on the reins, the other, the prosthetic, resting on his thigh. The arm had been quiet since the vault. But not silent. At odd moments, like during the last watch or when the shadows stretched longest, the palm would pulse—just once—like a second heartbeat. The feeling wasn't painful. It wasn't even unpleasant. But it was... knowing. Present. As if the arm was *aware* something was changing.

He didn't mention it.

Behind him, Duda sat higher in the saddle than usual, scanning the trail with quiet precision. He wasn't talkative either. Not since they'd left the ruined fort. He was thinking, and when Duda started thinking, people tended to end up bleeding.

After an hour of riding without a word, Clint finally broke the silence. "You figure it out yet?"

Duda grunted. "Figure what?"

"You've been wound tight as a whipcord since we cracked that vault."

"I don't like being played," Duda said flatly. "And this whole damn mission smells like a setup."

Clint didn't argue. The letter. The vault. The oddly specific trail markers that hadn't been there when the maps were made. Even the trapdoor lock—coded not just in spell-laced runes, but in a dialect only Savannah had recognized from a dusty old volume in Melville House.

It had all been too easy. Too guided.

"The Sunshell's real," Clint said. "That's not nothing."

"No," Duda agreed. "But someone wanted us to find it. Badly. That ain't good."

They rode on.

At dusk, they stopped to make camp. Savannah checked the wards around the artifact, refreshing them in quiet murmurs. Ahyoka stood nearby, her new spear balanced across her back. She watched the Sunshell like a wolf watches fire, wary but compelled.

261

Later, while the others slept, Clint sat beside the dying fire, cleaning the spellshooter with slow, methodical care. He wasn't expecting anything. He just didn't want to sleep.

The wind shifted. Just slightly.

Across the fire, Duda was awake, his eyes reflecting amber in the coals. He nodded once toward the wagon.

"We're bringing something back," he said. "Something old. Something dangerous."

Clint didn't reply. There was nothing to say.

But deep in his prosthetic arm, the palm pulsed again.

This time, stronger. Almost... eager.

# Chapter Thirty-One

The Sunshell was still hours from Copper Creek, packed in lead and cedar, nestled in the wagon Clint and Duda had dragged back from the fort. But even unseen, even wrapped and silent, it leaked.

Savannah felt it first. She couldn't sleep. Not really. Her body rested, but her dreams crawled with wrongness. A forest that screamed when the wind blew. A lake that rippled without wind. A face—not human, not beast—grinning up at her from beneath black water, whispering in a language she didn't know but understood all the same.

She woke up sweating. She didn't tell anyone.

Ahyoka knew too. She didn't dream, not like that. But she woke before dawn, throat tight, arms shaking, the spear she had carved clutched so hard her palm bled where a splinter had dug deep. She did not cry. She never cried. But she did not sleep again, and she spent the next hour working through drills with her spear until it sang.

Clint didn't feel wrong exactly. Not at first. But he caught himself staring into the fire and not remembering starting it. Or finishing it. Once, he found himself cleaning the barrel of his shooter with hands that weren't his own, breathing slow and steady, like he was waiting for something. Like someone else was inside him, waiting too.

He buried that thought so deep he hoped it would never come back.

The air changed. Birds stopped coming near the camp. Wolves howled, then fell silent. The children in town stopped playing. The laughter that usually echoed down the main street of Copper Creek never rose that day, or the day after.

A storm began to build—no clouds, no lightning, just pressure. People looked over their shoulders and didn't know why. Duda started sleeping in his chair, one eye open. Sharon Steed polished her badge and loaded her scattergun twice that day and told no one.

Somewhere beyond the horizon, something was hunting.

And the Sunshell—buried under blankets, wrapped in steel and salt and silence—hummed. Quietly. Just enough to make the floorboards vibrate when no one was walking. Just enough to keep the dogs pacing, growling at shadows. It wanted to be used. And something else wanted it used.

They gathered in the parlor of Melville House just after dusk. No one had summoned the meeting. No single hand had drawn it together. But by ones and twos, the survivors of Copper Creek's firestorm came—drawn not by obligation, but by instinct.

Duda arrived first, coat still dusty from the road, his hat in his hands and his face drawn like war maps. Savannah followed, silent, her hair braided tight against her skull. Her eyes flicked once to Ahyoka, who stood at the far edge of the room, back to the fire, her spear across her arms like an old soldier's rifle.

Clint came last, slower than the rest. He didn't say much. He didn't need to. His presence was weighted now, not just by pain or loss, but by purpose. His prosthetic, his left arm, clicked softly when he moved, and the room felt colder when he entered.

The Sunshell sat in its crate at the center of the room, untouched, and still wrapped in the layers they'd pulled from the vault. But everyone could feel it. Like a tongue pressed to a battery. Like something grinning with its eyes closed.

"I had a dream last night," Savannah said without preamble. "It wasn't mine."

Duda shifted but didn't speak.

"It came from the Sunshell," she said. "Or from whatever wants us to use it."

There was a beat of silence. Then Clint said, "The Wendigo isn't dead." It wasn't a question.

Savannah nodded. "The Concordium thinks it is. Already stamped it officially dead. But it isn't. Not dead. Just... hurt. Hurt bad enough it had to crawl away and hide. But it's not gone. Not yet."

Ahyoka finally spoke, voice flat. "It's healing."

Duda didn't react, but his shoulders flexed once. "You're sure."

"We're sure," Savannah said.

The fire snapped. For a long moment, no one spoke.

Then Clint said, "We don't have the luxury of waiting. If that thing gets strong again, there won't be a second shot. We either kill it while we can... or we die slower next time."

Duda exhaled. "We use it."

Savannah said, "But not here. Not in Copper Creek. Not anywhere near people."

Clint stood. "I'll take it."

All heads turned.

"What?" Savannah blinked.

Clint's face was calm. Calm like stone. "You need someone to carry it. To get it close. To make sure it works. That's me."

"No," Savannah said. "We haven't decided anything."

"I have." His eyes moved over them, slow and steady. "Mike would've done it. I'm doing it. It's what I'm for."

"You don't get to make that call," Savannah snapped, voice rising. "You're not a martyr, Clint."

"I'm not trying to be. I'm just... the Wall." He touched the metal arm. It buzzed softly in the silence. And this time, when no one stopped him, the quiet wasn't agreement.

It was goodbye.

# Interlude

**INTEROFFICE MEMORANDUM – FIELD OPERATIONS DIVISION**
*Classification: Omega-Level Review – Director's Eyes Only*

**To:** High Director Calvus Ardent
**From:** Commander Helena Marr, Senior Field Chief – Western Territories
**Date:** April 9, 1890
**Subject:** Copper Creek Event – Final Assessment and Field Status Update

Director,

You'll have the full stack of transcripts and sigil records by morning. This is the operational summary. Keep your advisors out

265

of it unless they know how to read damage reports with blood on them.

1. **Subject 32-B/SM-Prototype (Savannah Melville)** was confirmed alive and active after a decade-long lapse in surveillance.

2. She was embedded within Melville House under an assumed identity, facilitated by Senior SpellCaster Cyrus Melville. No alarms tripped. That's an internal failure. Audit your roster.

3. A high-level blood magic detonation occurred during the Wendigo incursion in Copper Creek. Result: complete neutralization of threat entity. Secondary result: Class-Nine magical fallout, visible from orbit, registered by six arcane satellites.

4. Enforcer Third Class Blander initiated an unsanctioned confrontation hours after detonation. Was warned. Ignored warning.
Outcome: physical, magical, and professional humiliation. One gutbuster round. Spectacular result. You'll have to read the incident report yourself if you want the details. I don't recommend it while eating.

5. Local witnesses include:
— One dozen licensed casters and Slingers from regional chapters (volunteers, first response)
— Crew of a Concordium rescue dirigible
— Several hundred unaffiliated mercenaries and travelers
— Captain Jack Tillman (yes, *that* Tillman)

6. Due to the visibility and volume of magical activity, **memory wiping** has been deemed logistically impractical and politically dangerous. Too many eyes. Too many rumors already moving.

7. Subject Melville is currently in the custody of Clint Black, SpellSlinger. He exercised traditional quarter in front of over forty magical witnesses. This makes her his legal and magical responsibility under the Accords. Whether you like

that or not doesn't matter. He followed the letter. Break it now and you'll start a war—one we'll lose in the court of public sentiment, if not in blood.

8. Subject Melville is dangerous. Controlled, but dangerous. More stable than expected. Power output is off chart. Recommend observation, not confrontation. Anyone sent after her should be cleared for extreme magical threat response and have the sense to *not get clever.*

9. The Wendigo is dead. That cost us dearly. We didn't kill it. She did. The locals know it. So do the Slingers. So do the Casters.

10. New Copper Creek is under provisional magical quarantine. Former territory is deemed nonviable due to ground corruption. A temporary Concordium liaison has been stationed at Outpost Twelve to monitor post-fallout behavior. Locals are rebuilding under unofficial protection of independent Slingers and volunteers.

**New Copper Creek** is, by all functional definitions, sovereign.

That's the situation.

**— Commander Helena Marr**
Senior Field Chief – Western Territories
Concordium Field Operations Division

The airship loomed like a copper-skinned leviathan over the loading gantry outside Copper Creek, engines chuffing and hissing in the pre-dawn cold. It wasn't a warship, but she was armored, fast, and big enough to carry ten armed men and their regrets. The Concordium crest on the bow had been freshly polished, but nobody believed it meant anything anymore. Not now. Not with what they were flying toward.

Clint stood near the ramp, gloved fingers flexing around the polished barrel of his SpellShooter. The prosthetic arm—silent now, watchful—rested loose at his side. The palm hadn't buzzed in hours. It was waiting. Like all of them were.

Savannah finished strapping down the last crate of spell supplies with steady hands and a hollow ache in her chest. She'd spent the night in silence, half-dreaming, half-praying, not sure who she was asking or what she hoped to hear. When she looked at Clint, she saw the wall already—unmoving, unreadable. She hated it, and she loved him for it.

Duda arrived last, riding up in a battered land-wagon with five of his best men in tow. They wore grey armor and blank faces, the kind of men who'd seen too many battlefields and survived by never blinking first. Duda climbed out without speaking, cast one glance at the ship, then looked to Clint.

"You sure about this?"

Clint didn't answer immediately. He adjusted the strap across his chest and met the older man's eyes. "I am."

Duda nodded once. "I'll be in the sky with you. Won't step into the kill zone unless I have to, but if this goes sideways, my boys and I will pull you out or put something down trying." He grinned, sort of. "Silver bullets all around."

"I know," Clint said. He meant it. That was the thing with Duda—you never had to wonder.

From the shadows behind the supply crates, Ahyoka stood watching. She wore a simple tunic and the ash spear she had carved. Her eyes never left Clint. There was something subtle in her posture, something coiled, and only Clint noticed she was standing the exact way Duda did when danger was near, weight on the balls of her feet, shoulders relaxed, eyes hard.

Clint caught her gaze. Neither of them smiled.

Steed appeared out of the morning fog, wearing her coat and her badge and the kind of weight in her expression that only

268

comes when you're saying goodbye to someone who won't be coming back. She stood near Clint and handed him a folded strip of canvas.

"What's this?" he asked.

"Map to the blast site. Wrote in the coordinates myself. Concordium wanted to use their charts, but I don't trust 'em to get the sun rising on time these days."

Clint tucked it into his coat. "Thanks."

"You get the bastard," she said. Her voice was hoarse. "I don't care what it takes."

Clint looked at the loading ramp, then at the town behind him. What was left of it. "Was always gonna to be me," he said softly.

Savannah approached at that, eyes glittering. "Clint—"

He turned, took her hand in his gloved one. "If it goes bad, you keep them safe. You build something out of what's left."

She blinked fast. "That's not what I want to hear."

He leaned close, kissed her temple. "It's what you needed."

The airship hissed louder, boarding lights flicking green. Duda climbed the ramp first, wordless, his men following in tight formation. Clint lingered a moment, taking one last look at Copper Creek. Then he turned to Ahyoka. "You coming?"

She nodded. Together, they boarded.

The ramp sealed. The engines howled. And as the airship lifted into the bruised purple sky, Clint felt the weight settle across his shoulders. The arm flexed once—metal fingers tightening—before falling still again.

It was time.

# Chapter Thirty-Two

The airship cut through the night like a whisper, the wind coiling cold around the hull as the landscape fell away beneath them. Lake Tahoe loomed in the distance, a black eye set into the mountains, vast and bottomless. Clint stood at the prow, one hand resting on the rail, the other resting on the butt of his SpellShooter. The newly mounted prosthetic—cool, copper-veined steel wrapped in runes and spells older than the Republic—gleamed under the moonlight. It did not hum. Not yet.

The Sunshell sat locked in the reinforced case at his feet.

He hadn't spoken much since they'd taken off. There wasn't much to say. Everyone aboard knew what this flight was.

Duda leaned against the bulkhead a few paces behind, arms folded, eyes closed but not asleep. He had the stillness of a wolf waiting for snowfall—tense, quiet, patient. His five best stood near the ladder leading down into the cargo hold, checking gear and weapons. None of them spoke above a whisper.

Only Ahyoka moved. She paced the far rail, barefoot, balancing easily as the ship swayed. Her expression was unreadable, but she kept glancing toward Clint. Her spear lay across her back, bound in twine. Her jaw clenched now and then, and Clint wondered what she saw. What she sensed. What she feared. She brought out a small pot, clay, ash, war paint.

Ahyoka crouched in silence, dipping two fingers into the mix of ash and clay. With slow, deliberate movements, she drew black lines beneath her eyes—one for each loss she carried. A single line traced from her bottom lip to her chin: not a threat, but a promise.

Across her brow, she dabbed three white dots with the edge of her thumb. They caught the light like distant stars. Her breath stilled. The night answered.

She rose without a sound, the obsidian blade at her side. She wasn't a warrior by tradition. She was one by choice.

He turned away from the rail as Duda came to stand beside him.

"You sure you're ready for this?" Duda asked, voice low.

Clint didn't answer at first. The mountains were visible now, snowy teeth rising behind the black pool of the lake. "No," Clint said. "But I'm sure I'm the one who has to do it."

Duda looked at him a long moment. "Mike would've said the same thing."

Clint nodded. "He did."

They stood together, watching the sky change shade by shade as the lake drew closer.

Behind them, the hatch opened. One of the Concordium crew leaned out. "Ten minutes. Wind's rough but manageable. You'll drop just east of the shoreline. No one's around."

"Understood," Duda said.

The man vanished. The door shut again.

Clint crouched, unsnapped the case, and looked at the Sunshell. It was smaller than anyone expected. A narrow capsule, bone-white, etched with veins of obsidian and pulsing silver script that refused to stay still. It looked like it was alive. Like it was dreaming.

Duda's men avoided looking directly at it.

"I keep thinking," Clint murmured, "about how I used to think dying for something made you a hero."

"And now?" Duda asked.

Clint glanced up at him. "Now I think doing it because you have to is what makes you real."

Ahyoka stepped beside them, quiet as wind. She looked down at the shell, then at Clint.

"You'll die," she said. Not cruel. Just clear.

"Maybe," Clint said.

Her gaze lingered on him for several seconds, then she touched her forehead in a slow, deliberate gesture—not quite a salute. More like... respect.

Duda nodded to his men. "Gear up. Final check. We drop in five."

The five split to stations. Ahyoka took a seat, still watching Clint. Duda moved off to check the drop harness.

Clint turned back to the case, then reached out and rested his metal hand against the shell.

The arm purred. Just slightly. Not sound. Not heat. A response.

Clint's spine straightened. Something was aligning.

And for the first time, Clint didn't feel afraid.


The airship touched down in silence beneath a moonless sky. Tahoe lay still below them, but not asleep—no, sleep belonged to the living. What lingered beneath that black glass water, nestled in the ancient stone and buried ice, was something else entirely.

The cave mouth gaped like a wound in the mountainside. Clint stood at the threshold, staring into the dark, his duster flaring gently in the cold updraft that oozed from inside. He could feel the Sunshell pulsing faintly through the straps of the case slung across his back. It didn't glow. It didn't hum. But it beat, slow and insistent, like a second heart.

They descended in silence.

The others followed—Duda, grim as ever, shotgun across his back and a thick knife on his hip. Ahyoka moved like smoke, flanking them with her spear low and ready. The five hand-picked men Duda brought were quiet professionals, lanterns shielded, weapons loose in calloused hands. Not one of them cracked a joke. Not one tried to fill the silence with idle talk.

The deeper they went, the worse it got. It wasn't just the cold—it was a *wrongness*, soaked into the stone. Clint had felt this kind of magic before, when unholy rituals left their stink behind. But this… this was older. Older than pain. Older than death.

He didn't know how he knew, but he was certain: this cave had been a temple. Not built by hands but made by something that needed worship. And the hands that built it probably were not human.

"Doesn't feel like just a hiding place," one of the men muttered, voice taut.

"It's not," Duda replied. "This is bait. We're the fish."

Clint said nothing, but he could feel the arm again—the prosthetic. It had been still all through the flight, cold and quiet. Now the palm buzzed faintly, as if it were tasting the air.

They found the first sign of the Wendigo a quarter mile in—bones, gnawed and snapped, scattered in a heap like a child's discarded toys. The jawbone of a human sat atop the pile, and someone had scratched a crude spiral into the wall beside it. The scratch was old, but not *ancient*. Clint leaned close. It looked like it had been carved by talon, not steel.

"The thing's been feeding," Duda said.

"Not just feeding," Ahyoka added. "Leaving a message. It wants us to know we're walking into its mouth."

They moved forward.

Tunnels twisted down in impossible directions. The rock changed texture every few yards—obsidian in one stretch, limestone in another, and once a jagged corridor that looked and smelled like cooled flesh. The deeper they went, the more Clint could feel the Sunshell resonating with the walls. It wasn't just reacting. It was *calling*.

"We stop here," Clint said at last, in the dead of a tunnel that felt more like a throat than a hallway. "I go the rest of the way alone."

Duda opened his mouth, then shut it again. He understood. He always did.

"Be fast," the old operator said. "If you're not back in an hour, we're lighting the cave and falling back."

Clint nodded. "You won't have to wait long."

Ahyoka didn't say a word. She just placed her hand on his shoulder, not like a goodbye—but like the stillness before a last stand.

Then Clint was alone.

The path narrowed. The darkness wasn't just *absence*—it was presence. Heavy. Watching. The further he walked, the more his limbs protested. Not from pain, not even fear—just pressure. Like walking through the ocean at the deepest trench.

And still, the Sunshell pulsed.

He reached a chamber, larger than any he'd seen. It opened like a cathedral, the ceiling so high it vanished into the gloom. The walls were pockmarked with recesses—some shallow, others deep and caved in. The air stank of rot and sulfur, and the floor was carpeted with fur and bone.

In the center lay the Wendigo.

It was huge—at least fifteen feet tall now, its limbs curled in on themselves like a sleeping spider. Its body pulsed faintly, slow as continental drift, and the ice around it steamed as if it were breathing cold.

Clint stepped forward. The Sunshell's pulse matched the creature's. And far, far away—though no sound echoed in the chamber—Clint *felt* something watching. *Waiting.*

He had no way to know what it was, but the sense of malevolent attention was unshakable. It had found them.

The mountain breathed.

Not with wind or echo, but with something deeper—older. The cavern beneath Lake Tahoe shimmered with heatless moisture, the black rock weeping condensation like the walls knew what was coming. Clint Black stepped carefully, boots crunching softly against shale. He carried the SunShell cradled in his arms like a sleeping god. The thing pulsed with a dull, rhythmic throb—slow, but eager. As if it could smell blood. As if it could taste the moment drawing close.

Ahead, the Wendigo slumbered.

Its vast, hideous bulk was half-fused into the stone, its chest rising and falling in a sick parody of peace. Clint stopped ten feet away, sweat prickling at his collar despite the cold. He could feel the malevolence in the thing, even unconscious. And the SunShell—it responded. It grew warmer in his hands, the engraved copper runes flickering red. Not from magic. From hunger.

He looked down at it. The ancient artifact had been designed for one purpose: obliteration. But its design was not entirely human. The spirit bound within it—whatever sliver of malevolent soul had been carved into the spell-matrix—it wanted out. And Clint could feel that desire crawling up his arms, threading into his spine. For a terrible second, he thought he wouldn't be able to set it down.

But Clint Black wasn't built to quit.

He knelt, slowly, and laid the SunShell beside the Wendigo's heart. Its surface hissed against the rock. He pulled his Shooter, loaded the inferno round—a shell meant to ignite the unignitable. It slid into place with a finality that felt like judgment.

Far above, Duda and Ahyoka ran.

The tunnels twisted and roared around them, reacting to the magical currents swirling in the air. Two vastly powerful magical sources were coming into close proximity, and the disruptions flowed outward like a magical waterfall of wind. Wind from the coming blast already stirred dust and whispers. Tiny fae lights blinked ahead like breadcrumbs laid in a nightmare. Duda led, one arm shielding his eyes, the other ready to kill anything stupid enough to get in their way. Ahyoka followed, close, fast, light on her feet despite the weight of her spear. Neither spoke. There was no time.

The airship's dangling ropes came into view.

Joey, their pilot, leaned over the railing. "Ropes up! We've got movement!" he yelled. Guards on the deck scrambled. The ship's engines groaned, heat building as the vessel prepared to lift.

Duda reached the rope first. He didn't climb, he launched himself, grabbing high, using brute arm strength to haul himself up. Ahyoka leaped after, nearly as fast. Behind them, the fae lights blinked out one by one.

Below, Clint stood alone.

He watched the Wendigo shift. It stirred. Dreaming of slaughter. Dreaming of Coldwater. Dreaming of Copper Creek.

He thought of Slay. Of the weight the man carried, of his quiet strength. Of the moment his body hit the ground with no warning, like the light had gone out in the world for good. "This one's for you," Clint muttered. He raised his gun. And his voice. "Wakey, wakey, you Wendigo bastard."

The Wendigo's eyes snapped open—two pinpoints of icy blue, burning with malevolence.

But Clint had already fired.

276

The inferno round struck the SunShell dead center. The shell ignited, then bloomed. Not fire. Not light. Cataclysm. The mountain shrieked. The walls boiled. Everything went red, then gold, then white as magic old as the world itself detonated. The Wendigo never moved. It didn't have time.

Above, the airship was flung like a leaf in a hurricane.

Duda and Ahyoka screamed, but they held on. The ropes lashed like whips. The hull cracked. And then they were over the lake, dragging through water like human fishing lines, until Joey fought the controls and managed to lift them up, higher, safer, away.

Smoke churned below. A crater now. No Clint. No Wendigo. Just silence.

Duda collapsed onto the deck, soaked, his face blank. Ahyoka sat beside him, silent, staring at nothing. After a moment, he reached for the farspeak token.

"Savannah," he said, voice rough. "It's done. He… he didn't make it." He paused. Cleared his throat. "We're coming home."

He clicked the stone off. Sat in silence.

The Wall stood to the very end.

# Chapter Thirty-Three

The crater still steamed. Moonlight filtered through a haze of ash and vapor, casting a ghostly glow over the scorched earth that had once been part of a mountainside. Nothing moved. The silence wasn't just quiet, it was final.

The airship banked low over the rim of the ruined peak, slow and cautious. Joey, hands tight on the controls, kept his eyes on the jagged terrain. Below, only blackened rock and molten glass spread in all directions—like the world had been burned clean of meaning.

Duda stood near the side rail, one arm looped through the rigging, the other steadying Ahyoka as she scanned the surface below. Neither spoke. Not since the blast. Not since the light that erased everything behind them had nearly dragged them into the lake.

"Set us down," Duda said finally. His voice was flat, rough. Like it had forgotten how to carry emotion.

Joey nodded once. No questions.

The airship dropped gently, skids scraping against warped stone. Duda and Ahyoka disembarked into heat that still radiated up through their boots. The ground crunched beneath their feet like shattered pottery.

They walked slowly—methodically—eyes tracing the path Clint might have taken. There was no hope in their movements. Just obligation. Just the stubborn kind of loyalty that didn't stop at death.

Ahyoka was the one who spotted it.

"There," she said quietly, pointing toward a small depression in the rock, half-filled with ash.

Duda followed her finger, knelt, and cleared the debris away with careful hands. It came free reluctantly, fused to the earth by whatever force had shattered the mountain. But beneath it—

A lump of metal. Misshapen, half-melted. Silver and dark steel twisted together with veins of copper ribboning through it. It was Clint's spellshooter—Rufus, or what was left of it.

Duda stared at the warped relic. Not saying a word. Not blinking. Just looking. He reached out and touched it.

It hissed.

He recoiled, teeth gritted, then stripped off his coat, wrapped the metal inside, and lifted it with both hands like it was sacred. Like it was the last piece of someone he couldn't bear to bury.

Ahyoka didn't speak. She just stood at his side, eyes fixed on the wrapped shooter. Her face was unreadable. But her hand rested lightly against Duda's elbow, grounding them both.

They turned together, walked back to the ship. Along the way, Ahyoka spotted a small piece of fused glass, alternately clear and ashy, with a bit of gold at the center. She placed the glass in her pouch, then started walking again, quickly catching up to Duda. They climbed back onto the airship.

No one asked what they found. No one needed to.

Joey lifted them into the sky again, turning the ship back toward Copper Creek, engines humming low against the wind.

And though the night stretched long, and the flight would last hours, not one voice was raised. Not a single word spoken.

They flew in silence.

Carrying the memory of a man who stood alone, in the dark, and chose to end a monster with fire and light.

And somewhere in the cradle of Duda's coat, the melted spellshooter still smoldered, quiet and heavy as grief.

The dawn came late in Copper Creek now. It crawled over the ridgeline like a thief, hesitant, painting the shattered earth with diluted gold. Smoke still clung to the timbers of half-finished roofs. The charred skeletons of old structures stood like witnesses, black against the morning. What had been Copper Creek was now something else—new bones, same scars.

The rebuilding had been steady but cautious. No one whistled while they worked. Every nail driven into the new frame of a building was measured, deliberate. The men and women who remained were not builders by trade—they were survivors, and they constructed not from hope, but defiance.

Children no longer played in the streets. They trained. They watched. Some learned how to cast, others how to load, but all of them had learned how to shut up and listen. The lessons left by the Wendigo were not wasted.

Savannah stood at the edge of Melville House, the new one, constructed with the same white stone and copper fixtures but with more warding etched beneath its surface. Her arms were folded tight, eyes on the town. She hadn't slept. Hadn't needed to. The new kind of magic humming inside her didn't always let her sleep, and even when it did, her dreams weren't quiet.

The sigil above the door glowed faintly green. Old magic. Dormitory grade. No one questioned that this was a Chapter House now. Savannah didn't hold court, didn't play the part of noble matron, but when she walked the corridors, even the visiting Slingers stepped aside.

The town had grown quieter in its strength. No one talked about "getting back to normal." No one believed in normal anymore. They believed in watch rotations. In stacked crates of iron shot and alchemical tonic. In locked doors. Copper Creek was alive, but it didn't blink anymore.

This wasn't peace. This was the eye of something larger. But for now, in the wind-whipped silence of the new dawn, the town stood.

And that was enough.

# Interlude

PERSONAL REPLY – ENCRYPTED CHANNEL
*Classification: Ultra-Restricted – Author's Eyes Only*

To: Commander Helena Marr
From: High Director Calvus Ardent
Date: April 10, 1890
Subject: Copper Creek Event – Strategic Review Acknowledged

Commander Marr,

I've reviewed your summary. Efficient, clear, and blessedly free of political varnish. That's why you still have this desk, and why I still read your reports before anyone else's.

I've approved the New Copper Creek designation. Present it as a field necessity, containment, contamination, resettlement, etc. The usual excuses. The real reason will remain confined to my office, and to yours. Maintain the perimeter. Maintain the silence.

Regarding Savannah Melville: your instincts remain sound. She is beyond retrieval. More importantly, she was under the protection of a man whose name should carry weight in every Concordium hall, though I expect it will not. Clint Black stood against something no man should face. He did not stand alone, but when the end came, he *stood*.

He bought us time. That is a kind of magic we never learned to measure properly.

I've already initiated the commendation protocols. Quiet ones. A plaque, maybe. Something permanent. Small things for big sacrifices—that's the way of it.

As for Blander, I'm aware of the incident. I read the transcript. Three times. Laughed once. That particular enforcer will recover in time, though his reputation may not. There are worse wounds than embarrassment. Some of them you don't bleed from.

I've also confirmed that suppression efforts are being quietly shelved. There are too many tongues and too many tales already spreading. Let the story breathe—truth is easier to manage when it's wrapped in disbelief.

On a different note:

There are signals beneath the ruins. Echoes that don't decay like they should. Something old is testing the seams, Commander. You and I both know the blood magic isn't the danger—it's just the symptom. The cause is *still moving.*

If the thing beneath Copper Creek wakes fully, it will not knock. It will *burn* its way through.

You are authorized to use any means necessary to keep curious hands from digging too deep. No relic-hunters. No academics. No crusaders. I'll handle the politics. You handle the ground.

If the wrong name gets spoken again, we're not going to need a tribunal. We're going to need a burial shroud big enough to wrap a continent.

Keep your boots tight. Keep your blade close. And don't trust anything that smiles in silence.

— C.A.
*High Director, Concordium Central*

# Chapter Thirty-Four

The dawn rose slowly over New Copper Creek, stretching across broken rooftops and scorched earth like a weary sentinel. Its light felt cautious—delicate—and yet it revealed what had been rebuilt, piece by piece, by hands that refused to give in. Charred timbers had been replaced. Warded windows now offered resistance as much as light. The town's skeleton had been reforged into something stronger.

The scorched rim of New Copper Creek still smoldered when the two riders appeared out of the haze—Leya and Gorran, dust-caked and road-worn, their expressions hollow with exhaustion and something heavier. They dismounted without fanfare, ignoring the curious stares of survivors rebuilding the ruins. They asked only one question: "Where is he?"

The silence that followed was all the answer they needed.

They found Savannah at the edge of the blast crater, seated cross-legged in the dirt, her gaze fixed on the raw earth where a single stone marked the grave. No name. Just a worn copper round pressed into the top, gleaming faintly in the shifting light.

Leya approached first, hesitating a few paces away. "We left the moment they released us," she said quietly. "Rode straight through. Barely stopped to breathe."

Savannah didn't look up. She didn't move. Her voice was flat, brittle. "You're two days late."

Gorran removed his hat and bowed his head. "We heard what he did. What he stopped."

Still no response. But Savannah's fingers curled in the dust, slow and tight, her whole body straining against something she wouldn't let herself feel.

Footsteps behind them broke the silence. Ahyoka and Duda stepped into view, both unsmiling. Duda crossed his arms, expression unreadable. Ahyoka stood still as stone, her gaze sweeping over the newcomers with a quiet, watchful weight.

"We came to stay," Gorran said, squaring his shoulders beneath the burden of unspoken judgment. "To teach. To help."

Neither Ahyoka nor Duda replied. But the message in their stares was clear: they were being measured, and no words would tip the scale.

Finally, Savannah stirred. She turned toward them, and for a moment her face was raw with grief and fury—but only for a moment. Her voice trembled once, then steadied. "If you'd been here days ago…" She let the words hang. They didn't need finishing.

Leya nodded, eyes downcast. "We know."

There was no apology. No absolution.

Ahyoka passed between them then, slow and deliberate. She didn't speak either, but the glance she gave Leya was not hostile, just sharp, considering. Duda followed a step behind, quiet as dusk, offering no reaction.

Savannah stood, brushing dust from her coat. She looked back at the two spellcasters as if seeing them not just as people, but as questions still unanswered. "Don't expect me to thank you," she said, already turning away.

"We don't," Gorran replied softly.

Savannah paused, spoke without turning to face them. "But I'll watch."

Then she walked back toward the fractured town, toward something unfinished, smoke still rising behind her, and wind curling over the copper grave marker.

There was a subtle shift in the air today. Word had trickled in that someone, somewhere higher up, was taking notice.

284

Equipment, rare spell components, new bullets crafted from rune-infused copper, all showed up on doorsteps without explanation, as if gifted by unseen hands. Rumors spread quickly: Accorded schools, UAT armories, and even secret factions within the Concordium had pooled resources. They remembered what it cost to stand against the darkness, and they'd made a choice—to back New Copper Creek. No one in the town had asked for it, but everything dawning here now carried purpose deeper than the usual frontier magic.

They even whispered about the gutbuster incident—how Clint Black had dismantled those Concordium enforcers without taking a life, and how that single act had become legendary in nights around the campfires. It was a warning, a rallying cry, and a laughing curse depending on who told the story. It also marked a turning point: New Copper Creek didn't just survive—it set its own rules.

But the truce with peace was fragile. When the Sunshell detonated under Lake Tahoe, it had splintered the veil between worlds over the entire territory, and the barrier was cracked. In the last week, fifteen miles north, the town of Coldwater was found—silently slaughtered, raided by something that left no tracks, no clues, no survivors. Nothing there now but lingering dread.

Savannah stood at the front of the new Melville House, watching the town awaken. The dormitory halls behind her were bearing their first students, some apprenticing in magic, others in defense. The sigil above the door pulsed soft green light, a quiet promise that this was a sanctuary, and a bastion. But she didn't smile. She waited.

No children were playing in the streets today. Instead, even the youngest carried awareness, locks they'd learned to snap open and closed, wards sketched in dust on doorframes, and eyes always moving. Those were the lessons of the past seasons, hard-earned and unforgotten.

From the corner of Savannah's vision, she saw Ahyoka training with Duda—steel on wood, silent footwork, accurate breath. She looked up at Savannah with a private flame in her eyes, ready, learning, growing. That bond was new and fragile, but deep.

Savannah knew this: if Coldwater could fall, they could be next. But there was something in the way the light bent this morning, an honest reassurance she couldn't name yet. Up the chain, someone had remembered them. And they weren't alone.

This wasn't peace. It wasn't even safety. It was a pause, a breath before the next fight. But right now, in the raw beauty of a hard-won morning, New Copper Creek stood unbroken.


Andrezj Duda had never been one for sentiment. He didn't keep journals. Didn't name his rifles. Didn't decorate graves. But when he walked the perimeter of New Copper Creek each morning, boots stirring dust that hadn't settled since the Wendigo died, there was purpose in every step. Not routine. Not paranoia. Intention.

The kind of intention a man gets when he realizes—without ever saying it aloud—that he's finally home.

Duda had once been the kind of man you hired to make your problems go away. He still was. But these days, his definition of "problem" had shifted. You threatened this town, its kids, it's weird half-trained Slingers, or the girl with the obsidian spear who followed him like a second shadow, and you became a name on a list Duda never had to write down.

That list was growing.

Since the Sunshell detonated, things had changed. Not just in Copper Creek, but everywhere. Word of the blast had spread faster than anyone could contain it, and strange things were surfacing. Creatures without names. Spells that bled backward through time. Magic that smelled wrong. And now, whole towns, like Coldwater, were going silent. Whatever came through the crack left behind by that detonation, it wasn't done.

So Duda sent letters. Not many. Just the right ones.

They weren't official. No call for bounty hunters or wizards. No banners or brands. Just a few carefully chosen words on thick paper, sent to men who understood what it meant when Andrezj Duda said, *I need help*.

And they came.

Quietly, in ones and twos. A big man with steel teeth and eyes like ice. A woman who used to be a healer before the war made her forget how. A pair of brothers who never said a word but watched everyone from opposite ends of a room. Not one of them asked for pay. Not one of them asked why. They were given a home and a purpose. None asked for more.

Sharon Steed deputized them all. Duda made sure they understood the rules. They didn't patrol the streets so much as haunt them, shadows on rooftops and boots under back porches. Nothing happened in New Copper Creek without at least one of them knowing it. Every alley had eyes. Every outcropping was sighted in. It wasn't paranoia. It was preparation.

Because Duda had buried enough people to know what came next. This wasn't over. Not even close.

But he'd also never given a damn about a place the way he did this one. He'd fought for causes before. Been paid. Been betrayed. But New Copper Creek had given him something he hadn't realized he was missing: purpose without pretense. A place to stand that didn't feel borrowed. Home.

And a girl who looked at him like he was more than what he'd done.

So Duda trained every morning with Ahyoka in the yard behind the new jailhouse. Spear and blade. Word and silence. She absorbed it all, not like a sponge, but like a furnace. Everything he gave her made her burn hotter. Sharper. And the purest metal comes from the hottest part of the forge.

Sometimes, she watched him too closely. Mirrored his steps with unnerving precision. But he let her. Because he knew the truth of it now: if he ever fell, she'd be the last line between this town and the dark.

And if anyone ever tried to take her from him?

Well. They'd better pray to whatever deity oversaw their version of Hell.


By mid morning, the streets of New Copper Creek buzzed with cautious optimism. Farmers, woodcutters, and craftsmen— people with rough hands and sharper eyes—filtered into town, drawn not just by prosperity but by whispers of something sturdier: a place to belong when the world was unravelling. They carried axes as easily as groceries, boots that had walked hard miles, and stories that trembled on the edge of fear.

They found in New Copper Creek a different kind of welcome.

A few blocks from Melville House, where Savannah had taken up unofficial duty as Chapter Mistress, a small but purposeful building was nearing completion. Its foundation sat deep in stone, its walls rising in clean lines of timber and copper. Within, a half-dozen apprentices drilled magic under watchful tutors from both the Slinger and Caster schools—none more important than Ahyoka, her obsidian-tipped spear resting within arm's reach as she absorbed lessons in wards and displacement spells.

Down the road, the new jailhouse stood finished: harsh lines of stone and reinforced copper steel grates, designed by Duda and Sheriff Steed. Inside, they'd sworn in the handful of "heavy hitter" deputies Duda had recruited—silent men with steady eyes and no agenda but protection. Their job was simple: guard, intercept, or eliminate threats before New Copper Creek ever knew danger walked among them.

It hadn't gone unnoticed among the new arrivals. Graying settlers, still a little cagey, had paused at the gates of Copper Creek—not the rough boomtown it once was, but a settlement with

288

backbone. Morning whispers turned to noon hymn become conviction: these weren't idealists or fools. These were people choosing safety over ignorance.

Savannah watched them with thoughtful eyes as she moved between households, teaching straightforward defensive spells and distributing earthen wards to protect wells and barns. She was quieter now, more deliberate. The old urgency remained—alive in her hands as she drew indigo glyphs in the dirt—but it was tempered by something steadier, colder and more resolved. She'd suffered through hell and come out stronger.

At the edge of town, Duda carved a new bullseye drill into timber with Ahyoka beside him. The pair wore matching sets of scars and quiet competence. Ahyoka moved as he did, simulated his stance and breath, till her spear forced the wood singsong just so. Duda let the tool slip from his hand without a word, pride hidden in the corners of his eyes.

Evening came with the scent of coffee and quiet contentment drifting through open windows. In the square, a modest ceremony was held in front of Melville House. Savannah read a missive from the Concordium:

## CONCORDIUM CENTRAL OFFICE – WESTERN ACCORDS REGISTRY
*Filed: April 14, 1890*
*Delivered via bonded courier under protected seal*

**To:** Savannah Melville
*New Copper Creek, Nevada Territory*

### RE: Post-Event Recognition and Wardship Clarification

Ms. Melville,

On behalf of the Concordium of Magical Oversight and Accordance, I write to formally acknowledge the changed legal and arcane status of the region henceforth referred to as **New Copper Creek.**

289

As of this filing, New Copper Creek is granted **Special Territorial Designation**, falling outside direct Concordium governance but under open observation, in recognition of both the region's unique magical volatility and the role you have played in its survival.

While no formal title is conferred, it is the determination of this office that, in practice and by right of action, you have assumed the role of **Warden Pro Tempore** of the territory. This is not a position granted, but one earned.

The following individuals are recognized by this office with **Posthumous Commendation of the Highest Class**:

• **Marshal Michael Slay**, for exceptional service in defense of the innocent and unwavering enforcement of the Accords.
• **Senior SpellCaster Cyrus Melville**, former Territory Warden and educator, for his personal courage, his final stand, and his lifelong dedication to balance over power.
• **SpellSlinger Clint Black**, for actions in direct confrontation with an apex-tier supernatural threat, and for the ultimate sacrifice in the preservation of lives far beyond the blast zone. His name will be entered into the Book of Broken Oaths, not for a betrayal, but as a reminder that some promises are kept with blood.

In accordance with Standing Protocol 19-G, a memorial record has been established in the Central Archives. Concordium personnel are instructed to grant due respect to the region, and to its current guardians.

No further agents will be dispatched without direct authorization from the High Director. Local disputes remain under your jurisdiction unless they rise to the level of continental concern.

Consider this a line drawn in quiescence, not in challenge.

**You hold the peace. You've earned the quiet.**

If ever that quiet is broken again, this office will listen—first.

Respectfully,

*— Lenera Vellum*
*Acting Diplomatic Secretary*
*For the Office of the High Director, Concordium Central*

As she was about to replace the message in the tube, another small parcel fell out. It was a handwritten note on heavy paper, with a dark wax seal. She opened it, puzzled.

**Savannah—**

Officially, you'll get flowers and legalese.

This isn't that.

I read the field logs. Watched the replay sigils. Read the casualty reports and the silence between the lines. I know what you did. I know what it cost.

I also know what it saved.

Cyrus once called you a storm with a heartbeat. He wasn't wrong. He also said you had the rare gift of knowing when to break things—and when to *leave them standing*. That's rarer than magic, these days.

Slay was a good man. Black was something harder to name. The kind of man you only meet once, and then only if you're lucky—or in danger. You walked through hell with both of them. You came out the other side.

Don't let anyone tell you how to carry that. Not even me.

If the wind shifts again—if the veil tears and something worse than truth gets through—you know where to find me. I won't send a committee. I'll come myself. And I will bring Hell.

Until then, keep the town quiet. Keep the shadows shallow. And if anyone from Central gives you trouble, tell them this:

*I said she's earned her ground.*

**— C.A.**

291

She reread the message and put it away in her robes. Tears swam in her eyes. She sat on a bench and stared out at the ruins of the town, old town, they were already calling it. At least someone understood what was happening. A weight had been lifted, and a new one placed.

New Copper Creek would receive dedicated supply convoys—spellbooks, enchanted gear, protective wards—unasked, unsolicited aid from both schools of magic, and from within the Concordium's more humane faction, who recognized what stood here. The crowd—townsfolk, Slingers, Casters, Ahyoka standing still as a sentinel—broke into applause.

But applause didn't drown out threats.

Aboard the Skyward Mercy, the command crew were gathered with Captain Ward. A Concordium vessel left them with a missive of their own, directing them to remain at New Copper Creek permanently. Captain Ward turned the message over in her hands, the formal lettering of the Concordium directive glaring up at her. "They think they're punishing us," she said, voice low as her bridge crew hovered nearby. "I think we've just found a real purpose. It won't be quiet duty. Not here."

Her gunnery officer, Lieutenant Harrow, let out a low chuckle. "We should get plenty of gunnery practice, at least."

She folded the missive and dropped it into her pocket without a second thought. She'd been thrown out of Concordium Command School for thinking—seriously thinking, something that didn't align with their handbook. Reassignment to Copper Creek? She'd take it. It beat endless mail runs between dusty outposts. "I can think of worse assignments," she said, ice in her voice turning to heat. "New Copper Creek it is. Let's show them what real duty looks like." And so, with a wry grin shared between officer and captain, the *Skyward Mercy* lifted from harbor—its new home unmistakably written among the shifting currents of western wind and conflict.

Later, as the airship settled back into Copper Creek's familiar envelope, Ward gathered her command team in the cramped briefing salon. Lanterns cast warm glows over maps and crew logs spread on the central table.

"Permanent assignment," she said, tapping a finger over the map's mark on Copper Creek. "That means medevac runs, supply drops, orbiting support. Multidimensional presence." She looked at each officer in turn—Harrow, Navix, even the newly assigned communications specialist who'd never seen a Ghost Shell in action—and let the gravity of her words settle in. "We're anchored by mission, not means. And out here, we make our own Justice."

They sat, a quiet respect in the air, rooted not in command protocol but in choice. Ward's order was unspoken they weren't just staying—they were choosing this fight. And whatever came next, Copper Creek would never face it alone.

As Savannah finished speaking, the sound of pounding hooves shattered the quiet. A lone rider tore into the square, his horse lathered with sweat, eyes rolling white. Dust chased him like something trying to catch up.

He dismounted fast and hard, stumbled, caught himself. His voice came ragged.

"Up near Tahoe," he said. "Something crossed the patrol line last night. Fast—too fast. No shape we could mark. No sound but the wind."

He paused, swallowing.

"We fired. Every damn man fired. Rounds went through like smoke—or maybe missed, but it didn't feel like a miss. Didn't slow. Didn't stop. By the time we got to where it had been…"

He shook his head.

"…nothing. Not tracks. Not heat. Not even the smell of something alive."

The square fell into silence.

Ahyoka straightened, every muscle tight. Her head tilted slightly, listening not with her ears but with the part of her that *knew*—the part gifted by Monster Killer, the part that felt when the world turned wrong. Her eyes narrowed, tracking something no one else could see.

Duda moved next. No words, just a slow pivot, hand on his sidearm, fingers loose but ready. His jaw clenched as he scanned the horizon. Not afraid. Not yet. But alert in the way a man gets when the old instincts scream, and the new ones lie.

He exhaled once through his nose. "Bad wind," he muttered. "Something slipped through."

No one asked what he meant. They all felt it.

Something had changed. Again.


The stars over New Copper Creek changed.

Not in their placement, not visibly—but to those who watched closely, who whispered spells under their breath or stared too long into firelight, something was different. The sky felt thinner. Hungrier. And it wasn't just the Wendigo, or even the detonation of the Sunshell that changed the world.

It was the cracking.

When the Sunshell burst—unleashed not by accident but by Clint Black's deliberate hand—it didn't just erase a monster. It ruptured the veil between the real and the forgotten, the seen and the whispered. And what bled through that rupture was not just magic.

Coldwater had been the first sign. Fifteen miles west, a small, solid town. Farmers. Trappers. A midwife who could read runes better than most professors. It vanished in a night. No signs of struggle. No blood left behind. Only the walls and doors pried open like unsealed coffins, and a smell of ash where nothing had burned.

Savannah had sent three scouts, two Slingers and a silent fellow named Enoch who never missed a track. Only Enoch came back. And Enoch came back *quiet*.

Whatever had killed Coldwater, it didn't leave tracks. Or rather—it didn't need to. It didn't step. It just *was*.

Word spread fast. Not rumors, not fear-mongering, but quiet truths spoken over campfires and warded doors. Settlers doubled their wards. Caster apprentices wore iron charms they'd once thought quaint. The new dormitory engraved copper inlays along its outer wall, symbols old enough to hurt the eyes of anyone with real power.

Inside the jailhouse, Duda ordered a second weapons locker installed—this one hidden, this one full of very particular things. Blessed silver. Obsidian-tipped bolts. Alchemical fire. Cases of silver jacketed rounds. And one gutbuster round—an antique. Not for humor this time, but in memory of the man who'd made that humiliation legendary.

Ahyoka trained harder than ever. She had stopped flinching when the spear cracked against her palms. She moved like something not-quite-human anymore, *almost*, but sharpened into something forged for a single task: protect the girl, protect the town, *stand in the breach*.

Some of the new settlers noticed. Most of them didn't comment.

They saw her walk beside Duda, as an equal, never behind, never before, just with. And when he spoke, she listened. When she moved, he watched. No one questioned it. No one dared.

Sheriff Steed swore in three more deputies—two old companions of Duda's from his stranger years. One had been a knife-for-hire in the Redlands, the other a conjurer with one hand and no tongue who spoke volumes anyway. She didn't ask their stories. She just nodded when Duda said, "They'll hold."

The dormitory held its first open session that week. Savannah, now called "Mistress Melville" by new apprentices who didn't dare shorten it, stood before two dozen students in the courtyard, rune chalk in one hand, a copper-threaded ward pinned to her coat.

She didn't teach with passion anymore. Not the way Cyrus had. She taught with *precision*. Every word had weight. Every hand gesture bled intent. Her power had become instinct, her lessons a map toward surviving in a world where the night didn't just hold monsters, it *birthed* them. Practical, Save Your Life Casting 101.

And all the while, whispers circled back from the wilds. Figures seen on ridgelines. Dead livestock found opened but not eaten. Glassy tracks across riverbeds where no man walked. A man at the edge of Coldwater's ruins saw something move *against the light*—a silhouette that didn't cast shadow but *drank it*.

Savannah heard all of it.

She took notes in a leather-bound journal Cyrus had left her.

And each night, before she let sleep take her, she drew a single glyph onto her skin, blood magic, careful, contained.

For when the darkness came again.

Then, one night, two Accorded riders arrived, exhausted, injured. They had lost a companion, a SpellSlinger who stayed behind so they could get away. Neither saw the thing that killed her, but they confirmed that she died. They asked for shelter. They weren't turned away.

The girl they spoke of, a quiet child with dark hair and a bright copper coin in her pocket, had told them to come. Said they'd be safe in Copper Creek.

The world had grown darker. But the town had *sharpened*.

Duda walked its borders by night. Ahyoka paced the rooftops by morning. And from the open door of Melville House, Savannah Melville read every breeze and every silence like they were ancient scripture.

When the next threat came, it would not find New Copper Creek unready.

It might not find New Copper Creek *at all*. It might vanish into fire and copper and never know what hit it.

Because this was no longer just a town. This was *the line*.

# Epilogue – The Thing That Waits

The ruins of Coldwater were still. Not quiet, because nothing in that place could be called peaceful, but still, like a corpse waiting to twitch.

Moonlight spilled across the bones of the town. Shattered windows stared like blind eyes. Wind whispered through broken shutters, but no dogs barked, no horses snorted in the distance. The wind carried only the faint stink of blood and scorched cedar.

In the dead center of town, where the old well had stood, something was… moving.

It wasn't a man. Not anymore.

The Skinwalker pulled itself from the ground, bones cracking and flesh whispering into place like paper catching fire in reverse. The form it wore was wrong — too long, too lean — but for now, it held. The empty eyes blinked once, black on black.

A mangled hand lifted. It clenched a twisted charm of rawhide and antler, pulled from the body of a Concordium scout who had dared to track what shouldn't be tracked. The charm dissolved in his palm, swallowed into the void between skin and muscle.

*Pieces return. Slowly. But they return.*

The Skinwalker turned its face north, toward the high ridges above Lake Tahoe. Toward what had once been the Sunshell's heart. It could still feel the burn — a wound in its essence. Something stolen. Something sacred.

And worse…

*A sliver. Buried in him. In the SpellSlinger. The one who laughed as he died.*

The Skinwalker didn't snarl. Didn't scream. It *smiled.*

*That piece will return to me.*

The air shimmered behind it — faint distortions, like figures almost coming into focus, but never quite solid. Things with too many fingers. Shapes that should never fit the human eye. Not yet.

Not *yet.*

*The walls weaken. The wound widens. The light they unleashed tore the veil, and now…*

It stepped across the ash-streaked stones. One of its feet left behind a perfect footprint, still steaming.

*They think they've survived. That they've rebuilt. That Copper Creek stands.*

It lifted a finger, drawing a sigil in the air with bone-nail and something darker than blood. The symbol hung for a moment, then burned itself into nothingness.

*Let them build. Let them train. Let them pray to little gods with copper badges and iron rifles.*

A breath. The first breeze Coldwater had felt in days.

*I remember what was taken.*

It looked toward the horizon, where smoke from New Copper Creek curled against the sky.

*And I remember who took it.*

The Skinwalker's shape unraveled slightly, not dissolving but spreading. Echoing.

*Let them rest. Let them heal.*

The shadows leaned toward it, like disciples kneeling.

*When I rise in truth, I will rise with fire.*

And far away, in the hills, something ancient and unquiet stirred in its sleep — not the Skinwalker, but something older. Something *drawn* by what had begun. A plan coming to fruition, a plan from a being who thought in terms of millennia, not years.

Because the veil was thinning.

And monsters do not walk alone.

# Afterword

The book you hold in your hands is not the book I intended to write. SpellSlinger was originally going to be very different. But, like many great characters, Clint had a mind of his own, and chose his own adventure. I hope you enjoy it as much as I enjoyed the writing. There are many more chapters in this story. You will meet many of the Accorded, should you choose to read further. I hope you do. For more stories, in world lore, or simply a behind the scenes look, visit my Patreon page and join. I have both free and paid tiers, plus access to exclusive swag!

Patreon/EricGarnerJohnson

Eric Garner Johnson